News of his father's death brings Dominic d'Estainville back to Moonshadow—his family's plantation in Georgia—after three long years. But Moonshadow, his rightful inheritance, has been sold, and to obtain it Dominic must marry Veroníque, the new owner's daughter. Veroníque agrees to the marriage for her dying father's sake, knowing that a future as the unloved wife of d'Estainville will bring her nothing but heartbreak, for she has loved Dominic all her life.

While the American Civil War threatens Moonshadow from without, a more bitter contest is fought inside its walls as Veroníque battles to win the love and trust of a husband who despises her.

By the same author in Masquerade

FRANCESCA
MADELON
GAMBLER'S PRIZE
A PRIDE OF MACDONALDS
THE COUNTESS
MARIA ELENA

Moonshadow

Valentina Luellen

MILLS & BOON LIMITED
London · Sydney · Toronto

First published in Great Britain 1981
by Mills & Boon Limited, 15-16 Brook's Mews,
London W1A 1DR

ISBN 0 263 73644 X

Set in 10 on 10 pt Times Roman

Photoset by Rowland Phototypesetting Ltd
Bury St Edmunds, Suffolk
Made and printed in Great Britain by
Cox & Wyman, Reading

CHAPTER ONE

It had been over three years since Veroníque had last seen Dominic d'Estainville. She had been seventeen then, in love for the first time when, without a word, he had disappeared from his home at Moonshadow a few months before the Southern States were plunged into bloody conflict with those in the North.

During the long years which followed, she convinced herself she had put him out of her thoughts and her life forever, but now he was back and she knew there would never be anyone else to take his place. The sight of him standing at the rail of the battered steamship, that bright spring afternoon in March 1864, aroused memories she had pushed to the furthest recesses of her mind. He was taller than she remembered, but his hair was still as thick and black, the proud, strong face as darkly sunburnt and arrogant, the self-assured air even more noticeable as he surveyed the crowded wharf with narrowed gaze.

He wore no coat, and his shirt, blackened by smoke and grime, was torn in several places, revealing the strong muscular chest beneath. There was a bloody gash across his forehead.

He stood watching preparations for the unloading of the battered cargo being brought up on to the shattered deck, indicating towards several large, leather-bound trunks that were his and should be left for the moment. The brace of silver-mounted duelling pistols thrust into the waist of his black trousers made him look like some triumphant buccaneer coming home with a great prize, Veroníque thought. Which in a way, he was.

The *Southern Star*, or what remained of the grey-painted steamship with its iron-clad superstructure and revolving gun-turret on the upper deck, was the first ship successfully to run the Union blockade in over six months. People had been gathering since early morning, excitement rising to fever pitch as it neared land. Merchants and speculators had come to bid for what was left of the cargo in the battered holds. Women, in home-spun dresses, waited silently for the latest news of the war and the men who had left them to fight. A few wounded soldiers rested on crutches or on the arms of some of the many ladies of the town who now spent their days raising money for the Confederacy and tending the injured daily being ferried back from the front.

Bull Run—Shiloh—Gettysburg! The names were written with the blood of the thousands who had died in these places.

It was a miracle, but half the cargo still remained intact. Desperately needed supplies for people on the verge of despair. People who days before had prayed with no hope of deliverance, now reached out with smiling faces and words of gratitude, touching the bearded faces, the arms and bodies of the men who had given them another chance to survive.

A chance for them, but never again for the *Southern Star*. Onlookers fell back to allow the horse-drawn ambulances nearer to take on the dead and wounded as the ship began to list badly. There was a moment of panic as it shuddered and sank lower into the water. A woman in the crowd screamed as packing cases were thrown violently about the decks and over the rail into the water.

Dominic d'Estainville swung around towards the Negro staggering up from below, caught and flung him over one shoulder. Willing hands reached out to bring them both to land and take his burden from him.

'Father.' Veroníque laid a gloved hand on her father's arm, grimacing as she noticed another hole in the fine white lace. They would stand no more patching and they were her last pair. 'Isn't that Micah—the darkie who disappeared the same time as Dominic? You always said they were together.'

'So I was right after all.' George de Brissac stood up in the rig, staring at the ebony features of the man being helped in their direction, then raised a hand to attract the attention of his companion over the heads of the crowd. 'Damn Dominic! He causes the biggest scandal this county has ever known by half-killing his father, and in a fight over a slave at that, jilts a fine young woman of good family background only four weeks before the wedding, and then takes himself off to Havana, stealing one of my field-hands in the process. Now he's back as cool as you please, like the prodigal son, and probably expecting the same reception.'

'I doubt that very much. Dominic has too much pride,' Veroníque returned, folding her parasol as the tall figure of Dominic d'Estainville approached the rig. One arm still supported the Negro, who was limping badly.

As he drew closer she could see the wound across his forehead was at least several days old and the blood had dried. The dark eyes which surveyed her were shadowed with tiredness, yet a familiar mocking gleam crept into them as they swept her from head to toe, in a scrutinising look that took in every detail of her appearance. The long hair, as black as a raven's wing, falling loosely down beneath the ribbon-trimmed sunhat. The green cotton check dress and white gloves. The finely shaped features shaded beneath the floppy brim, the high cheekbones and softly curving mouth, and eyes as blue and brilliant as a sapphire.

Veroníque had inherited not only a passionate love of horses which had abruptly ended the life of her vivacious mother when she was only a child of three, but also reflected the striking beauty of the French Countess whom George had taken as his second wife. She had blossomed during Dominic's absence, like a firm cotton seed flowering beneath the warmth of Georgia sunshine. She knew that by the way his eyes lingered. His first sight of her in three years, and she was wearing last year's dress and gloves with holes in them.

Damn the war and the Yankees, she thought savagely, and damn him to hell for coming back!

'Veroníque! If I had known I would be greeted by such an apparition of beauty, I would have washed and shaved.'

There was no amusement in the soft, drawling voice, nevertheless she knew he was laughing at her. He always had. As children growing up together, their relationship had been turbulent and unpredictable. Yet when Dominic went riding, it was always Veroníque he chose to accompany him. On those days when she rode at his side through the pine trees and across the fields they had shared something neither had ever been able to put into words.

In the summer of 1860, he had finished his last term studying law at university, and come back to Moonshadow for a holiday before joining a law firm in Atlanta. It was about this time that Melissa had caught his eye for, as far as she knew, no one had held any interest for him, not even the girl his father had arranged he should marry. It had been a marriage favoured by both families, although apparently not by Dominic himself.

In those days she had been a silly child, idolising a man unaware of her existence half the time, Veroníque thought. Now she was a grown woman, stronger of will, hopefully wiser. Still in love with him, but determined this time that her heart would not control her head.

'Welcome back, Dominic.' She almost said 'welcome home', but caught her father's warning look.

'George! My God, it's good to see a friendly face again.' Dominic's voice changed as with his free hand he reached up to grip George's outstretched hand. It contained sincere pleasure—almost relief, she thought. 'How did you know I was on the *Southern Star*?'

'I didn't. Veroníque and I were on our way back to the house when we heard a ship was coming in. Nowadays Atlanta doesn't see that many. We came out of sheer curiosity. You look exhausted—put that darkie up with my coachman and climb in with us. You need a hot bath and a change of clothes. You will stay with us, of course. Point out your trunks and Jacob will fetch them.'

'First a large drink and then some sleep,' Dominic drawled, helping his charge up towards the waiting driver. 'Are you all right?' he asked the injured man, whose face was contorted in pain. The fingers clutching a bandaged shoulder were wet with fresh blood.

'Yes, Mister Dominic.'

Veroníque's eyes widened in surprise at the cultured voice. The man called Micah who had run away from her father's plantation, like most of the coloured field-hands had been illiterate. It was against the law to give schooling to slaves. How like Dominic to provide the forbidden learning, she mused, moving her hooped skirt aside as six feet of lean bone and muscle lowered itself into place beside her.

Motioning the driver to move off, George de Brissac sat

back in his seat and looked enquiringly at the man opposite. Considering the shock Dominic's unexpected return had given him, Veroníque thought he was remaining surprisingly calm. Her heart was beating so loudly she was sure everyone could hear it.

'How was Havana? That is where you have been, isn't it?'

'Havana was—profitable. After I left here I travelled for a while. England—France—and then I found myself on the way to Havana with the prospect of settling down with another plantation, which is what I did. It was small to begin with, but it grew with time and hard work and I sold it for a good price. I reckon I've made enough to keep Moonshadow on its feet until this damned war is over.'

'There is something you should know,' Veroníque began. He loved that place above everything, even Melissa. She wanted to soften the blow if possible, but he gave her no chance.

'My father is dead. Yes, I know. Why else would I have come back? Moonshadow is mine now. I've waited a long time for this moment.'

'The place has been sold. It no longer belongs to the d'Estainvilles,' George said heavily, and his face became as grey as his thinning hair.

Dominic said nothing, but close against him in the jolting rig, Veroníque felt him tense as the sudden shock slammed into him. Never in his wildest dreams could he have imagined coming back to this! The bronzed features hardened, the narrowed gaze turned on her father chilled her. The voice, insolent in its questioning, challenged the words to be repeated.

'What did you say, old friend?'

The term was meant as an insult. George knew it and grew even paler. He was a slightly built man in his middle fifties, a good head shorter than Dominic, who had always made him feel insignificant.

'The plantation was in debt when your father died. It was inevitable—the war . . .' George began and then shrugged. '*Bon Dieu*, why do I defend myself because you are angry? I would be too—coming home to find my inheritance gone. But it's no one's fault, except perhaps your own. You should not have gone away. You broke Phillipe when you turned your back on him and he never recovered. With Sarah gone and the realisation that you were not coming back, he began to drink heavily. Your mother did nothing —just watched and waited . . .'

'If you were not a friend . . .'

'You would kill me for telling you the truth?' George interrupted with a sad smile. 'For saving Moonshadow from twenty or more creditors? Giving your mother enough money to leave with her head still held high? Your father and I were good friends for many years. It is not my way to turn my back on a friend—or his widow.'

'My mother—gone away.' Dominic's voice was harsh and bitter. 'Where?'

'She, too, has a talent for leaving no trace. Twelve months ago she told me she was going to friends in Richmond, but she never arrived. I'm sorry, Dominic.'

'Why? She should have been kicked out of the house long ago when my father first discovered what a whore she was.'

'This is neither the time nor the place to discuss such a matter,' George said coldly. 'Did you leave your manners behind you in Havana?'

Dominic looked into Veronique's embarrassed face and the dark eyes were almost black in the sunlight. She had never seen such eyes: it was as if they could look down into her very soul.

'So *la belle princesse* now rules Moonshadow,' he said in a tone that for all its softness, had a bite of steel in it. She was mistress of his domain. How that must ruffle the eagle's feathers!

Fierce colour flooded into her cheeks at the use of his pet name for her. He had always called her that when he wanted to provoke her. *La belle princesse*, aloof, untouchable, just because she had chosen not to join in the other children's boisterous games, preferring to sit with Paul and read Molière or Shelley. *La belle princesse*, not worthy of his attention, only his scorn.

'You are welcome to stay with us at Pinewood until you can make other arrangements. Isn't he, Father?'

'Don't you mean Moonshadow? Charity beneath my own roof? God in heaven, I never was a man who took kindly to people handing out favours,' Dominic snapped.

'Do you think I came back for that? I haven't slept in three days. I've seen men blown apart by Yankee guns, watched them dying on the bloody decks because there was no doctor to tend them. Eighteen dead and Lord knows how many wounded. Four Micah and I killed when the cowardly swine wanted to surrender.'

'You killed men like that—brave men?' Veroníque whispered, horrified. 'Such men have kept Atlanta alive. Heaven knows, there are few of them left.'

'Men like that?' he mimicked cruelly. 'Men like what? Scum who panicked when the ship was holed, refused to obey orders and knifed the Captain and two of his officers when he wouldn't run up a white flag! I hardly knew the man, but I liked him. I promised him I would get him and his ship back here if humanly possible. Do you know how I got this?' He touched his forehead and immediately his mouth tightened in pain. 'And Micah his wound? They came at us in the dark, like all back-stabbers, only they didn't know the knife is my weapon too. I was better than they were.'

'How horrible!'

Veroníque could feel no pity for the men he had killed, although she knew she should. She could only feel relief it had not been him. Her gaze was drawn to the front of his shirt. Tight against his chest she could just see the thin black strap which held in place the six-inch throwing knife, sheathed in leather beneath his left arm. She remembered how proud he had been of the handmade rig which Micah had given him on his twenty-second birthday. He had bought the knife the following week in Atlanta and proceeded to frighten the life out of everyone with his skilful handling of it.

The carriage halted before the de Brissac house on Washington Street, a two-storied house with a slate roof and a high white fence surrounding the small, well-tended garden, just coming to life with colourful spring flowers. The original iron railings had long since been taken away to be melted down as part of the war effort.

Dominic's face was expressionless as he helped Veroníque on to the red dust of the road and handed over her parasol. His thoughts were suddenly elsewhere, making her feel both she and her father were unwanted.

'Does Dr Barton still live on Oakway?' he asked, about to resume his seat. 'Micah needs attention.'

'My dear boy, you will find all the doctors are in the hospitals and far too busy to see a coloured. Bring him inside. I have a quadroon woman who will know what to do. You need attention more than he does,' George replied.

Dominic considered the suggestion for a long moment, his brows drawn together into a deep frown, and he looked about to refuse when Micah began to ease himself out of his seat. He slipped and would have fallen if Dominic, lithe as a panther, had not leapt forward to break his fall with outstretched arms. Veroníque saw the look which passed between them, a look which conveyed that the bond between them went far deeper than that of master and servant.

'You are still weak. Hold on to me.'

'It's all right, Mister Dominic. I can manage.'

'The hell you can. You—Jacob! You look as strong as an ox. Carry him into the house and make sure that woman in there takes good care of him. If she doesn't, she will answer to me.'

'Find Tante Michelle,' Veroníque added, and Jacob nodded and started up the path, staggering a little, for all his powerful build, beneath the weight he carried.

'Do not give orders to my servants,' George said, in an authoritative tone that surprised even him.

'I—apologise,'—this accompanied by a half-smile.

'You have not forgotten, I hope, that Micah still belongs to me. When he disappeared the same night as you, I guessed he had taken it into his head to follow you. I always did dislike the way you allowed him to hang around.'

'We will settle his ownership when we talk of Moonshadow,' Dominic returned, standing to one side to allow Veroníque to enter the house. She was aware of his eyes following her as she reached up and removed her hat. Of the smile which touched his mouth as he slowly considered her standing in a shaft of sunlight from a side window, as if seeing her for the first time. His voice was all velvety charm as he answered her father, yet the words sent a chill of fear through her. It was like being touched by a cold gust of wind. 'I intend to have them both back, you realise.'

'Are you proposing to buy the place from me?' George asked, hoping his tone betrayed none of the hope suddenly rising inside him.

'Why not? I have the money.'

'Confederate money is useless, Dominic, you know that,' came the grim answer. 'I've lost so much I shall be forced to put this house up for sale soon. I've two years' cotton stored at Pinewood, but it's worthless until the blockade is lifted.'

'My money is all in gold,' Dominic returned.

'Yankee gold!' Veroníque said accusingly. 'Keep it.'

'I assure you it buys more than worthless paper money. I sweated blood for what I have. If it gives me back Moonshadow, then I don't give a damn what anyone thinks.' Again that softness was back in his voice, but his eyes were like ice as he stared into her indignant features. 'The place belongs to me. It is my rightful inheritance. I mean to have it back and I don't much care how I go about it. The sooner both of you get that into your heads, the better it will be for all of us.'

And with that parting shot, Dominic d'Estainville sauntered casually into the sitting-room, helped himself to a large glass of George's best Bourbon, and relaxed into a chair to await the unloading of his luggage.

He spent over an hour soaking in a hot tub, slowly consuming the rest of the bottle he had brought upstairs with him, while one of the housemaids put away his clothes. After she had gone he sprawled across the double bed and slept. He awoke late in the afternoon and once again, his first thoughts were of going home.

Moonshadow was the only thing in his life that meant anything to him. It was wife and mistress rolled into one. More challenging, infinitely more satisfying to possess. It had been in his family for over fifty years, built by his ruthless, ambitious old grandfather, who had run off with the prettiest girl in New Orleans. Eloping, of course, without the permission of her very autocratic Spanish parents.

Her dowry had set him up in the shipping business, but later on he and his wife had moved inland, together with his business partner, Antoine de Brissac. Thirty miles on the far side of the Macon, on the banks of a small river which had broken away from the mainstream, a new plantation was born out of uncultivated soil. A fine house raised where tall pines once stood. Moonshadow! A monument to Grandfather d'Estainville. To his strength of will and mind—his determination.

Ten miles away, in total contrast, as were the characters of the two men—Pinewood. A present for the new bride of Antoine de Brissac. Built in love. Given in love.

Like the de Brissac family, Grandfather Luc d'Estainville had come originally from the Basque country, which nestled in the shadow of the French Pyrénées. A wild, untamed country which produced equally proud, unpredictable men to whom danger was, and always would be, a challenge not to be ignored. It pleased Dominic to think he had grown up in his grandfather's image. The old man had been the only one to really understand him. Apart, that was, from his nanny, Sarah.

Now both had gone out of his life, and he had returned to face the consequences of the past alone. To reclaim Moonshadow and look down his nose at the upper Georgian society and laugh quietly to himself as the old man used to do. He knew that nothing anyone said or did could touch him. He was an island, and Moonshadow was his fortress.

He began to doze again, only to be roused by the sound of the door opening. Veroníque peered in, then entered, carrying a tray of sandwiches and coffee.

'I did knock,' she said, as he sat up.

'Sorry, I was half-asleep. That looks good.'

'Hot coffee and ham sandwiches. Father said you probably hadn't eaten today.'

'He's right.'

Veroníque avoided his gaze as she advanced into the room. She was in control so long as she did not look into those eyes. It had taken her nearly an hour to compose herself after their last encounter. As she put down the tray the toe of her slipper kicked against the empty Bourbon bottle. She stared at it in disgust, making no attempt to pick it up.

'I would prefer more of that to coffee,' Dominic murmured, reaching for a sandwich which he ate with relish.

'Then I suggest you ask one of the servants to bring it up to you,' she replied with great dignity, and turned towards the door.

'Where are you running off to? Stay and talk to me for a while, I have a lot of news to catch up on.'

She glanced back at him, her eyes widening at such an outrageous suggestion under the circumstances. Dominic wore only his trousers and a pair of boots. A clean shirt and coat lay across a chair beneath the window, beside the harness containing his knife. With a laugh he sprang from the bed, reaching instinctively first for the harness. Over the years he had worn it as some people might wear a lucky charm.

'George was right, my manners are still in Havana. You can turn your back if you wish.'

Veroníque ignored the jibe and sat down, helping herself to one of his sandwiches. A sensible young woman would have left him then and there, but she felt anything but level-headed in his company.

'Was it so different in Havana?' she asked after a while.

'How do you mean?' He slipped a white silk shirt over sunburnt skin, did up the two lower buttons and then sat down again to pour himself some coffee.

'You may have had need of that then,' she motioned to the now concealed knife with a nod of her head, 'but not here. There is no one beneath Father's roof who wishes you harm.'

'You are right, of course, but I have grown used to having it with me. How is Micah? Is he being well looked after?'

'Tante Michelle has rebandaged his shoulder. She is well skilled in the art of healing.'

Now he looked like the man she had known before, Veroníque thought. The expensive shirt, and the high leather boots, and the clothes she could see through the door of the half-open closet, were of the best quality. Melissa would only need him to crook his little finger.

'Why did you go away, Dominic?'

She caught sight of the bitterness which crossed his face before it creased into a lazy smile. He had never been one to reveal his innermost thoughts.

'Surely you have all the facts after three years? I had an

argument with my father, during which I nearly killed him—over a Negress. I could hardly stay around here after that, could I?'

'Sarah had been with your family for years. We all knew and loved her, you especially,' Veroníque persisted. 'I still cannot believe she tried to kill your mother.'

'Well, she did. You have been too well brought up to mention the fact, but you know damned well that Sarah had been my father's mistress for many years, and mistress of Moonshadow far more than my mother ever was. He idolised her, as I did, and my mother hated her. For years she must have been waiting for the day she could have her revenge. That's why, when I was away and could do nothing about it, she sold not only Sarah, but Micah, her son—knowing what that would do to me.

'My father didn't have the guts to go against her. He didn't possess Gran'père Luc's stomach for a fight. By the time I was on my way home, Sarah had run away from her new master and gone to Micah. They reached Moonshadow before I did and my mother turned the dogs loose on them . . .'

Dominic could not keep the fury out of his voice. It lurked so near the surface, heating his blood to a dangerous level as soon as memories of that terrible day returned.

The memory of his father falling to the ground beneath the merciless blows from the wicked, plaited horsewhip wielded by his own son—the howl of the dogs pursuing Sarah and Micah into the woods—her agonising screams as she fell with one of the savage hounds sinking his teeth into her arm . . .

'You almost beat your own father to death.' Veroníque's voice sent the past spinning back into the dark recesses of his mind. For the sake of his sanity it had to remain there.

'So I did.' No added explanation, no remorse in that soft drawl, no pity in the bleak eyes which looked at her. 'By the way, whose idea was it to sell Moonshadow?'

'Your mother's.' Veroníque still failed to understand his dislike of the very elegant, beautiful woman who had always greeted her most hospitably when she visited. 'Your father died owing a great deal of money to everyone. My father, the bank, the merchants. The place was left to you in his will, but your mother said she was unable to trace you. Did she try, or was there too much bad feeling between you?'

'The last thing she wanted was for me to return as master of Moonshadow.'

'She wanted to leave, but with so much money owing the only way was to sell the plantation. Why Father bought it is still beyond me. Trying to keep one place going in such difficult times is bad enough. But two . . .'

'Then he'll be pleased if I take it off his hands.'

'He has already had an offer which appeals to him—from Paul Loring,' Veroníque said, and watched Dominic start at the name of the boy who had been a childhood friend to them both.

'So—the writer wants to be his own boss, does he? Well, he will have to find somewhere else. There should be plenty of people wanting to sell up, with the Yankees about to come through Georgia.'

His casualness about the nearness of the Northern army took her breath away. Did nothing frighten him? Her eyes followed the movements of the slender hands which selected a cheroot from an engraved silver case and lit it. They could be gentle, cruel, destructive, loving, whichever he chose. She loved him, but she was quite convinced she would never understand him.

'So Paul is planning to settle down, is he?'

'Of course, you don't know! He joined the Fifth Georgia Cavalry . . .'

'Paul with a sabre in his hand instead of a pen! I don't believe it!'

'He's here in Atlanta, in hospital. He lost an arm at Chickamauga,' Veroníque broke in quietly. She would never forget the pale-faced boy who had ridden off to war with his friends, so proud and confident in his grey uniform with its gold braid, despite the fact that he abhorred fighting and its consequences and knew nothing of the horrors he would have to face in battle.

They had brought him back to Atlanta on a stretcher, gaunt-featured, bearded, and minus an arm. The boy had become a man who had survived death and yet still carried it in his soul.

'My God,' Dominic ejaculated softly. 'Poor kid . . .'

'Even as a child, you know how difficult it was between

him and Melissa. It's worse now. She has a brother who is a cripple, and you know how she hates any kind of deformity. She won't even visit him in hospital. It's one of the reasons I encouraged him to look around for somewhere else where he could get on with what he really wants to do. He's talking about writing a book about the War; about us, the people of Georgia, and what is happening all over the South so that others will know what we are really like.'

'Hard-working folks, toiling from dawn to dusk to feed and clothe our families. Not living in big houses, gorging ourselves on chicken and ham while the overseer flogs our black slaves in the cotton fields,' Dominic returned sarcastically. 'Somehow I think it will be a long time before anyone wants to know about the South again. If we are to survive and retain what our forefathers left us, then we will damned well have to fight for it all by ourselves.'

'If you feel that way, why don't you join the army too?' Veroníque ventured to ask.

'And leave Moonshadow to fall into the keeping of a one-armed man of artistic temperament who will let the fields go to grass while he writes his masterpiece? Never! I'll fight if the bluecoats come, but in my own way and on my own territory. Are you going to marry Paul? He always was sweet on you.'

'Of course not.'

'Why so indignant? Hasn't he asked you?'

'It's not that way at all between us.'

'That means he has found someone else. Never mind. What does Melissa think of her brother's idea?'

'You can ask her that yourself at dinner.' Veroníque was watching his face closely, searching for some reaction to her words. 'She's come to collect Paul and take him home. She isn't too keen to have him around the house, but he's threatened to discharge himself from hospital, and the beds are needed so badly that the doctors thought it best he goes home to convalesce.'

She had half-expected Dominic to be pleased at the news, but he registered no emotion as he rose to his feet and walked across to the window.

'Did she ever marry?' was all he asked.

'The year you went away. Martin Beauville, the banker's

son. He was with Paul at Chickamauga, only he didn't come back.'

'Dead?' Dominic asked, turning. Still there was nothing to read in his expression.

'Yes.'

'Melissa was always a strong-willed woman. She will take death, like everything else, in her stride.'

'Don't—don't you love her any more?' Veroníque was puzzled by his lack of sympathy.

'Love? My dear child, I was never in love with Melissa, or she with me. We—amused each other.'

'What a horrible thing to say!'

'Should I lie and say we were madly in love? That's not my way, and between us, if I remember, there was always truth, no matter how painful. I sometimes used to hurt you deliberately, just to make you cry. Did you know that? You were the only girl I knew who cried real tears and never used them as a weapon. And they are a very powerful weapon to a vulnerable man, believe me. I wonder if you would know.'

'Did—did you . . .' Veroníque found it hard to put into words what she had been longing to ask ever since they met. 'Do you—have a wife? A family?'

His dark eyes blazed with sudden sardonic humour. The cheroot slanted from his lips impudently.

'No, I never took a wife. There were always ample diversions to keep me amused.'

'Like Melissa kept you amused,' Veroníque said, and her voice was all iced sweetness. She had always thought it was the other way round—what a wrong conclusion that had been. In what other ways had she been mistaken about Dominic d'Estainville? She stood up, not liking the change in his manner.

'Good God, I haven't shocked you, have I? I apologise, *ma belle*. I thought you had grown up. But not that much, eh? Run along before one of the servants tells George I have been trying to compromise his very beautiful, but still so innocent little girl.'

Dismissed like a child! Veroníque bristled and stood her ground. He came away from the window and was standing before her before she became aware of his moving. Hands on hips, he studied the slender figure before him with an insolence of expression that told her she was being systematically undressed.

'Oh, you beast! *Cochon*!' She spat the words at him and fled from the room with burning cheeks. Not twenty years old and in full control of herself, but once again fourteen, running to escape the mocking echo of Dominic's laughter.

CHAPTER TWO

FROM the window of his bedroom Dominic looked down into the street and realised he was seeing Atlanta as he had never seen it before. It had always been bursting with life, a bustling go-ahead kind of a place, and he had never much cared for it, even less now in time of war.

Soldiers in grey uniforms were everywhere. During the drive from the jetty they had also passed blue-coated prisoners-of-war, ambulances and supply wagons which choked the narrow streets with red dust. People jostled each other on the sidewalks, their faces drawn and tired. It had become impossible to obtain new materials and so many were dressed in homespun clothes. Necessities like spools of thread, buttons, even hairpins could no longer be found in the shops.

Across the rooftops, the tall chimney-stacks of new factories belched black smoke into the grey-blue sky. Atlanta had become not only a hospital base for the wounded from the front, but the nerve centre of the Confederate struggle to survive.

The place had become full of old men and women, wounded and widows. Overworked wives struggling to feed what family remained. Pretty girls destined to mature before their time, to see death and suffer privations never intended for man nor beast, let alone cossetted Southern womanhood.

Dominic had kept up with the war news in Havana, dreading the day he might learn that the Yankees had set foot on his land. Over his dead body! That's how they would take Moonshadow. It was no idle threat.

It was dusk when he turned away from the window and lighted the oil lamp to dress for dinner. Around his neck he fastened a dark green, silk cravat and over the ruffled shirt, a plain but well tailored grey broadcloth coat to match his trousers. In the mirror the reflection which faced him was the personification of a gentleman of quality. Poor Veroníque! It was startling to think he could still shock her after three years.

She was quite the elegant lady now, still maintaining the old way of life despite the threat from outsiders who knew nothing about the people who lived in the South except the fact they owned Negro slaves. He had admired her for that. She had grown more lovely over the years. He found the fact oddly disconcerting.

'Am I really pretty, Tante Michelle?' Veroníque asked the Creole woman who was helping her into a dress of midnight blue silk. She hoped the addition of several rows of delicate Brussels lace around the neckline helped to disguise the fact that she had worn it before.

A pair of liquid brown eyes frankly surveyed the girl before her for a long moment. Veroníque's long black hair, swept back from her face, was caught up in curls on the top of her head and secured with large tortoiseshell combs. She had lost weight over the past few months and the dress now clung more snugly to well rounded breasts and a tiny waist which scarcely needed a corset to accentuate its smallness.

'Pretty,' Michelle repeated, and her face broke into a smile. She was a tall woman in her thirties, the daughter of a quadroon woman George had bought on Gallatin Street on one of the rare occasions he took his wife back to visit her parents in New Orleans. Veroníque valued her friendship, the advice she offered and sometimes gave without permission.

'*Ma petite*, you are beautiful. You are growing into a fine lady, just like your mother.'

'I am twenty now,' Veroníque said. At the time of her mother's death she had been only three. Old enough to miss her after the accident, to remember the sound of the infectious golden laughter which had filled the house, but young enough to accept Tante Michelle in her place.

'Twenty years old! My now, isn't that a great age.'

'Perhaps not to you, but do you realise most of my friends have married long ago? Some have families of their own.'

'But you did not want to marry, did you, *mignonne*? You

chose to listen to your heart and wait for the dark-haired one with the devil's eyes.'

Fierce colour burned in Veroníque's cheeks. She meant Dominic!

'Why do you say that about him?' she asked curiously.

'I knew the old one—*le grandpère*. They are alike as twins those two. Ruthless and too fond of a pretty face. My mother always used to say a real man meant being half devil, half saint. I think your Monsieur Dominic has more than his fare share of *le diable* in him.'

'Is that so bad?'

'For him? No. For the poor unfortunate woman who loves him? *Dieu!* He will make you very unhappy, *mignonne*.'

'Tante Michelle, he means nothing to me.'

'Is that why you came out of his room this afternoon looking for all the world as if you had been struck by a thunderbolt? You passed right by me like a blind person. What did he say to you?'

'It isn't what he said,' Veroníque confessed, growing hot at the remembrance of Dominic's eyes on her. Did he look at every woman that way, or keep such provocation for her alone? 'It—it was the way he looked at me.'

'The way a man looks at the woman he desires, perhaps?'

'No—not me! He has never felt like that about me.'

'That was three years ago. Now you are a woman and Monsieur Dominic is aware of the fact.'

'I wonder what it would be like to be kissed by a man who is part devil?' Veroníque murmured, turning once again to look at her reflection in the long wall mirror.

Michelle's brows curved into a quizzical frown as she saw the expression on Veroníque's face, understanding, as a more experienced woman of the world, the yearning to be in the arms of a handsome lover. But she was perturbed by the choice. Veroníque was an unawakened child when it came to love. Such a man could raise her to the heights of ecstasy, or destroy her.

Dominic came downstairs and turned towards the parlour, pausing to light a cheroot as he heard the sound of a woman's laughter coming from the other side of the door. He recognised it at once. Apparently the death of her husband had not unduly concerned her. He stepped forward and opened the door.

'Dominic, my dear! George has just been telling me of your exploits.'

The soft, husky voice came from the direction of the high-backed sofa beneath the window. The woman it belonged to was beautiful. Perhaps striking was a better word. Flame-red hair surrounded clearly defined features, high cheekbones, and dark violet eyes. Full red lips deepened into an inviting smile at the silent man who stood in the doorway. She did not rise to greet him, just extended a slender white hand where numerous rings flashed and sparkled, and waited for him to go to her.

It had always been that way, Dominic remembered as he moved across the room to take hold of the long, tapered fingers. As he stared down at the sensuous mouth, he found himself wondering how many men she had taken to her bed since he had left.

George de Brissac stepped away from the writing bureau in one corner of the room, a sheaf of papers in his hands.

'If you will both excuse me, I must write a very important letter before dinner. Help yourself to drinks, Dominic.'

Melissa's head was tilted on one side as she looked up at Dominic, and he knew she was silently laughing.

'Poor George,' she murmured. 'Do you think he has left us alone on purpose?'

'Would you care for a drink? Sherry, isn't it?'

Dominic poured her a glass of the golden-brown liquid, not waiting for an answer, and a large Bourbon for himself.

'That was hardly the kind of greeting I expected from an—old friend,' she said, her full lips drooping petulantly.

'You're an old, married friend,' Dominic returned with a slow smile. 'Besides we don't want to shock George beneath his own roof, do we?'

'I don't think you ever knew my husband, Martin Beauville.'

'I know the name, but I can't put a face to the man. Veroníque said he was killed at Chickamauga. My condolences, although I can see you don't need them. It's lucky you didn't lose Paul too. How is he?'

'He still has one good arm, and that's all that seems to matter to him. His writing—he can still do that, you see.

That stupid, useless idea of writing a book about the war. Who wants to hear about death—and battles—?'

'Haven't you ever thought that idea in his head might be the only thing keeping him sane just now?' Dominic cut in harshly. 'You always were a selfish bitch. Your own brother, and you don't give a damn about him, do you?'

'He feels the same way about me. Besides, he'll be like some fragile ornament around the house. He changed after you went away. It was bad enough before, when he either had his head stuck in a book or between his hands with a mammoth hangover, after the two of you had just come back from Atlanta. But at least we could still talk then.'

'It may be the war.'

'What does it matter anyway?' Melissa shrugged her shoulders, indicating that she cared very little what the reason might be.

'Whatever possessed you to get married?' Dominic could contain his curiosity no longer.

'Why? It was the uniform, I suppose. All that gold braid and the polished sabre. I knew it was a mistake the moment he put the ring on my finger,' she said, fingering the gold wedding band she wore almost contemptuously.

'But luckily the war saved him from finding out what a faithless little cat you really are,' Dominic answered with heavy sarcasm.

'My, we are glad to be back among friends, aren't we?' Melissa's tone matched his own. 'George has obviously told you about Moonshadow. You can come and stay with me at the Folly until you decide what to do.'

'I'm in no doubt as to what to do. I want the place back, it's mine. Besides, what would everyone say about my visiting you, a widow not yet out of mourning?'

He did not care what people thought, and knew she felt exactly the same way. It was a queer kind of honesty, Dominic thought. He shared something like that with Veroníque; honesty, but of a different kind.

Melissa rose to her feet, putting down the glass she held. As was the custom for all widows for a period of at least two years, she was dressed from head to toe in black. Despite the sombreness of her attire, the outfit, buttoned high to the neck, did more for her than it would for most other women.

'I haven't told you how pleased I am to see you again.'

She halted in front of him, her body close but not touching his, and the aroma of her perfume drifted once again into his nostrils. Her fingers reached for the top buttons of the dress and unfastened them, revealing it to be a tight-fitting jacket, so cleverly put together that it made the whole garment appear to be in one piece. Laughter, uncontrollable laughter began to rise in Dominic's throat as it came off and was tossed carelessly across a chair. Beneath, the low neckline of the plain bodice, curved over full breasts and milk-white shoulders. It would have sent the matronly ladies of Atlanta into hysterics for a whole month had they witnessed the scene.

'Well?' Melissa's arms slid up to his shoulders. She, too, was openly laughing now. 'It's black, isn't it? Welcome home, Dominic.'

'It's good to be back.'

Her offered mouth was eager against his. He heard her moan softly as he held her tight and allowed his lips to wander over her throat, her shoulders, but as he kissed her he realised that he cared very little if their relationship continued on its old level. Moonshadow could make his heart ache, but not a woman.

He lifted his head and saw Veroníque watching them from the doorway, her face an ashen mask. She swayed back as if to leave, then with a supreme effort regained her composure and stepped into the room.

'Did you knock this time?' he drawled.

Melissa disengaged herself from his embrace, in no particular hurry despite the new arrival.

'This is my home, or have you forgotten?'

Veroníque's eyes were centred on the daring neckline, registering displeasure. Melissa slipped on her jacket, fastened the buttons and then took up her drink again, and sat down as casually as if she had been interrupted in the middle of a boring conversation, not a passionate embrace.

Dinner was a pleasant, relaxed affair. Despite the growing shortage of food, for most supplies now went to feed refugees and wounded, they ate well, and George produced a bottle of vintage port for the occasion.

They talked only briefly of the war, for it was hard to imagine the Yankees sitting a hundred miles away when the four of them wined and dined in such a congenial atmosphere. They returned to the comfortable parlour and Dominic found himself gradually relaxing and talked freely of the sugar plantation he had built up near Havana.

Veroníque sat beside her father on the chaise-longue, listening intently. Never once did she allow her expression to betray the agony of mind she experienced as he related the shelling of the *Southern Star* by a slower but heavier-gunned Federal ship. He could have been killed! Badly injured! Lost overboard! Yet in the telling of the story his voice remained calm, as he merely related facts which were past and no longer important. He was home, and she knew that nothing else mattered to him.

Dominic was aware of Melissa trying to catch his eye. She had been bored for the last hour and was anxious to leave, but he ignored her, more concerned over George Brissac, who since dinner had become unusually quiet and pale. At first he had attributed it to the vintage port, but now he was not so sure. The pallor in the usually ruddy cheeks was almost unhealthy. Even as he tried to make up his mind whether the man was tired or drunk, George rose to his feet, noticeably unsteady.

Veroníque saw him sway and jumped to her feet, but Dominic was there before her to support the crumbling figure.

'What is it, my friend? Are you ill?'

'A little tired. It's very late.' The pale blue eyes which lifted to Dominic's face were shadowed with pain, conveying a silent plea for help.

It was his heart again! Veroníque thought worriedly. That tired, stubborn old heart, survivor of so many tragedies.

'Will you help me take him upstairs, Dominic? Melissa, call Jacob, please, and tell him Father needs him.'

Together they helped George to his room and laid him on the bed. Veroníque wanted to send for the doctor, but her father would not allow it.

'I think you should,' Dominic said firmly, unfastening the tight cravat at the older man's throat. 'You are not well and we both know it.'

Veroníque knew it too, he thought, as he straightened and looked at her. In a few minutes she had suddenly aged.

Her cheeks were almost as colourless as her father's and the lovely sapphire eyes had lost their lustre.

'Nonsense. Nonsense, it's nothing. I will be myself in the morning.'

'You have been overdoing things,' Dominic told George. 'Rest when you get back to Pinewood.'

'Rest?' Veroníque echoed, and her sudden brittle tone made him stare at her in surprise. 'How can he rest with two plantations to care for? It's almost time for the spring planting, yet most of the fields at Moonshadow haven't been cleared yet. He's worn himself out trying to keep that place going, and Pinewood has suffered because of it. And all because your father was his friend. He bought Moonshadow out of a sense of honour, and it's ruining him. The sooner Paul has it, the better!'

Dominic's eyes glittered dangerously at the outburst, but she was too distraught to notice, or to care.

'Daughter—don't,' George protested feebly. 'Dominic is not at fault.'

'Isn't he? The d'Estainvilles, from the time of *Gran'père* Luc, have always thought they were God Almighty. They give their orders and expect everyone else to jump to obey. They live out their lives according to their own set of rules and despise others more tolerant. They even think they can walk away from all responsibilities and pick up where they left off the moment they return.'

'You mean me, of course,' Dominic broke in harshly. What had got into the girl? He had never heard her talk this way before. 'I had little choice whether I stayed or not.'

'A man would have stayed . . .'

The words were out before she realised what she was saying. For a horrifying moment she thought Dominic was going to strike her. His hand was raised and behind it were the blazing black eyes of the devil himself. Hot tears rushed to her eyes. She wanted to apologise, but the words stuck in her throat. No! It was the truth. He ran when he should have stood his ground.

Jacob appeared in the doorway, looking from one angry face to another, and hesitated until Veroníque motioned him to enter.

'Miz Beauville wants to know if you is takin' her home, Mr Dominic. It's gettin' late and she don't like going home alone with so many strangers in town nowadays.'

'I'll go straight down,' Dominic said with a nod.

Veroníque was ahead of him as he reached the top of the stairs. His hand on her arm brought her to an abrupt halt.

'Let me go! I want to get Father some warm milk,' she gasped indignantly, but the fingers coupling her wrist stayed firm.

'How bad is he?' Dominic's tone defied argument. She stopped struggling against his grip and looked up at him, and he saw her soft mouth quiver.

'He saw Dr Barton about six months ago. It's only a matter of time. Now do you see what Moonshadow can do to him—is doing to him?'

'What about overseers?'

'We have one at Pinewood naturally, but that's all. Everyone has joined the army to fight and there's even talk of conscripting the Negroes. I go there when I can, especially since Father's first attack. He doesn't think I know how serious it is . . .'

She broke off, regretting her choice of words. She was no longer angry at him, only disappointed. If he had not come back Paul would have bought Moonshadow, married if she nagged him enough, raised children in that large old house and made the walls echo once more with the sound of laughter. Dominic would change that, the way the d'Estainvilles changed everything to suit their own selfish desires.

She had never realised she felt so strongly about them before. From somewhere she had found fresh courage to face up to his taunts, a new battleground on which to fight him. And fight him she would, for the happiness of those dear to her.

'I didn't realise it was that serious,' Dominic answered. 'If it was not, *ma belle*, you and I would have a reckoning for that little scene just now.'

'What would you do, Dominic? Spank me like a naughty child? Or tell me to run away and read my poetry?'

'You are too grown up for either.' He felt her stiffen and knew she had sensed his meaning. The old devilry rose up in him once more, the irrepressible urge to shatter that outward show of composure. Whenever he had made her angry, her defence was to retire behind a barricade of icy silence, at which he hammered mercilessly with barbed comments and mocking laughter until it began to crack and finally crumble, and the tears came. Although he never admitted it to Véroníque, he was always sorry afterwards, and the remorse he experienced made him lash out at her with doubled enmity the next time. He bent his head until his face was barely inches from hers and immediately felt her grow tense as she prepared herself for the kiss which never came. 'I shall be back around twelve. Why don't you wait up for me?'

Her reaction was not what he expected. She tilted her head back so that she could see his face in the glow of the wall lights directly above them, and there was a smile on her lips, as if she was actually considering the suggestion, even knowing full well the implication behind it.

'I think not, Dominic. We are collecting Paul from the hospital tomorrow. Father thought our company might ease his return home. One of us should retain a little strength in case he needs help, don't you agree?'

He had never known her to use such a tone before, so disinterested in what was, after all, a most outrageous suggestion for someone of her strict moral code. If he had not known better he would have sworn she had heard dozens of such proposals before. This was not the girl who had met him at the ship, or talked with him in his room and run from him because he had offended her sense of propriety. This was a woman! And it had taken him nearly twenty-four hours to discover the fact.

Veroníque's voice, softer and containing a sarcasm which did justice to the d'Estainville training she had been forced to endure as a child, was in his ears again.

'Thank you for the offer of company, Dominic. Perhaps another time, when we are not so preoccupied with other problems.'

With great dignity she lifted his hand from her arm, walked back into George's room and closed the door behind her.

'Well, I'll be damned,' Dominic declared. There was no mockery in his voice, no amusement on the dark, sardonic features as he slowly went downstairs.

He had looked into Veroníque's lovely face and the smile there had been one of derision and contempt. His kind of smile! Her words were his kind of words, meant to inflict pain, and should never have been uttered from lips meant only for endearments and kisses. For the space of a heartbeat Dominic d'Estainville had looked at his own image—and he had not liked what he had seen.

Paul Loring was twenty-six. He looked at least ten years older than that, Veroníque thought as she watched Dominic help him to board the train which was to take them as far as Macon. From there they would continue on to the family home by carriage. During his months in hospital he had lost so much weight that his grey uniform hung on him like a sack. The left sleeve of the jacket was folded back beneath the stump of his amputated arm. Although Paul was almost six feet tall himself, Dominic's tall frame seemed to dwarf him in the narrow compartment.

'Come and sit beside me.' Paul stretched out a hand and drew Veroníque down beside him. Dominic sat opposite, beside George who, although pale, seemed to have recovered from the night before. 'Where's Melissa? She'll miss the train if she doesn't hurry.'

'I saw her talking to friends outside,' Veroníque returned. 'She sees so few people at the Folly, she's probably catching up on all the latest gossip. Are you comfortable? Michelle has a rug if you are cold.'

'Don't fuss over the boy,' Dominic drawled, and she looked at him coldly. She had heard him come in as the grandfather clock on the landing chimed two. The knowledge that he had spent nearly three hours with Melissa angered her, when once it would have reduced her to tears. From inside his coat Dominic produced a small silver flask, unfastened the top, and motioned Paul to take it.

'A shot of brandy is what you need, not mothering. You'll get enough of that when you get home and Alice descends on the place. I bet you a five-dollar gold piece she'll be waiting when we arrive.'

He was aware something was wrong the moment he had spoken. George gave a sharp intake of breath at the name of his eldest daughter by his first wife, who had died before she reached thirty. Paul's fingers curled so tightly around Veroníque's hand that Dominic saw her wince with the sudden pain, and her face drained of colour, the blue eyes blazed contempt across the space which separated them.

Alice had been the plain one, the one who stayed at home, content to learn sewing and cooking and plan for the day she would be a wife and mother. Alice, the little mouse, who ran the house while her pretty sister dwelt in the limelight of admirers and of a father who doted on her every word. What had Alice done for her name to produce such reactions? Dominic wondered, but was too wise to press the matter at that moment. Veroníque shared Paul's love of literature, but before he left, Dominic had been aware of a new relationship for Paul with the older, wiser Alice. Now it seemed that Veroníque had made the most of the gifts endowed by her mother. Not only had she stolen Paul back, but she had her eyes on Moonshadow as a future home. Veroníque de Brissac was accustomed to the best of everything.

'I take it you intend to stay at the Folly?' Veroníque said icily, totally ignoring the reference to her sister. How like Dominic to touch on the one subject no one dared speak of, she thought. Her father looked ghastly, and Paul's fingers, clutching hers, had gone white at the knuckles.

'Dominic is coming back to Pinewood with us for a few days,' George replied, and she could only stare at him in horrified surprise.

'I'm glad of that. You can come over and tell me what an adventurous life you have led since we last saw each other,' Paul said, and for the first time in many weeks, Veroníque saw the ghost of a smile touch his gaunt features.

Paul swallowed several mouthfuls of the brandy before returning the flask with a grateful nod. Immediately his hand sought Veroníque's again as it lay in her lap, like a tiny child seeking reassurance. She turned and smiled at him. Dominic's lips tightened as he turned to look out of the window, deliberately shutting his mind against the implications the pair of them presented. Paul in Moonshadow! Paul and Veroníque in Moonshadow!

The train moved slowly out of the depot. It had begun to rain, turning the dust in the streets into thick red mud, but he did not even notice. He felt a strange sense of elation as the houses began to disappear behind them and Atlanta, in all its hectic chaos, was lost to view. He was going to see

Moonshadow again! He became oblivious to George chattering at his side, despite the fact he managed to maintain a coherent conversation. His expression became unreadable, but in the depths of his eyes a spark was kindled as, with the passing hours, familiar landmarks began to present themselves. He was going home!

CHAPTER THREE

THE de Brissac plantation was linked to Moonshadow by a mile-wide section of thick pines, and tall trees also ringed the white Georgian-style house. From where he sat on the verandah enjoying a cup of black coffee, Dominic could just see the rows of cottages at the end of the garden, noticeably shabby and in need of repair. Most of the barns and outbuildings required attention of some kind too.

It had been late by the time they reached Pinewood. Veroníque had suggested upon leaving the train that the journey had overtired Paul so much that he should not continue to his own home until the following day. After settling the extra guests in their rooms she had gone directly to bed, insisting her father also retired.

Despite the long journey, sleep eluded Dominic for the best part of the night. He had been given one of the large, comfortable rooms which looked out over the back paddocks and the short cut to his old home. How often he had come that way as a boy. Moonshadow was less than six miles across those darkened fields. . . .

He had been washed and dressed for over two hours before he heard the house-servants beginning to stir the next morning. When he went down he found George alone on the sunlit verandah and joined him for coffee, refusing anything to eat. It was only eight o'clock, so he was not surprised that Melissa and Paul were still in bed. Neither, he remembered, had ever been early risers.

'I'd like to borrow a horse,' he began.

'To ride over to the house? Why not take Veroníque with you?'

'Let her rest; she's probably tired after yesterday.' Somehow Dominic could not imagine Veroníque giving him a guided tour. She had made it quite clear that she resented not only his return, but also his presence at Pinewood, believing it was the first step in a deliberate plan to get back what had been taken from him. Which was the exact thought in his mind as he rose to his feet.

'Mademoiselle Veroníque went out an hour ago,' Michelle declared, catching the tail-end of the conversation as she brought a fresh pot of coffee.

'There was some trouble, she said, with Gifford.'

'The overseer,' George explained as Dominic glanced his way enquiringly. 'Stephen Gifford. He's been here about eighteen months. What kind of trouble, Michelle?'

'It would seem Monsieur Gifford has again been using his whip to excess, this time on a young pregnant girl. She has been living with him, apparently. Mademoiselle was very angry.'

There was nothing in the woman's tone to betray her dislike of the overseer, but for a brief moment as she turned to go back inside, Dominic was aware of the hatred mirrored in her brown eyes. If Gifford didn't take care he would end up one dark night with a knife in his back, he mused.

'How is Micah's wound?' he asked.

'For such a strong one, it was only a scratch. Do you wish to see him?'

'Later. Thank you for your help, Michelle. It is appreciated.'

'Veroníque shouldn't have to deal with such matters herself,' he said, turning to stare towards the slave quarters.

'I no longer tell my daughter what to do around here,' George sighed. 'She has become very independent these last twelve months, because I have been too ill to take personal charge. She took over for me as a son would have done. She has been my strength, Dominic. Such a timid little thing she was once, with her nose always in a book. Now she runs this place for me. I am truly a lucky father.'

'You'll feel the loss when she is married,' Dominic murmured and the older man looked at him in surprise.

'Who is there left for her? All the young men are soldiers now.'

'Why, Paul, of course. Isn't that the reason he wants Moonshadow?'

'Perhaps. They have become very close again since he was wounded, but he is not the right man for her. A one-armed cripple! *Dieu*! How can he protect her when I am gone?' George's groan was suddenly harsh. 'His money would keep Pinewood going, settle most of what I owe. Why, in God's name, don't I sell?'

'It would grieve me to have to call him out. Paul is my friend, but this I will surely do if you sell him Moonshadow, *mon vieux*,' Dominic said in a flat tone.

He stood with his back against the verandah rail, hands thrust deep into the pockets of his trousers. Against the deep sunburnt skin, the scar on his forehead showed white and taut as he fought to keep the growing anger out of his expression.

George leaned back in his chair, folded the paper he had been reading and put it to one side, hoping Dominic did not notice the tremor already in his hands.

'I doubt if you will be prepared to meet my price.'

'Damn it, you know I will. I've already told you I have funds in gold.'

'You don't understand me, Dominic. I am quite prepared to give you Moonshadow.'

Dominic blinked at him, slowly raised himself up to his full height. His hands clenched into tight fists. What in thunder was the old man playing at?

'Give it to me, when you are desperate for money?'

'To some people, money is not everything. I am a sick man, Dominic. I could die at any time. Death will release me from the prospect of having to face my creditors; to watch this house built in love, where I lived with Veroníque's mother, go to someone else, its contents sold off piece by piece. The memories I have defiled by strangers. If Paul bought Moonshadow I could delay that moment and give Veroníque a chance to be a lady again, perhaps find someone worthy enough to marry, who would cherish her as I did her mother.

'Unfortunately I don't have that much time. I am being pressed for payment from all directions. I love my daughter above all things. I won't see the sacrifices she has made for me these past months go to waste. I must know she will be adequately protected after I am gone.' George de Brissac took a deep breath and lifted his head to look up at the man facing him, forcing out the words he had been rehearsing since he saw Dominic on board the *Southern Star*. 'Take

Veroníque as your wife and I will give you Moonshadow as her dowry. What do you say?'

'No.' Dominic's answer came back with such explosive force that George cringed beneath the anger, the crushing contempt, in that single word.

'In heaven's name, why not?' The refusal was beyond his comprehension. Never before had he seen Dominic so emotionally shaken.

Dominic did not answer. He was beside himself with rage, and cursing under his breath he spun around on his heel and strode off down the driveway. George was mad. The thought of death had turned his mind! No, he was sane, seeking to protect the daughter he had spoiled and pampered because she was the image of her mother; determined, even at the edge of the grave, to leave her in the charge of someone else. From what he had seen of her over the past two days she was well able to fend for herself.

As he turned a corner, he saw two figures a few yards away across the yard. Veroníque and a great ox of a man with a face to match. Her wrists were held in one hairy paw, another was fastened in the thick cloud of loose black hair, while the man's weight forced her back against the side of one of the baling sheds. She was struggling against his grip like a wildcat. Even from where he stood Dominic could see the fear mirrored on her lovely face, hear her gasping for breath beneath the force threatening to crush her. There was no one else in sight! Why didn't the little fool scream for help?

In five long strides he had crossed the space between them, moving so swiftly and silently that neither were aware of his presence until steely fingers fastened themselves on to the nerve at the base of the man's neck.

Veroníque was released so abruptly that she lost her balance and reeled backwards into the dust, bruised and dazed.

The advantage of surprise compensated for the other man's extra strength. Dominic's fist thudded into his chest as he turned, bellowing abuse. He grunted and doubled in pain. A savagely wielded knee caught him beneath the chin and he was sent crashing backwards against the wooden shed. Veroníque watched him slide to the ground and lie there unmoving.

'Thank—thank you.' She tried not to stammer as Dominic wheeled on her, but found she was shaking so much she could not help it.

He lifted her to her feet, brushing the dirt from the pale yellow blouse she wore, with impersonal fingers. As she lifted a hand to push back her dishevelled hair, he saw red marks on her wrists.

'Damnation! Why didn't you yell? I take it this is the overseer, Gifford?'

She nodded, wincing as he examined her bruised wrists.

'I—I thought I could handle him. I never thought . . .' she broke off, realising what could, and probably would, have happened if Dominic had not appeared.

'That he'd tumble you like one of his black wenches? You still don't know very much about human nature, do you, Veroníque? If you're going to play at being the boss-man of this plantation, you'll have to learn how to use that authority, or the fact that you're a woman is going to be a definite disadvantage.'

Veroníque realised that this time he wasn't laughing at her, but honestly trying to give her good advice. She had known from the beginning that Stephen Gifford disliked taking her orders. His insolent manner should have been a warning. She managed to stop trembling at last, and steeled herself for the sarcasm she felt sure Dominic could not contain for much longer. *La belle princesse* struggling to fend off the advances of a common overseer . . . !

'The darkies take my orders,' she said.

'A few of them happen to think you are a fine young lady. They respect you and so they obey you. The others probably hate your guts and your father's, but they know if they show it they'll get a whipping, so they do as they are told and curse you behind your back. People are the same the world over. There's good and bad in all of us, white or black.'

'Did you learn that in Havana?'

'No, strangely enough, I discovered it at Moonshadow. It just took me a few years to realise it, that's all.'

At Dominic's feet, Gifford stirred. As he came up on to his knees blood seeping from a gashed mouth and swaying unsteadily, the toe of Dominic's boot sent him crashing backwards again. He looked up into eyes that held murder.

'Don't move. I'd love the excuse to kill you. I've a good mind to anyway, for putting your dirty hands on this girl.'

'Dominic, no!' Aware of his temper, Veroníque was suddenly afraid. 'Just send him away.'

'Are you sure?' What was it she saw in his eyes? For Gifford there had been a threat. For her—what? An ultimatum, perhaps? Without an overseer she could not manage Pinewood by herself, let alone cope with Moonshadow. Dominic took a cheroot from his pocket and scraped a match on the side of the shed to light it. Over the brief flame she was aware of his narrowed gaze—intensely unnerving.

'What is more important to you? Your virginity or your pride?'

Only he would have dared issue such a challenge, backed by all the arrogant confidence of the d'Estainvilles.

'Send him away,' she repeated.

'You can get up now, Gifford. Collect your things and clear off,' Dominic ordered, stepping back.

He was perfectly relaxed, the cheroot hanging from lips that hinted at a smile, hands hanging loosely by his sides. The huge man stared at him as he gained his feet, sensing a silent invitation to defy the order, together with the knowledge he would be beaten to a pulp if he tried.

'You'll regret this, d'Estainville. You've played God long enough. As for you . . .'

Veroníque was chilled by the man's harsh tones, the hatred in his eyes as he looked at her. She stepped quickly to Dominic's side, slipped her arm through his and was reassured by the firm pressure of his hand as it covered hers. Gifford swore at them, and then turned and almost ran from their sight.

Dominic looked down at the tousled head which barely came up to his shoulder. He could feel her trembling, and almost gave way to the urge to take her in his arms and offer comfort.

'I lost my temper with him,' Veroníque explained. 'I shouldn't, I know, it only made matters worse. He said the most terrible things to me . . . how he was going to . . . to . . .' she broke off, sudden colour flooding into her cheeks.

'You should have let me give him a sound thrashing. I've

seen his kind before, like mad dogs.'

'He had been drinking, and he wasn't armed. You have a knife.'

'There's no need to worry about a murder charge being added to my other misdemeanours. I'd have used my bare hands.'

'Does nothing ever frighten you?' Veroníque asked, unable to accept, as one who had never seen death, the calmness with which he spoke of it.

'Are you all right?' Dominic demanded. Veroníque had suddenly turned so pale he thought she might faint. 'I should have asked that first, shouldn't I?—like a considerate Southern gentleman, but I find this independence of yours damnably annoying, *ma belle*.' He stared pointedly at the tight silk shirt she wore, tucked into a thick leather belt encircling her tiny waist and the divided riding skirt which reached down to her ankles, almost hiding the well-worn riding boots. 'I take it you are trying to look—businesslike? I'm sorry; you fail miserably. Any man in his right mind would find you infinitely more attractive in that outfit.'

'I can hardly ride about the place in my one and only best gown, can I?' Veroníque found that the top button of her blouse had been torn off in the struggle. Conscious of his smile, she drew it together to conceal the rise of her breasts.

'I like my women to be all soft woman,' Dominic drawled.

Her determined efforts to shoulder the responsibilities that her father could no longer manage touched even his hard heart, but he did not acknowledge this to her, fully aware she would not accept his praise as being totally without malice. Their relationship had never been one of meaningless words and false compliments. As it was, she took offence at his remark and came away from him as if he had suddenly become white-hot.

'I may not come up to your requirements, but then I was never included in your circle of female devotees,' she said. 'Without an overseer I can't manage Pinewood, and well you know it. How dare you look down your nose at me because it's more important to me to keep the plantations going, instead of taking tea with the local gossiping hens. Our boys at the front need food—I'm helping to grow it—to supply horses—to grow more cotton, to ensure that when the war is over Pinewood will be able to survive. My grandparents came here from Savannah. They are buried over there behind the house, together with Alice's mother and mine. Do you think I'm going to let anyone take this away from us—Yankees or creditors?'

Dominic had seen the same show of fire in Atlanta when she had decried the d'Estainvilles. For the space of a heart-beat they were kindred spirits. She with fierce colour in her cheeks, eyes flashing; he quiet, questioning, waiting for her to realise that at that moment in time there was no difference between them. Waiting and watching, and at last seeing the dawning of realisation in her expression, an acceptance of his right to fight for what belonged to him, that was as great and as just as her own.

'I think we understand each other now, *ma belle*,' he said softly. It was a moment of truth for them both. Such a moment, he knew, might never happen again. 'You need help with Pinewood, I agree. Micah can take Gifford's place.'

He was matter-of-fact again, his mind already racing ahead to assess the problems.

'But—but—he's black,' Veroníque protested.

'He's competent. We ran the place in Havana together. By the way, he's a free man. I gave him the papers before we came home.'

'He's devoted to you, but he wasn't yours to set free. Father bought him from your mother, Dominic, and because he followed you when you left, he's a runaway slave.'

'He's a free man. The choice is yours. Micah as overseer—or run the place yourself.' He was unsympathetic towards her plight. The one moment when he might have weakened had passed.

'It isn't a choice. It's an ultimatum,' Veroníque cried bitterly.

'Why don't we ride over to Moonshadow together and take a good look at the place? You did offer me your company the other night, if you remember?'

'Very well. Give me a few minutes to change this filthy blouse and wash my face. Why don't you pick yourself out a horse? The chestnut might suit you.'

'Fine. No frills and silk though. I like you as you are.'

Veroníque could find no answer to that surprising statement. A compliment from a d'Estainville—whatever next? She sensed he was watching her as she walked back to the house, but when she reached the verandah and looked back, he was nowhere in sight.

'*Ma petite*, what has happened to you?' George came out of the library as she passed, and stared at her dishevelled appearance in horror.

'It's all right, Father. I'm not hurt. Gifford attacked me, but Dominic gave him a sound beating and sent him packing. He has promised Micah to work in his place. We will manage.' Veroníque went into his arms and kissed his lined cheeks. 'Promise me you won't worry.'

'Has Gifford gone?' George demanded harshly. Years ago he had hanged a slave who had only smiled at his wife.

'Yes.' Veroníque hugged him, tried to reassure him she was not hurt.

'I'll send Jacob out with the dogs just to make sure. Look at those marks on your wrists,' he said, and caught her hands in his, examining every tiny blemish on the white skin.

George had never been able to accept that Veroníque did not like to be treated as a fragile piece of china. Her mother had readily accepted it, often demanded it. Poor Veroníque! What she needed was a husband to remind her of the more important things in life. He had not seen her with a book in her hands for weeks. How she had loved to read!

'Dominic and I are riding over to Moonshadow,' she told him.

'Moonshadow!' George echoed. 'He told you, then?'

'Told me what? What have you been arranging with him?' Veroníque's face clouded with apprehension as she visualised all her well-laid plans disintegrating.

'I have offered the place to Dominic,' he said.

'So that's why he wants to go out there! He made me believe he was concerned for us. He doesn't change, does he? You can't let him have it! Paul needs it. You have practically accepted his offer.'

'He has no right to it.'

'Dominic forfeited all claims to it when he went away,' Véronique cried.

'He's back now. He's the last of the d'Estainvilles and it is his birthright. I never told you this before, but before Phillipe died, I made him a promise: at all costs I would return Moonshadow to Dominic. Why else do you think I bought it?'

'Phillipe should have found out where his son was. Written to him—asked him to come back. If he felt so strongly about the inheritance, whatever was between them should have been unimportant, even after the terrible thing he did.'

'You're wrong, you know. There could not have been peace between them. Phillipe lived in the shadow of his father, who despised him for allowing Elizabeth not only to trick him into marriage, but also flaunted her many affairs in their faces. The whole county knew she was unfaithful, and only Grandfather Luc's terrible threats of revenge could still the tongues which might have wagged. After he died, Phillipe shut himself away at Moonshadow and ignored them all. He had only one love left—his little quadroon, Sarah.'

'But Dominic,' Veroníque said, puzzled, 'was the apple of his father's eye. Phillipe loved him as much—as much as you loved mother—as much as you love me.'

'There was a time when I thought so too, but you see, Dominic was unfortunate enough to grow up in the image of Luc d'Estainville. I admit, the talk about his mother, and the knowledge that his father's coloured mistress was actually living in one of the cottages on the plantation, couldn't have helped to contain the d'Estainville wildness in him. Poor Phillipe! At times it must have been like looking at his own father.'

'Then why, at the last moment, did he do everything in his power to ensure Dominic inherited the house?'

'Because in the end, love for his son was stronger than the fear he had known for his father. Love is the driving force in many lives, *ma petite*.' George broke off, unable to find the courage to tell her that his last wish would be to see her married to the last of the d'Estainvilles. 'Dominic will be wondering where you are. Go and change quickly, now.'

Veroníque washed and changed into a fresh, dark-coloured blouse. As she was fastening it she caught sight of herself in the mirror, and paused to consider the slender figure there. The boyish attire accentuated every curve of her hips and breasts. Dominic was right, she admitted begrudgingly, no one would believe her capable of delegating authority. The knowledge was infuriating. She knew the plantation and its needs better than any overseer. If only she had been born a boy, or with Melissa's strength of character! No Negro ever dared question *her* orders.

It was still hard to forget the sight of her in that outrageous black dress, her arms locked about Dominic's neck. He never discussed their relationship. At least he was a gentleman in that respect, she thought as she tied back her hair with a piece of ribbon, and hurried out of the room.

Dominic was waiting by the stables. Her own horse had been saddled, and he had selected the chestnut as she suggested.

'When it comes to horseflesh, your judgment is impeccable,' he chuckled, seeing her quizzical look. 'Come on, I'll race you to the woods. That's if you're still as good a horsewoman as when I went away.'

'I'm better.' Veroníque took up the challenge without hesitation. In this at least, she could hold her own against any man.

He was ahead of her on the long-legged stallion as they reached the paddocks. Both horses went up and over, clearing the top bars with inches to spare. Veroníque checked her mount suddenly, veered behind him and then gave the filly its head as she raced towards a narrow opening in the tall pine trees. Dominic wheeled to follow, momentarily forfeiting the lead, but as they reached the woods they were once again level.

He saw her face, alight with pure enjoyment as she flattened herself over the back of her horse and became one with it. The ribbon came loose from her hair and the black cloud billowed out behind her in the wind.

The trees began to thin out as they sped towards the hill overlooking the other plantation. Dominic's horse faltered. For a moment he thought it had put its foot in a hole, then it recovered and galloped on, but in that brief moment Veroníque had surged ahead, using every ounce of skill she possessed to coax the maximum from her mount. When he came out into the open, she was reining in on the slopes of the hill.

'I reluctantly concede defeat.'

'Shall we call it a draw? I haven't enjoyed myself so much in years,' Veroníque offered breathlessly.

'Were you fathered by a wind spirit, *ma belle*? Why else are you carried to victory each time we race?'

'To teach the last of the d'Estainvilles humility perhaps?'

He was breathless too, laughing. It was the first time she had seen him so completely relaxed. Suddenly the old charm was working on her again, the easy grace with which he had stolen so many female hearts, and antagonised an equal number of male egos.

'You've called me *ma belle* several times since you came back. I used to hate it.'

'I've never called anyone else that,' Dominic answered quietly. She became aware of the laughter fading from his face. He dismounted and held out his arms to her.

She slid from her horse into them, her face upturned to his, and saw the dark eyes, narrowed against the brilliant sunshine, gleam suddenly. The next moment her soft mouth was crushed beneath his.

Since the day she had first realised she was in love with him, Veroníque had tried to imagine what it would be like to be kissed by Dominic d'Estainville. Nothing could have prepared her for the fire which swept through her body the moment his lips touched hers. It was the fulfilment of all her dreams. The other women who had passed through his life, including Melissa, no longer mattered to her. He had noticed her . . . perhaps in time . . .? Without warning she jerked her mouth free and pushed away his arms.

'No, Dominic . . .'

'So I am still the *bête noire* who offends *la belle princesse*.' There was an odd note in his voice as he stood looking at her.

'Now you are being hateful again.'

'It was your choice. I was quite happy kissing you.'

'The way you have kissed hundreds before me,' Veroníque retorted, a faint blush of colour mounting in her cheeks. It had been so wonderful. If only it had meant something for both of them, not her alone! 'You make love to any woman who takes your fancy, and they are forgotten directly afterwards. I won't be one of the nameless multitude, Dominic.'

'A pity! Your father would have liked us to get together.'

'Father?' She stared at him open-mouthed. 'He told me he wanted to give you Moonshadow. What didn't he tell me?'

'We must talk,' Dominic said curtly and turning on his heel strode off up the hill. She followed hesitantly, then dropped on the soft grass where he sat, and looked at him expectantly. 'George is willing to give me the place—as your dowry.'

He made no attempt to soften the blow. He wanted it to hit her as hard as possible so that she would fly at him in anger and erase the memory of the innocent he had held in his arms and wanted as no other woman in his life before. Instead those sapphire eyes widened and she looked at him as if he had taken leave of his senses.

'Marry—us! But he needs money desperately! He can't afford to give it to you.'

'Hell! He knows I'd deal with any creditors. Why not? I'd have all I want.' Damn the girl, why did she always think of others before herself? She had more sides to her than a diamond.

Veroníque sat back on her heels and her eyes lifted over his head to the top of the hill. From there they could look down on Moonshadow, the envy of every plantation owner in the county. Marry Dominic! The idea was too preposterous even to consider. Yet if he had loved her, offered one kind word, she might have been tempted.

'I don't suppose you'd consider the suggestion on a purely business level?' Dominic asked sarcastically. 'A marriage of convenience, I believe, is the correct term. I should get Moonshadow, and George would get his money.'

'And me, Dominic? What would I have?' For one mad moment she considered the idea, but then sanity reached out to grab at her fanciful dreams and crush them. To be his wife, but not share his bed. To bear his name, but not his children. To live in his fine house but as a stranger. All so that he could have Moonshadow, which he abandoned to others of his own free will in the first place.

'You would have a fine house, the biggest in Pinetree

County. The d'Estainville name . . .'

She interrupted him with a shrill laugh.

'Believe it or not, there is more to a marriage. I shall love the man I marry, Dominic. I don't want the kind of life my father had with Alice's mother. I never knew her, of course, but Alice once told me they never loved each other. He went to her only for the sake of children. How can two people make love, without love in them? It defiles something that should be pure and wonderful.'

Dominic, with a sigh, produced the silver flask she had seen on the train, but no answer to her question. How could he, who had made love to numerous women without loving one of them in the way she meant, explain hunger of the soul and body to someone who had never been touched by such basic instincts? He took a long drink and then held it out to her.

'You've just seen me drink to the only woman I've never been able to fool.'

Veroníque shook her head. He shrugged his shoulders and tucked the flask away in his shirt. Then he sprawled out full length, his hands clasped behind his head. The sun was behind her, framing her in brilliant yellow light, like some golden angel in a stained-glass window.

'You have never really tried,' Veroníque said at length.

'I wouldn't use you that way, *ma belle*. Even I draw the line at some things, so don't look so surprised.'

'There are times, Dominic d'Estainville, when you are a very nice person.'

'A real Southern gentleman. It does me no damned good at all.'

'I think I like you better now than when we were children. Is that because we are grown up, do you think? More tolerant of others; perhaps understanding them a little better?'

'I don't know. We are friends then, despite everything?'

She laughed softly. She looked even more lovely when the lines of tension were wiped from her young face.

'Friends? Oh, no. That would be far too dangerous. Sparring partners.' She was enjoying teasing him, as he used to tease her. Pleased he did not mind.

'We were always that. We could be friends, *ma belle*.'

'I am not Melissa,' she reminded him. 'I take my friendships seriously. Will you marry her?'

'Men like me make women like Melissa their mistresses, but we don't take them as wives.'

'You say some terrible things sometimes, do you know that?'

'The worth of a virtuous woman is above rubies.' Dominic quoted the words from the Book of Proverbs with all the solemnity of a lay-preacher. Then, his mood swiftly changing, he sat up, demanding, 'Where is Alice?'

The question had a more startling effect on Veroníque than his proposal of marriage. Her expression grew guarded and she deliberately avoided his direct gaze.

'Why are you so interested in my sister?'

'Because at the moment I am installed in her room, am I not? Yet there is nothing there to show it ever belonged to her, or in fact, that she even lived in the house. There's not one picture of her in the drawing-room, the library or the study, where I know George used to keep several. Why?'

'She has—married—and gone away. Her name is not allowed to be mentioned in front of Father.'

'What on earth did little mouse do to earn such enmity?'

'She married—a seaman. A dreadful, rough man, over two years ago now. Father completely disowned her. She lives in Savannah, so I believe. She wrote to us only once, but Father burned the letter before I could get hold of it.' Veroníque told the lies with the coolness of an accomplished professional. If he knew the truth he might also realise why she so desperately wanted Paul to have Moonshadow, and that did not fit in with her plans.

He accepted the explanation without comment and did not believe a single word.

They rode down to Moonshadow, past deserted fields where the red soil waited patiently for the plough, hungry for the new cotton seeds it would nurture and cherish until it was time to push them forth into the warm Georgia sun.

Veroníque watched Dominic's face become an expressionless mask as they continued towards the house. He looked at her, silently demanding an explanation, and haltingly she told him that as his money dwindled, her father had sold the slaves from Moonshadow, leaving between fifteen and twenty to keep up the grounds, not even enough to clear one field in time for the spring planting.

'He told me this morning he had made a promise to your father, Dominic, that no matter what it cost him, Moonshadow would revert to you,' Veroníque said. She tried to keep the bitterness out of her voice, but it crept back and he looked at her sharply.

'You don't approve?'

'He said it is your right. I don't agree. Right has to be earned, like respect.' She ignored the tightening of his mouth. That mouth which had so gently kissed hers was now a forbidding line. Yet still she stood her ground.

'We are penniless. If you were any kind of a man you would be fair with Father, let him sell to Paul, save his face and our home.' Her moods could change as swiftly as his. All the love she had felt for him such a short while ago vanished with this new confrontation. 'My father is dying. Have you no heart?'

'If I were any man at all I would take you to task over your choice of words,' Dominic said coldly. 'If you don't shut up I might just pull you off that horse and show you how much of a man I am; more than you've ever had to deal with before, that's certain.'

The threat quietened Veroníque. She allowed her horse to slow its pace until he was in front of her as they rode down the cedar-lined driveway, where the air was heavy with the perfume of wild honeysuckle.

Dominic was aware of every muscle in his body growing taut. There it was, framed against a background of pines and sweet-smelling magnolia trees, wisteria still climbing the white-washed walls. It was a six-columned house of the old Colonial style, two stories high with large bay windows looking out over the enormous lawn. In his grandfather's time he would have been greeted by a crowd of servants, the kitchen boys, housekeeper, maids, butler, stable lads, all rushing to welcome him back. Grandfather Luc would have been sitting in his favourite rocking chair on the verandah, probably yelling at a bright-eyed little darkie boy chasing chickens across the yard.

All was silent now. Silent, but full of memories that came crowding in on him until he felt beads of sweat trickle down the back of his neck. With something that sounded very like a groan to Veroníque, he slid from his horse and moved, like a sleepwalker, towards the front door.

As he reached the steps, the door opened. Veroníque caught her breath, half-expecting to see the ghost of Grandfather Luc waiting to welcome him, but she saw instead Micah, beaming unashamedly at the approaching man, heard him say quite clearly: 'Welcome home, Mister Dominic.'

'How did you get here?' Dominic asked in surprise.

Looking past him through the open door he saw his trunks piled in the mirrored entrance hall.

'I came over in the rig, Mister Dominic. Mister George sent me with your things. He thought you would prefer to stay here, seeing as you have decided to help him run the place. By tomorrow the old house could be quite habitable again.'

Veroníque froze. Once Dominic was reinstalled in Moonshadow, nothing short of an earthquake would move him.

'Well, I'll be damned,' Dominic chuckled. 'The old fox! He really was serious after all.'

He sounded amused, but there was no laughter in his expression. He was being pushed towards an abyss he had deliberately gone out of his way to avoid, yet with every one step he took back, circumstances pushed him three closer. If he didn't watch out he would not only end up with Moonshadow, but with Veroníque too!

He turned slowly and looked at her and saw her flinch. It was as if she sensed it too, the inevitable return of a d'Estainville to Moonshadow no matter how fiercely anyone fought to prevent it. Triumph blazed out of his eyes bringing her back to her senses. Without a word, she turned her horse around and rode away from him.

CHAPTER FOUR

It was past midday when Dominic returned to Pinewood. As he walked from the stables towards the house, he could see a carriage in the driveway and Jacob loading it with cases, aided by several small boys. He remembered that Melissa and Paul were leaving before lunch.

He had gone through Moonshadow, ripping off covers, opening shutters and windows, allowing fresh air and sunlight into the cold, darkened rooms, and starting a fire in the huge chasm of a fireplace in the drawing-room. The moment he did that it was as if the house came alive again, and welcomed him.

He knew he would never be able to put into words what he felt as he stood with his back to the flames and allowed his gaze to wander over familiar objects; the high, button-backed chair beside him where Grandfather Luc always used to sit. In one corner stood a rosewood piano, brought from France, a present from him to his parents on their sixteenth wedding anniversary. It had rarely been played. Beneath the window was a long velvet chaise-longue where his mother used to sit and sew. The memories lingered still.

There was only one d'Estainville now, and he suddenly found himself wondering what he would feel like in this house, with a wife, and a child playing at his feet. An unknown hunger gnawed at his stomach. It was not difficult to imagine Veronîque as mistress of Moonshadow. She had qualities his mother had never possessed, like patience, charm and pride. Old Grandfather Luc would have approved of those things, and of her too.

'Come and have a drink,' George said quietly from the direction of the library, as Dominic drew level with the open door.

'When Veronîque came back she was in tears.' Dominic stood with his back against the door watching his companion pour out a large Bourbon. George gave it to him with a curious look. 'You told her of my offer, then. I thought the idea did not appeal to you.'

'Isn't that why you sent Micah to the house with my things? To persuade me?' Dominic returned harshly. 'Damn you!'

'Persuade you—is that possible?'

'You know how much I love that place. You decided to kill two birds with one stone, didn't you, *mon vieux*? Keep your promise to my father and find a husband for Veroníque. You made an unfortunate choice selecting me.'

'Don't try to make excuses for not wanting to get married. I am interested only in Veroníque's happiness, someone to protect her when I am gone. You have ambition and drive like your grandfather. It would be a pity if the d'Estainville line died out with you.'

'You fight dirty,' Dominic snapped, tight-lipped. That very thought had been uppermost in his mind since seeing Moonshadow again.

'I use whatever ammunition is at my disposal, especially when there is a fifty-fifty chance of me losing the battle. What is it, Dominic? Is there someone else? In Havana, perhaps?'

'No.' Dominic poured himself another drink, swallowing it more slowly this time. With surprise mounting inside him, he watched George also refill his glass with sherry. Noticed too, that the decanter which had been full when he left the house was now almost empty. 'You don't usually drink this early in the day.'

'Does it matter? Does anything matter any more?'

'Veroníque?'

'Yes, only her. She must never have cause to associate with men like Gifford again, Dominic. She is a lady, like her mother. I was about to send her off to France when the war began. She flatly refused to leave me alone here to be murdered in my bed by blue-coated Yankees, as she put it.'

'She hates my guts,' Dominic said crudely. 'It won't work.'

'It is something I must have settled,' George insisted, 'before she takes it into her head to do something silly, like marrying the Loring boy. You know how close she has always been to Paul. They share the same interests. Only you have ever roused her spirit, the fire her beloved mother possessed. For the sake of what I have done for you, Dominic, let me die in peace. Take her, please. Why is it too much to ask?'

'You know why,' Dominic said, in a tone heavy with apprehension.

'Because of that stupid lie your mother put about to spite her husband? God, man, no one ever believed that.'

'My father's mistress was a quadroon. He spent more time with her than with my mother. You and I both know the story was a lie, but the mud still clings, George. There are those who still believe what she said, that I am Sarah's son, not hers. I don't give a damn for other people, I never have, but think, for heaven's sake! How would Veroníque stand life with me, with that accusation hanging over our marriage.

'I have never believed the story either. It was your mother's hope, I'm sure, that Sarah would be sent away. Your father loved Sarah too much however. Veroníque is no fool, Dominic. It made no difference to her when you were children, did it? Think! Everything you have been forced to deny yourself over the years can belong to you again.

'I am offering you your rightful inheritance and a beautiful woman to share it with you, give you fine sons to carry on your name. You over-exaggerate. What that she-devil Elizabeth told everyone is sure to be forgotten by now. Can you afford not to accept this chance? What will the years ahead hold for you without the thing you love most? I wish I'd had a son,' George sighed, 'but it was God's wish that I had two girls, and one of them destined to bring disgrace to my name.'

'I am no credit to my father,' Dominic said heavily.

'No? To your grandfather then. He was an old devil, but my God, he knew how to enjoy life. Your father never did learn, not even with Sarah's expert instruction.'

'Damn you,' Dominic swore. 'You'll surely go to hell for this. We both will.'

'You have my offer. You know the price. I want an answer.'

'Veroníque will never agree!'

Goddammit—no! With the last of his will-power Dominic fought against acceptance. If only he had not returned to Moonshadow and stood there alone, master of all he surveyed. If only he had not held Veroníque in his arms and been stirred by her loveliness, her innocence. George was swaying slightly as he topped up their glasses. He was beginning to feel the effects of what he had already consumed. Even Dominic could feel the fire of the whisky burning deep inside him.

'To my daughter and future son-in-law. I shall leave this earth a happy man, and the sooner the better. This waiting grows tedious,' George said, an unfathomable smile on his face.

When Jacob knocked on the door an hour later to tell them Paul and Melissa were leaving, he found both men still drinking steadily. By that time George could scarcely walk in a straight line.

Veroníque came downstairs as he reeled across the hallway towards their departing guests. She had changed out of her riding-habit into a plain blue cotton dress and Tante Michelle had soothed her agitation and bathed her forehead with ice-cold rosewater.

'How could you? You know he isn't supposed to touch alcohol,' she said in a low, fierce whisper as she reached Dominic's side.

'Let him enjoy what little time he has left.'

'What have you been talking about?'

'What do you think?'

A few feet away Melissa gave a surprised exclamation and Veroníque turned, an icy hand clutching at her heart. She saw that her father was smiling. Paul looked startled—then he stepped forward, extending his hand towards Dominic.

'You always were a dark horse. Congratulations to you both. You are a very lucky man, Dominic.'

'Father,' Veroníque began, then words failed her. She allowed Paul to kiss her affectionately on both cheeks, heard Melissa offer her congratulations in a honey-sweet tone, and knew full well that she did not mean a word of it. She watched Paul and her father walk out to the waiting carriage, and then lifted her eyes to Dominic's face.

'I did ask you this morning,' Dominic reminded her.

'But—you didn't mean it.' She did not want to remember that wonderful moment on the hill.

'I made you a serious proposal. You chose to refuse it.' It was on the tip of his tongue to confess that he had meant what he said then, but the coldness of her expression deterred him. Let her think what she wanted.

'A marriage of convenience you called it. Convenient for you—and only you,' Veronique returned.

'My dear, you look positively stupefied,' Melissa murmured. 'Am I to understand you don't want to marry Dominic and live in that lovely house? You'll be the envy of every woman for miles.'

'The most talked-about, don't you mean?' Veronique came back scathingly. 'The woman Dominic d'Estainville was forced to marry because it was the only way he could get his home back! What a fine trio we make. The last of the d'Estainvilles, his unwanted future wife, and his mistress.'

Melissa's laughter echoed around the hall.

'At least you will know where he is, my dear.'

'That's enough,' Dominic snapped. 'If you have anything else to say, Veronique, I suggest it is said to me—in private.'

'I am the key to Moonshadow, and now you have me . . . for all the good it will do you.' Veronique's contemptuous tone lashed him unmercifully. 'There is nothing more to be said, is there? Goodbye, Melissa. I hope you have a safe journey home. Dominic will see you to the carriage. I have work to do.'

With that she picked up her hooped skirts and walked away towards the kitchen, her face an expressionless mask. As proud as a d'Estainville, Dominic thought.

Dominic returned to live at Moonshadow the following day. Veronique did not appear to say goodbye.

The next two weeks he spent buying slaves and equipment, sufficient of both to begin ploughing the fields immediately. The weather was good, so he gambled and began early. He knew George wanted him to go to Atlanta and have the change of ownership papers drawn up and legalised by the family lawyer, but although he was as anxious to get it over with, he stubbornly refused to leave until his work had begun in earnest.

He had the old cottage, where Sarah had lived, levelled to the ground. The sight of the ruin had been too painful. He stood beside Micah watching it crumble. Both men had their own thoughts. Neither spoke. Afterwards Dominic got on his horse and rode away towards the Folly and did not return until well after midnight.

It had been Dominic's intention to take Veroníque to Atlanta with him to try and ease the frosty atmosphere which existed between them, but when he arrived at Pinewood to collect her, he found that George was confined to bed with a heavy cold and she refused to leave him.

He would ask Paul to go with him instead, he decided. It would give him an opportunity to find out exactly how close he was to Veroníque.

Dominic had only seen her once or twice since he went home, and on each occasion she was aloof and distant.

She had made it quite plain she had no interest in any of the wedding arrangements. She would not allow any invitations to be sent out, insisting that she wanted only Paul and Melissa as witnesses at the ceremony, and she refused to look at the beautiful negligée and nightdress Michelle had made for her, using watered silk from an old ball gown. All the lovely things she had collected over the years, as most unmarried girls do, were packed in an oak settle at the bottom of her bed, untouched.

For days she had cried herself to sleep. She no longer did that. What was the use? Dominic would marry her as surely as he had regained Moonshadow and there was not a thing she could do about it, except show her contempt for the mean, underhand way he had gone about it. She had convinced herself that it had been his intention to go through with the marriage from the very beginning, even when he had first held her in his arms and made her want to tell him of her love.

'I want you to have this,' Dominic said.

She looked at the ring lying in the palm of his outstretched hand and did not move, even when he stepped closer and took her left hand and slipped it on to the appropriate finger. Coldly she looked down at the initials *V.E.*, emblazoned in emeralds and diamonds in the gold mount. Veroníque d'Estainville!

'I can't take it,' she cried and tried to pull it off, but it was too tight and Dominic's hand was over hers, warning her not to try again. 'How can you spend money so extravagantly when the South needs every dollar?'

'You don't like it?' He looked taken aback, as if the idea had not entered his head.

'I—I—it's lovely.' She could not say otherwise, although she desperately wanted to, 'but . . .'

'My grandfather brought it with him from the old country. It belonged to his mother. It's purely coincidence that the initials are yours. I think it's rather a nice touch.'

'Very well, Dominic, as it has been in your family for so many years I will accept it. Thank you.'

'Will you tell your father I'll call here on the way home with the documents he wants, and that I'll arrange for the minister to be here on the nineteenth of next month?'

He saw the colour begin to fade from her cheeks, but could not bring himself to speak kindly to her. It was best that she knew where she stood from the start. He did not have Paul's patience—or George's plausible tongue.

'Could—couldn't we think about a later date?' Veroníque protested. 'It's too soon. Such a short engagement is positively indecent. It's not as if you are rushing away to fight. People will think . . .' she broke off, realising fully for the first time what would be thought of her marrying a man of Dominic's reputation in such haste. They would think she had been seduced!

'As this is a time of war, and the future for everyone is very uncertain, they will simply think we want to be together,' Dominic returned coldly, recognising her train of thought. 'Should anyone say otherwise, I'll call them out. Goodbye, *ma belle*. I'll see you in a few days.'

Paul and Dominic stayed at the house of George de Brissac on Washington Street, which Paul announced he would be buying in the near future. It was his intention to remain in Atlanta if the Yankees arrived, and keep a chronicle of daily events. The enemy forces were only thirty-five miles from the city itself and people no longer deluded themselves that there was a Southern general alive who could hold them back.

Since the beginning of May the Confederate army had retreated sixty-five miles, most of the time in heavy rain which turned the countryside into a quagmire of thick, red mud. No one who watched the wounded and sick being brought back to Atlanta held out any hope that the greatly reduced Southern forces, in desperate need of rest, decent clothing, food and fresh stocks of ammunition, could do anything but fall back to Atlanta and dig in.

That evening, all business transactions successfully completed, Dominic and Paul went on a tour of the waterfront area, visiting places they had often frequented as students.

'You,' said Paul Loring, who was very drunk by the time they arrived at the third bar, 'are a right bastard. Here you are about to be married to the prettiest girl in the county, and you're ogling that brassy-haired wench by the bar.'

'It takes one to know one,' Dominic returned good-humouredly. 'You haven't taken your eyes off her either since we came in.'

He pushed the bottle across the table. Paul attempted to refill his glass, failed miserably and ended up with most of it on the dirty pitted surface. He glared at Dominic, who accomplished the feat without spilling a drop.

'I'm going to tell you a secret.'

'No secrets. Share a secret and you lose a friend. I don't have that many I can afford to lose one.'

'You're still sober,' Paul accused.

When he had first been wounded and had been carried into one of the foul-smelling hospital tents, his left arm shattered and useless, the doctor had ordered him to be given whisky to deaden the pain of the amputation which was to follow, for all anaesthetics had been used up long ago. He had recovered from his drunken stupor on a cold stone floor, with only a thin blanket covering his shocked body. The pain had been unbearable. An orderly, unable to stand his screams at night, had found him a bottle of whisky which he proceeded to drink like a madman. Since then, whenever the stump became painful—and it was strange how that arm could hurt when there was no arm there—or his sleep was plagued by nightmares of that horror that had been Chickamauga, Paul had sought solace in a bottle. He had been drunk for two weeks since returning to the Folly, shut away in his room alone, needing nothing but the oblivion—the peace he could get from raw liquor.

He looked into the tanned features opposite and grinned stupidly.

'Get drunk, damn you. Like me. It's the one thing I've learned to do well.'

'If this is what you intend to do in Atlanta you won't be in any condition to write a single word,' Dominic returned.

He was beginning to feel good. A little drunk, and enjoying it. The deeds of Moonshadow, signed, witnessed and duly sealed, were safe back at the house. The years of waiting were over. Even Veroníque was no longer a problem. At least at that moment he didn't consider her one, because he told himself—and with the best part of a bottle of Bourbon inside him, actually believed—that they could live two separate lives at Moonshadow. He would use whatever money was necessary to settle George's debts so that the old man could die in peace, and she could go on running Pinewood if it was that important to her. Perhaps it might even prove a bond between them.

'You're right,' he agreed, in a tone so low he could have been talking to himself. 'I am a bastard. Shall we stay here, or go on? Those two in the corner are beginning to get definite ideas about us. I don't know about you, but I'd prefer to spend the next couple of hours with a bottle.'

'God, my arm hurts,' Paul said. 'Let's have another bottle, Dominic. I need to talk and you're the only person who will understand. I'm as much a bastard as you. Do you know that? I've turned my back on the girl I loved—deserted her . . .'

'Veroníque? So I was right in thinking you two had become more than just bookworms together?'

'No—not her.' Paul looked at him almost angrily. 'Alice.'

'You *are* drunk. Why don't you admit you would have married Veroníque if I hadn't come back?'

'She's like a kid sister to me—as Melissa used to be. She meddles too much in my affairs, bless her soft little heart, but she means well. God, when I think of what I have done . . . to her . . . to Alice . . .'

Dominic decided it was better to humour him in his present condition, rather than to try and reason with him.

A fresh bottle was brought across on his signal by a blonde-haired girl. Thick powder and rouge plastered over her cheeks diminished the not-unattractive face and made her age impossible to determine. Somewhere around eighteen or nineteen, Dominic guessed. The sweetheart of a soldier who had not come back—or a wife grown tired of waiting. There were too many of both in Atlanta that May.

'She reminds me of someone,' Paul said as the girl moved away. 'Of little mouse . . .'

'Alice? Good God, man, has the smoke in here affected your eyes? That little tramp looks nothing like her!'

'Not the hair, or the face, but the eyes. That terrible look of—rejection . . .'

Paul cupped his chin in one hand and stared across the table, oblivious to the fight which had just started up behind his chair.

'I let her down, you know, Alice. She needed me . . . I let her down. . . . She had a child, do you know that? She tried to tell me it was mine. I really loved her, Dominic, but I can't remember. God, I can't remember. I'd have married her, cared for the child, but she kept insisting it was mine . . . and I don't know . . .'

'Alice was never a liar.'

'She would never let me touch her, so how could I have fathered her child? She had to hear the sound of wedding bells before I was allowed to kiss her. All that pretence, while there was someone else in the background. She came to me in the end though, didn't she? All sweet and doey-eyed, pretending to be the injured party. Still waters run deep. . . .'

His voice trailed off into incoherent mutterings. He picked up his glass and stared at it, before deliberately tipping the contents on to the floor.

'What about Veroníque?' Dominic suggested quietly. 'Surely she knew the truth.'

'She's convinced the child is mine because Alice says so. What does she know? Ever since I lost this arm she's been on at me to buy Moonshadow and settle down—even think of marriage. Don't you see what she's after? Damn her meddling! She wants Alice and me together. She almost had it, too, before you came back . . .'

'You would be fathering another man's child,' Dominic replied, leaning back in his chair to light a fresh cheroot.

His eyes issued a challenge. 'It's been done before—and successfully.'

'No Moonshadow, no child, no Alice. What the hell have I got to offer her, even if I knew where she was?'

'Let's move on,' Dominic suggested. 'The air in here stinks.'

'I'll take you somewhere special.' Paul reeled towards the door and out into the fine rain which had been falling all day. Dominic followed, and they leaned against the side of the wall for a moment, enjoying the fresh, clean air. The rain was cool in their faces and Paul was momentarily revived. He glanced around and then waved a hand in the direction of a side street. 'Down there. I know a place, clean and comfortable, and it has the most accommodating girls in Atlanta. The woman who runs them provides the best money can buy.'

'I think you would be better sleeping alone tonight,' Dominic chuckled. 'I'm starting back early in the morning.'

'First we must pay a visit to Madame Elizabeth,' Paul urged.

In the half-light of the street lamp Dominic's mouth grew suddenly taut as a thousand ghosts leapt out at him from the shadows.

'Elizabeth?' he repeated slowly. Coincidence—it had to be. She was long gone from this part of the country with money George had provided. By now she would have snared some rich fool to provide for her needs. She had no reason to stay. Reason enough! With Phillipe dead she had total freedom at last, and enough hate in her to want to drag the d'Estainville name into the slime of the gutters after her. 'No,' Dominic said in a fierce whisper. 'Tell me I'm wrong, Paul.'

He knew the answer before Paul spoke, and the knowledge settled over him like a cold, enveloping blanket of fog, blinding, choking, pushing him relentlessly towards yet another deadly precipice.

'You're about to be married, Dominic. Can't the two of you make it up? Forget the past. After all, she is your mother . . .'

CHAPTER FIVE

THE house Paul stopped outside was in a narrow side-street. A single light over the door guided the two men through the mists drifting around the rows of warehouses which led to the waterfront. It was a part of Atlanta where the poorer folk lived in hovels not fit for a dog and thought themselves lucky to have a roof over their heads. Where soldiers, back from the fighting, sought to forget the horrors they had seen with women and drink, and Southern gentlemen sought refuge from their frigid wives and a standard of living they could no longer maintain.

It was the kind of place she would choose, Dominic thought, looking at the paint peeling off the door. Squalor—the exact opposite of everything she had known at Moonshadow. But as Paul pushed open the door and they stepped inside, he was surprised to find he had been totally wrong.

They stood in a small, thickly carpeted hallway, surrounded by mirrored panels. Like Moonshadow, Dominic realised, and cursed the woman who dared install such an insult to his home. The paintwork was a pale neutral colour, the lighting subdued. It gave the impression that they were about to step over the threshold into some comfortable family parlour. A door opened in front of them. A heavily built man stood there, a Negro woman beside him.

'You gentlemen looking for anything in particular?' the man asked.

He scarcely looked at Paul; his attention was centred on Dominic, studying his face, the cut of his clothes, especially the silk shirt and cravat. In a time when the appearance of even the most wealthy men had begun to show some sign of wear and tear, here stood a man who could obviously pay his way without worry. As a prospective customer, Dominic saw he was acceptable.

'My friend and I are in need of a little relaxation,' he drawled. He was aware of the big man stiffening as he reached into his pocket and noticed the bulge in his coat pocket. Madame Elizabeth's bouncer, no doubt. She might have need of him later on. There was a smile on his face as he spun a twenty-dollar gold piece into the oustretched hand of the Negress. Only Paul knew that lazy smile meant trouble. 'I think that should cover our entrance fee.'

'Lisette will show you to a room, gentlemen.'

The bouncer moved aside and they passed through the door and up a flight of stairs to a room on the first floor.

Throughout, the house looked well maintained and that surprised Dominic. So, even at gutter level she still liked her comfort, did she?

'Tell Madame I wish to see her,' Dominic ordered. The Negro woman turned in the doorway and looked at him in surprise.

'Madame 'Lisbet don't see customers, mister. You tell Lisette what you want—blonde—redhead—I fetch. The best in the house for you gentlemen.'

'She'll see me. Tell her I'm a rich eccentric recently returned from—Havana, and before I look at any girls she has to offer, I want to make sure there is no sickness in this place. Here, take this for your trouble.'

The woman pocketed the gold piece he slipped into her hand with a knowing grin. After such a handsome bribe she cared little that he might be telling the truth.

'I—am drunk,' Paul murmured, falling into the nearest chair.

Although well-worn, most of the furniture was comfortable and the bed looked clean. Such luxuries in a house of this kind would cost the customer dear, Dominic thought as he leaned against the wall behind the door. Unfastening his coat, he reassured himself his knife was still within easy reach. Tonight, strapped to his left forearm, he also wore another legacy from his Grandfather Luc, a slim, deadly stiletto made in Italy, so small as to fit beneath his tailored coat without a tell-tale sign of its presence.

He heard the sharp staccato of a woman's heels on the wooden floor, looked through the crack in the door as it opened, to satisfy himself she was alone, then kicked it shut after her. In the silence which ensued he took his first good look at Elizabeth d'Estainville in three long years.

The woman who faced him was in her late forties, yet beneath the severely cut gown she wore, the lines of the plain colour broken only by a white scarf at her throat, she retained the figure of a girl of twenty. She had always been proud of her figure, Dominic remembered, but by God she was ageing now, and it could not be concealed by the skilful application of rouge and powder. Her hair was dyed, too—darker than its original colour.

'So! You are the man from Havana. I should have guessed.' Elizabeth looked slightly amused by the attempt to deceive her. Dominic stepped in front of the door, barring her retreat. 'That won't be necessary, I'm not staying, and nor are you.'

Her coolness threw him off balance for a moment, then his face hardened as he prepared for battle.

'You and I have things to discuss.'

'We have nothing to discuss, now or ever. I have only to raise my voice and there will be two very unpleasant men in here to deal with you—and your drunken friend.'

'And they will both be dead before they touch me,' Dominic warned, and his cold gaze narrowed. 'I'm not above killing you either. I've thought about it often.'

'Why have you come back?'

He had the satisfaction of seeing her begin to grow uncomfortable. She had seen his temper unleashed before and he guessed she would not risk it again. From the chair Paul watched them in silence. He was having difficulty in staying awake and wishing he had taken Dominic's advice and gone straight back to the house.

'Well?' Elizabeth demanded harshly. 'What do you want here?'

'Answers to my questions. What happened to Sarah after I left?' The enquiries both he and George had made had proved fruitless.

'How in heaven should I know? I hope she's rotting in hell.'

'If she is, then you may be joining her sooner than you anticipate,' Dominic returned. 'She wasn't caught, then? Veroníque said you had gone after Micah and then burnt her cottage when you found he had run off. Poor Mother! So in the end your revenge was spoilt, wasn't it? No

Micah—no Sarah—no son to take out your spite on.'

'Don't call me that—you're no son of mine. You belong to her, to that coloured bitch.'

'Don't bore me with that old lie again. You ask why I came? To see how you looked in your natural surroundings. Grandfather Luc was right. You're a whore. *Una puta*! And where you belong at last, in *una casa de putas*.' Dominic spat the insulting Spanish words at her contemptuously and she flinched visibly.

'Get out.' Elizabeth flung a shaking hand towards the door. 'Out, or I'll have my boys throw you into the gutter. A truly royal place for the last of the d'Estainvilles. Your one-armed friend won't be able to help you. Look at him—asleep. He always was a timid fool.'

'I won't need any help and if you raise your voice one semitone higher, I'll put a bruise on your face that'll keep you indoors for a month. You know I'll do it, too. A pity my father didn't beat you occasionally, it might have kept you in line. It wasn't him I should have whipped that day, but you. You look afraid. Do I frighten you? Do I sound like Grandfather Luc as well? The old man taught me good. I can hear him laughing in his boots right now—looking at you and knowing you're finished. Looking at me and seeing a new future for the d'Estainville line.'

'You—you are married?' The implication behind his words rocked Elizabeth on her feet.

'I soon shall be—to Veroníque de Brissac. I'm sure you remember her. Don't worry, I'm not here to collect congratulations. I wanted you to know I'm back, not only in Georgia, but in Moonshadow too. You've failed all around, haven't you? You wanted to destroy everything Grandfather Luc built. Father knew that; knew that even though he'd left the place to me in his will, it wouldn't be safe. You thought when you sold it to George it had passed into other hands for good. Well, you were wrong. He promised Father that Moonshadow would stay in the d'Estainville family. He bought it to keep in trust for me until I came home. Even in death father beat you. Nothing mattered to him, not even the fact I tried to kill him. Nothing, so long as a d'Estainville rules Moonshadow.' In the light of the oil lamps Dominic's expression mocked the silent woman before him. 'I'm home now and I'm about to take a wife. My children will live there, and their children. All d'Estainvilles . . .'

Elizabeth suddenly drew herself up and said in a malicious tone:

'What is your little bride going to say when people begin to whisper in her ear, shun her, because she's your wife?' An unpleasant smile masked her features. 'I'm going to drag you down into the gutter with me and enjoy it.'

Dominic's fingers were suddenly entwining themselves in the thin silk scarf she wore. Before she had time to cry out, he had tightened it around her throat. Her eyes bulged with pain and horror. Long nails sank into the back of his hands, but only served to make him increase the pressure.

'No—Dominic—I—I didn't mean—it.'

'Don't be afraid, I'm not going to kill you. This is simply a warning. If you breathe that damned lie again to anyone—anyone, do you hear? I'll come back and finish the job, and there will be a dozen witnesses to testify I was miles away at the time of your death. Do I make myself clear?'

Elizabeth nodded vigorously. She had no breath to speak. He flung her away from him across the bed where she lay whimpering as she loosened the scarf from her neck.

Dominic bent over Paul and shook him into wakefulness. A pair of sleepy, bloodshot eyes looked at him reproachfully.

'You were wrong about this place, you know. It's one of the worst places I've ever been in. Come on—I'll carry you.'

'The hell you will. I've lost an arm, not a leg,' Paul returned ungraciously.

He tottered towards the door, unaware of the woman on the bed, and out into the hall. Dominic paused to look back, for the last time he hoped, into the face of Elizabeth d'Estainville. The naked hatred in her expression as she glared across the room at him had a more sobering effect that the cool touch of the rain. She would do anything to drag him down to her level, despite his threat.

He expected her to call for help the moment he followed Paul, but all remained quiet behind him. Collecting his companion from the bottom of the stairs where he was clinging perilously to the bannister rail, Dominic opened the door and the two of them went out into heavy rain.

Elizabeth got up as she heard the sound of the front door closing noisily. With hands that trembled she rearranged the silk at her throat. Dominic's fingers had been like iron on her windpipe. For that he would pay, and for his insults, and for daring to come back and install himself in Moonshadow as if nothing had happened. George de Brissac had tricked her. Men—they were all alike! She would not forget him either. So Dominic thought he had won—that she was finished! Well, she would soon show him differently.

She went to her own room at the top of the house and summoned two of her most experienced employees. One was the man Dominic had already met, the other was a thin, small man of dubious descent who had brought three young women to Elizabeth one night and spent most of the week in her bed.

As the wife of Phillipe d'Estainville, for ever under the watchful gaze of Grandfather Luc, Elizabeth had been forced to curb her natural desires and submit to her husband whenever the occasion suited him. Look pretty, but not pretty enough to catch the eye of another man. Be a good hostess and mother, but at all times remember who she was!

It was an existence which almost drove Elizabeth mad. Not until the old man died and Sarah came to her husband's notice, did she have any freedom.

Sarah ruled Moonshadow. Sarah cared for Phillipe, ministering to his every need, with the tender care and love Elizabeth denied him. A hate began to fester within her. It grew quickly, consuming her like a raging fire until the only thought in her mind was to destroy the husband who had abandoned her for the arms of a coloured wench.

She sat back in the chintz-covered chair in her sitting-room and sipped at the glass of sherry Henri Dolman had given her. The two men stood silently waiting to hear why they had been summoned. She kept them waiting, enjoying the power of that moment, savouring every last second of it.

'The man who has just left here, together with the one-armed drunk. You saw them, Pearson?'

'Yes, Madame.' It was the heavy-set man who answered,

addressing her as everyone did in the house, simply as Madame.

'I'm not interested in the cripple. The other one—annoyed me. I want him taught a lesson.'

'Is that all?' He did not question his orders. This would not be the first time he had maimed or killed for her. She paid well and he had his pick of the girls whenever he chose. It was sufficient for a man of his somewhat limited requirements.

Elizabeth nodded, dismissed them with a wave of her hand, and went into her bedroom. She looked into the lined face of the woman standing by the bed.

'Did you see him when he came in?'

'Yes.'

'Good. I was hoping you did. He didn't see you, though, did he? Wouldn't have recognised you if he had. You're as fat and ugly as an old sow, and I laugh every time I see you. Look at yourself in the mirror . . .'

When the woman did not move Elizabeth grabbed her by the arm and thrust her in front of the wall mirror. She stared hard at the implacable reflection watching her.

The years had not been kind. The softly tanned face which had first caught the eyes of Phillipe d'Estainville had been hardened by fear, poverty, degradation beyond the comprehension of most decent people. The slender figure he had adorned with dresses of the finest watered silk had long since lost its appeal, except to the men Elizabeth carefully selected and paid to commit the final humiliation upon the body of the woman who had taken her place. One hand hanging loosely by the side of the cotton skirt was horribly scarred and deformed, the result of a savage attack by one of the hounds unleashed on her on the personal order of Elizabeth d'Estainville.

'Shall I prepare Madame's bath?' Sarah asked, shutting her eyes against the distortion confronting her.

This was not the first time Elizabeth had forced her before a mirror to taunt and humiliate her, never knowing that the words fell on deaf ears, and the reflection in the glass was not of a tired, abused woman of colour, but of a girl of twenty in a pale green dress of the finest silk. In her arms she held a child and at her side was a man who looked at her with love in his eyes—who bent to kiss her cheek and whisper, 'How is my son today?'

Not once, since the first day Sarah had knocked on the door of 17 Pelican Street, penniless, half-dead from hunger and weakened by a brutal beating from a white man who had dragged her into an alley the night before, had Sarah betrayed one iota of expression before this woman. She had tried to run away when she recognised the face and realised the cruel blow fate had struck, but had been dragged back to live—no, not to live, to exist—in the service of Madame Elizabeth. She fetched and carried, performed the menial tasks of the lowest servant, aware she was now the object of revenge for the woman she had usurped. No job was too dirty, or humiliating. She did them all without protest, knowing she would be beaten if she refused.

Had Elizabeth ever known the vivid threats whispered to the dark night sky and diamond bright stars, the sharpened bread knife beneath a loose floor board in Sarah's tiny attic bedroom, caressed with the same intense feeling a child had once been caressed, she might not have felt so secure.

By the time they reached the corner of the street, Dominic was half-carrying Paul who had decided to give passers-by a rendition of poetry. As Dominic's knowledge of *The Ancient Mariner* was strictly limited to the first line, he was unable to join in. Besides, he was too interested in keeping a wary eye on the two men who had been following them since they left the house of Madame Elizabeth.

He had been right not to trust her! The heavy rain was turning the narrow road into a river of mud, hindering their already unsteady progress. By now Dominic was stone cold sober, soaked to the skin and dangerously angry. Sensing danger, he risked a glance over his shoulder and found the men were almost upon them. Paul gave a startled exclamation as he was pushed unceremoniously away from his companion against a wall. He flung out his arm in an attempt to steady himself and slithered to the ground in several inches of slimy rubbish.

Dominic had a vague impression of a huge shape bearing down on him, and recognised the bouncer before he was borne backwards, his head spinning from a savage blow on the head. As he tried to gain his feet, someone kicked his legs from under him and he went down again and stayed there, momentarily feigning unconsciousness.

'Search him,' a voice ordered. He felt his coat ripped open and his weapon removed. So also was his wallet. Thank God he had left the papers for Moonshadow back at the house! Elizabeth would have loved to get her hands on those. He had no doubt that the large man was the same one he had seen at her place and that she had sent them after him.

A kick in the ribs sent him rolling over on to his face in the mud, two more landed in his back. They didn't mean to kill him, he realised, or they would have used his knife. She wanted him hurt, crippled perhaps, helpless to defend himself, as Sarah had been the day she ran from the dogs.

Pearson had straightened, a grin on his face as he watched Henri rifling Paul's pockets. For a moment his attention was distracted from the still figure at his feet. Dominic rolled over on to his back, his fingers already grasping the hilt of the stiletto. The blade entered just below the big man's heart and he died without knowing what had happened.

Paul suddenly began to fight like a madman. Henri Dolman seized him by the front of his shirt and began banging his head quite deliberately, almost lovingly, against the stone wall. Dominic swore and reached for the knife Pearson had dropped.

Henri wheeled and saw him, crouching on his knees, one hand against his bruised ribs, the other balancing the wicked looking knife. Henri let go of Paul, stepped back, and caught sight of Pearson sprawled in the mud a few feet away. In two long strides Dominic had covered the space between them and his blade pricked the skin of Dolman's throat.

'Go back and tell her you failed. Tell her one day soon I shall be coming for her,' he said quietly. 'This is on account.'

The blade travelled upwards so swiftly that Dolman could not have moved, even if he had found enough courage to do so. He screamed in agony as it sliced across one cheek.

Dominic watched him back away, the fingers he held to his face stained with bright red blood. As the man turned and ran, Dominic bent over Paul and lifted him to his feet. He was a dead weight and blood was oozing from a wound at the back of his head. 'You crazy fool!' he groaned. 'Why didn't you stay out of it?'

A shaft of light suddenly cut across them. He looked up and saw a woman standing in the doorway of one of the houses, heard her gasp as he drew back from Paul's body and she caught sight of the blood, his torn clothing, the still form of Pearson.

'Don't scream—I mean you no harm,' he said quickly. 'My friend is hurt. We were attacked.'

He didn't wait to be asked in, simply carried the injured man towards the house.

'I'll pay you well for your help,' he added tersely and the woman stepped back, allowing him to enter.

The room he was in smelt damp, and there was only one light to guide him to the narrow bed in a far corner.

'Put him down,' the woman said. 'No, don't touch him. I'll see to him. Sit down, Dominic. Rest yourself.'

Dominic's startled gaze pierced the gloom, but the woman's face was in the shadows as she put down a bowl of water beside the bed and bent over Paul's inert body. She unfastened his shirt and began to bathe his face and neck.

'It's only superficial, but that's more than enough on top of what he has already suffered.'

Her voice, vaguely familiar, was tinged with pity. She straightened and he gave a soft exclamation as the light fell on her. The last time he had seen her had been at a summer barbecue at Pinewood, prevailing on the guests to eat some of the delicious pastries and sweetmeats she had baked herself. Her hair was pulled back from her face now, straggling untidily over her shoulders. There were dark grey shadows beneath her eyes which made her look ten years older. The calico blouse and skirt she wore hung on her wasted figure like a sack. The first wave of pity Dominic felt was swept away by the surge of anger which followed swift on its heels.

'This seems to be my night for surprises,' he said. 'What the devil are you doing in this hole, Alice?'

'I live here—with my son.' The woman's tired features brightened with a smile. 'Hasn't anyone told you of my terrible behaviour yet?'

The amusement in her voice startled him until he looked into her eyes and saw the sadness there and realised she was putting on a brave front for his benefit. What was it Paul had said? That terrible look of rejection . . . Now he knew what he had meant.

'Veroníque told me you had married—a seaman,' he began.

She shrugged her shoulders and turned back to cleanse Paul's head wound.

'He died last year, running the blockade in a ship rather like the one you came back in. I saw you. I was at the back of the crowd.'

'In heaven's name, why didn't you show yourself? Veroníque was there—and your father.'

'He refuses even to mention my name, let alone see me. Sit down Dominic, I'll be finished here in a moment, then I'll make some coffee. Please, don't be embarrassed, and don't look at me like that. I don't want pity from you, of all people. What happened outside? What did you mean, this is your night for surprises?'

'Paul and I were doing the town. Perhaps you haven't heard, but I'm going to marry your sister, and her dowry is Moonshadow. You might say we were celebrating.' It was as near the truth as he intended to go and he hoped for some reaction, but there was little.

He was sure he saw Alice stiffen and waited for her to make some comment, knowing full well that his possession of the plantation deprived her of a home, a future with Paul. But she said nothing. Dominic watched her bandage Paul's head and was struck by her control. The mouse, too, had grown up. Three years were such a short time out of a life span, and yet in that short while so much had altered, so many people had changed. And Alice—Alice had become an outcast, apparently by choice.

'There. Now for coffee.'

The stove was antiquated, but freshly blacked. The tiny room screamed of poverty, yet made a pathetic effort at comfort, with patterned curtains at the single window. The bed was practically falling to pieces, and there were no sanitary facilities. A curtained recess led off to one side. Alice's back was towards him as he quietly rose and stepped across to it, lifting it aside. Beyond, the tiny recess held a cot and a sleeping child, perhaps two or three years old. A single candle burned on the makeshift table beside it.

'My son, Michael,' Alice said behind him, as she put down a mug of coffee. He turned back, saw that there was only one and raised his eyes to hers questioningly. 'It keeps me awake,' she said.

'You little liar, it's all you have.' The flimsy excuse did not deceive him. He was only too aware of the poverty all around him. Reaching into his pocket he brought out several coins. Alice paled visibly and stepped back, her expression growing hostile.

'Don't you dare give me money.'

'Damn your pride! The boy needs food, doesn't he, and I see little around here. No coffee, no bread, no fresh vegetables. You weren't meant for this, and we both know it. Take it—it's only money. Let me tell your father where you are.' There was no time to be gentle. 'He's dying . . .'

'Yes, I know. Don't look so surprised, Dominic, I know everything that happens at Pinewood. Veroníque sees to that.'

'So she is playing matchmaker! Trying to get Paul to buy Moonshadow for you and the child.' Dominic looked at his unconscious friend with a frown. 'What am I missing, Alice? When I went away, I thought you and Paul might settle down together, that he loved you. Did Veroníque take him back? Is that the reason you left home—ended up here, married to a man you didn't love?'

'You have no reason to say that.'

'Why? Because she's your sister? I'm reading between the lines, my dear—correct me if I'm wrong. Well, I'm waiting. Did Veroníque take Paul from you?'

'No. No, Dominic, you are so wrong. Who do you think brought us together in the first place? Who has been keeping me since I became a widow eighteen months ago?' Alice sprang to the defence of her younger sister with a ferocity that made Dominic's eyebrows rise.

'Go on.'

'There is little enough money to spend on Pinewood, let alone idle luxuries—and I am a luxury,' Alice continued in a fierce tone. 'Veroníque found me here in Atlanta a few months after my wedding. She'd been searching for me since I left home, without Father's knowledge. She's been giving me money ever since. It isn't much. There isn't much to go around these days, but it helps and it's out of her own pocket too.'

'And you take it because she owes you?' Dominic queried, deliberately being cruel in the hope that all his questions would finally be answered.

'Like you, my sister would not owe a cent to anyone because it would place her in their debt. No, she owes me nothing. I owe her my survival, and Michael's. A year ago I wanted to die. Did she tell you that? I tried to take my own life. I thought if I was dead, father would take Michael back to Pinewood and care for him—love him as a grandfather should. She wouldn't let me die. She found me before I had time to do it properly, stayed with me in this hovel for almost two weeks, cared for me and Michael as if he was her own. Don't you ever speak of her in that tone again, Dominic! My sister has moved heaven and earth to bring Paul and me together. I've told her how hopeless it is, but she won't listen. She's obsessed with the idea that Paul still loves me, needs me.'

'He needs someone. Look at him! One arm and a head full of idiotic ideas of staying here in Atlanta—to write a great epic,' Dominic drawled sarcastically. Her acceptance of the situation annoyed him. What was it he wasn't being told?

'And what's so wrong with that?' The smile was back on Alice's face as she looked down at Paul and he knew she still cared. So what kept them apart? 'He's coming round. Perhaps you had better leave. I don't want him to see me. He thinks I live in Savannah.'

'Why? The child?'

'I don't want your pity, Dominic, nor his. What I did I must pay for—by myself. Perhaps one day . . . No, perhaps not. What use is there in dwelling on the past?'

'Let me leave something for the boy then?' Dominic said.

He gave her no chance to argue. Stepping back into the recess he laid three gold coins on the table, sufficient for Alice not only to buy food for them both, but find fresh lodgings until he could decide on some way to get them back to Pinewood where they rightfully belonged. The sight of the sleeping child touched him, for he knew he might never stand at the bedside of his own son. Hesitantly he reached out and lightly touched the tousled hair—and instantly froze. Just visible beneath the hairline at the base of the child's neck was a bright pink birthmark. He had seen an identical one on Paul's back, and Melissa's was on her right breast. Michael was a Loring—Paul's son! Paul fervently believed otherwise—swore he had never touched her—and Alice was content to keep it that way. What the devil was going on?

'Dominic, quickly.' Alice's urgent tones drew him back to the other room. She slipped behind him as Paul stirred on the bed, her thin face suddenly full of anguish. 'Take him away, please, and say nothing of me.'

'You're a fool,' Dominic said roughly. 'If I had my way . . .'

'This is none of your business. Stay out of it. Enough people have been hurt. Marry my sister, Dominic. Make her happy. She deserves it.'

The curtain dropped into place behind her, leaving him with the semi-conscious Paul, who was attempting to sit up, alternately cursing his aching head and the arm he no longer possessed. Dominic forced the remainder of the coffee he had left into him and managed to get him on to his feet. All the way back to the house he carried in his mind a picture of Alice's tortured expression.

It was growing dark when Dominic arrived at Pinewood the following day. He had delivered Paul, nursing a hangover, to his home, declined Melissa's offer to stay to dinner, and rode straight on. Jacob showed him into the study where George sat behind a large, carved rosewood desk, gazing at the papers scattered across its polished surface. As Dominic sprawled into a chair, he pushed them suddenly away into a top drawer, locked it and looked across to where he sat.

'When I am gone, everything you will need is here,' he said slowly.

'Don't be morbid. You are not going to die for a while yet.' Dominic's narrowed gaze centred on him thoughtfully. 'Did you know she was living in Atlanta?'

'It didn't take long for the news to reach me. I haven't seen her, you understand. My debt was paid when I bought Moonshadow. I thought it best to say nothing to you.'

'Dammit! I don't mean Elizabeth. I'm talking about Alice. I can't believe you have abandoned her, George. If only you saw where she lives . . . and the boy, your grandson . . .'

'Would you like a drink?' George's harsh tones abruptly curtailed Dominic's explanation of Alice's circumstances, and he broke off with a frown.

'What's wrong? You must want to know how she is. Good God, man, she's your own flesh and blood.'

'I have only one daughter, Veroníque, who you are about to have trouble with,' George returned. Dominic took the glass held in his direction.

'What exactly does that mean?'

'Veroníque and I had words this afternoon. She wants the wedding date put back until August. I refused. She now refuses to marry you at all. You'd better go and talk some sense into her.'

Dominic took an envelope from his pocket and tossed it on to the desk.

'Everything is as you wanted. The papers are there too for the Atlanta property, for Paul to sign whenever he likes. You kept your word by my father, *mon vieux*. I will keep mine to you. You have my solemn oath.'

So she was trying to back out now, was she? Little fool! Surely she had enough sense to realise he would allow nothing to stand in his way, Dominic thought as he made his way upstairs and knocked on the door of Veroníque's room.

'Monsieur Dominic,' Michelle said, opening the door, 'what can I do for you?'

'Where is she?' was all he said.

'Mademoiselle has a headache. She has retired for the evening,' came the polite, but final answer, and the door was quickly closed in his face. As his hand fastened over the handle he heard the key being turned in the lock.

Three strides took him to the door of Veroníque's sitting-room. He slipped inside. The communicating door was open and he could see Veroníque sitting before the dressing-table, believing that the locked door protected her against her unwelcome visitor. Her thick black hair was loose about her shoulders, so long it reached almost to her waist. She wore a pink wrap, over the top of a white silk nightgown. Dominic paused by the communicating door wishing she was not so disturbingly beautiful—so desirable. It had been easy to make plans for two separate existences at Moonshadow, not so easy to accept they would work as he looked at her and saw fire and ice offered to him in a most tantalising form.

Leaning against the wall, he folded his arms and waited for her to catch sight of him in the mirror, in no hurry to precipitate that moment.

Michelle saw him first and touched her mistress on the shoulder. Veroníque spun around and the colour fled from her cheeks at the sight of the silent onlooker, then returned to stain them with fierce colour as she got up and firmly belted the robe around her.

'Have you taken leave of your senses, Dominic?' she demanded coldly. 'Get out. I am about to go to bed.'

'I was concerned about—your headache. Michelle, go and fetch your mistress some hot chocolate.'

'You will do no such thing. Stay here,' Veroníque ordered.

'Get out, Michelle, and close the door behind you.'

To Veroníque's dismay, the woman obeyed him, but as she reached the door, she looked up into the hard, brown face and said quietly:

'If you lay one finger on her to hurt her, Monsieur Dominic, you will not live to see your wedding day.'

'I could have you whipped for such a threat,' Dominic returned. He would never have ordered the beating, and she knew it. The years drifted away. It was like looking at Sarah all over again, remembering the day when she had faced Elizabeth d'Estainville with the same defiance.

Veroníque sat down before the dressing-table, not looking at him. 'Well, what is so important you have to invade my room, like—like . . .'

'A rejected suitor? Isn't that what I am? What nonsense is this that you won't marry me?'

'Not next month,' Veroníque protested. 'It's too soon. Be reasonable, Dominic. I can't—I won't, leave Father—not now. You've seen what is happening to him, the way he has begun to drink. It's—it's as if he's trying to kill himself.'

'*Ma belle*, he has the right to spend his last days any way he chooses,' Dominic replied quietly. He had come prepared to assert his authority, but that desire disappeared in the face of her genuine distress.

'And I, surely have the right to be with him?' Veroníque's eyes as she looked up at him were swimming with bright tears. With a soft expletive he caught her hand, carrying it to his lips, and the gesture was so out of place that she could only stare at him in amazement.

'Dominic, please. It's so little to ask,' she pleaded, determined to press home the argument while he was in this strange, receptive mood. 'You have Moonshadow, and after all, that's what really matters. Father needs me. When—when he is gone . . . I will marry you whenever you say.'

'He has given you into my care. I won't delay the date one day longer than I have to.'

'You don't have to pretend you want this marriage, because I know you don't,' Veroníque protested. 'You have the only thing you want.'

Her voice faltered. He thought, for a brief moment, that she looked afraid. Without knowing why he sought to reassure her.

'As you say, I have what I want, plus the attentions of a captivating mistress. Is that what you wanted to hear?'

'Then our marriage . . .' She could hardly bring herself to say the words, but she knew she must. 'It will be . . . I mean, we will have our own lives to lead . . .?'

'There is only one other thing I want in this world. Perhaps one day I will tell you what it is,' Dominic murmured, but did not offer further explanation. Nevertheless she felt infinitely relieved.

He was all she wanted. Perhaps one day they would open their hearts to each other. 'Thank you.' She could hardly believe he had given in. What had happened to mellow him so?

He still held her hand, but she made no attempt to pull away. His eyes studied her in silence—black bottomless pools. She could not begin to imagine what thoughts ran through his mind. If he kissed her, she thought . . . Oh, if only he would. There was gentleness in him tonight—and compassion.

'I saw Alice last night.' He felt her hand tremble as the shock of his words hit her. 'I tried to tell your father in the hope he would bring her home. The boy too. He looks a fine lad.'

'You saw Michael?' Veroníque whispered. 'How? What were you doing in those terrible little black streets, crawling with vermin . . .' Her eyes caught sight of the long, deep scratches Elizabeth had made along the back of his hand. They were clearly nail marks.

'Paul was showing me the sights again. We were jumped by a couple of toughs. He was knocked unconscious, but he's all right now. Don't worry.'

'Alice—she—she didn't see him? Oh, no, Dominic. She'll think I broke my word and told him where she was. She'll run away again.'

'I don't think so. What really happened to her, *ma belle*? Tell me the truth.'

Veroníque's lips trembled. With an effort she composed herself comforted by the pressure of his hand on hers.

'Do you remember the last party which brought us all together?' she asked.

'Yes, here at Pinewood. Christmas 1860. Paul didn't want to come because his father had just died, but you persuaded him.'

'He drank heavily that night—delayed reaction, I suppose, and then ran upstairs in a terrible state. I went after him, but he was wild, uncontrollable, crying. . . . Alice came. She took him to her own room and I left them. I didn't see her again until morning. She told me they had slept together, but that Paul remembered nothing. He thought he had passed out . . . he could only remember Melissa plying him with large drinks all evening, and he had a mammoth hangover. When she became pregnant Alice told him the truth. Melissa overheard and she openly ridiculed the idea. She said Paul had been too drunk to do anything like that. Paul's rejection of her was too much for poor Alice to take. She ran away. Three months later the war began and Paul enlisted. Almost as if he believed she hadn't lied and couldn't accept the fact he had driven her away.'

She shivered as the memories caused pain.

'Go on,' Dominic prompted. 'How did you find her again?'

'Purely by chance. It was one of the times Father and I stayed in Atlanta. I was taking bandages to the hospital when I saw her looking for a doctor because Michael was ill. She took me home, if you can call it that. She had had a terrible time. At first she had gone to an aunt in Savannah until the truth came out and gossip forced her to leave. She went to Atlanta and found work as a cook—you know how good she is—until the baby was born. The little money she saved was soon gone. She couldn't afford to pay her rent and she was turned out on to the street. If Joe Tanner hadn't found her when he did, she would have died. Michael too.'

'Is that the man she married?'

'Yes. She spoke well of him. A rough man, but kind. He gave her his name and she looked after him. He was killed in a blockade ship.'

'She told me. She also made it quite clear she wants nothing to do with Paul.'

'In her position I might well feel the same way. Could he look at her now, in that place, and feel the same? She always asks me. I tell her, yes—that he still loves her. And then she reminds me of his arm, how he must feel lacking as a man, and that she would be an added burden. Sometimes she's so stubborn I want to shake her.'

'Moonshadow offered you a way out of your dilemma?'

'At first. But the harder I pushed Paul, the more determined he became to fight against the suspicion that he had been wrong all these years. I didn't mean any harm, Dominic. I love them both so much. To see them happy—and father with a grandson on his knee before he dies . . .'

'I understand.' Dominic slipped a finger beneath her chin and tilted back her head. 'Do you know for a while I thought you were a selfish little bitch . . . wanting Moonshadow for yourself . . . and Paul . . .'

She looked into his eyes and saw they were no longer void of emotion. She knew only too well what he was thinking as his arms went around her, drawing her up against his chest, and she was powerless to fight against the lips which took possession of hers, demanding surrender.

The sound of a single shot shattered the silence, brought them apart, sent Dominic wheeling towards the door. As he reached the stairs he heard Veroníque's agonised cry behind him.

'Father!'

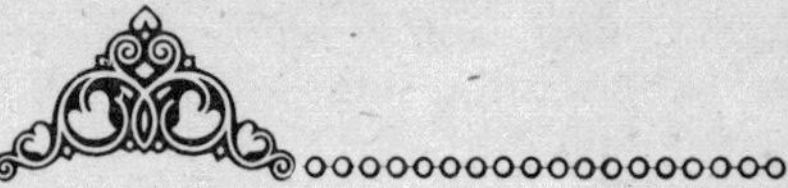

CHAPTER SIX

GEORGE had been drinking steadily all day. Consequently his hand was far from steady when he put the muzzle of the pistol against his temple and pulled the trigger. He was not quite dead when they reached him—Dominic first, instinctively knowing what he would find when he entered the library—Veroníque close on his heels, her lips moving in a soundless prayer.

She fell on her knees at her father's side, cradling his shattered head against her breast, tears spilling down over ashen cheeks. Blood soaked the front of her wrap and the nightdress beneath.

'A doctor,' she moaned. 'Send someone for a doctor.'

'It's too late for that.' George's glazing eyes looked into Dominic's shocked features. 'Take her away . . . be good . . . to her . . .'

'By God, you planned this all along,' Dominic cried.

He was cold-bloodedly leaving Dominic with no alternative but to carry out the dying man's wishes. It was a thing of honour between them.

'You will find out why . . . in . . . in the desk . . . keep your word . . .'

Blood began to seep from the corner's of George's mouth. Desperate fingers clutched at Dominic's sleeve, dragging him closer.

'Swear it . . .'

'Father, don't talk . . . it isn't important,' Veroníque begged.

'You are wrong,' Dominic said quietly. 'It is very important.' He gave a brief nod. 'You have my word, old friend. It will be as you wanted it.'

The clutching fingers grew lax and fell away, and the heavy lids closed for the last time over the pale blue eyes. Veroníque continued to cradle him against her like a mother trying to comfort a fretting child, unaware that he was dead. It took Dominic and two of the houseboys to disengage her. As the realisation dawned on her she began to scream, struggling against the efforts to restrain her. She became hysterical, totally uncontrollable. Dominic's clenched fist struck her beneath the chin and she folded in his arms like a rag doll.

'Well, don't stand there like gaping black apes.' He laid her on the couch and wheeled on the sea of faces crowding at the door. He singled out Michelle, pushing her way to the front. 'I want the rig harnessed and at the front door in five minutes, you are taking Mademoiselle to Moonshadow. Pack an overnight bag and bring a coat. Someone fetch a blanket.

He covered George with a blanket brought by one of the maids, standing in silent respect for a moment over the body.

'I hope you have found your peace, my friend,' he murmured, lapsing into the softly intonated Creole French which was, at times, more natural to him than any other tongue.

'He is with Mademoiselle's mother. Such peace is to be envied,' a voice remarked at his shoulder. He turned and looked at Michelle, annoyed that she had not only overheard, but understood.

'See to your mistress,' he said curtly. 'I've sent a boy for the sheriff. I'll stay here until he arrives, then I'll follow you to Moonshadow.'

'Is that wise, Monsieur Dominic? Would it not be better to bring Mademoiselle Loring here?'

'Damn you, what do the proprieties matter now? Veroníque is in a state of shock. She can't stay here in this house. Get something warm around her. The rig should be ready in a few minutes. Now, Michelle—if you want to stay with her.'

The woman stared into the angry, narrowed eyes and nodded. This one was not to be argued with. What a man! Just like Gran'père Luc.

Remembering George's earlier words, Dominic took his keys and unlocked the desk. He found more than he anticipated. He had expected heavy bills, but was not prepared for the staggering amount which began to accumulate as he scanned briefly through the sheaf of papers. By present day standards he had returned home a rich man, and careful placing of his money, coupled with the fact it had been in gold in the first place, meant he could lay hands on it again with comparative ease. But once these debts were paid! George had omitted to tell him that Pinewood itself was under the threat of foreclosure from the bank. It would be an effort to keep the place going even when the mortgage was paid off.

Veroníque was barely conscious as he carried her out to the rig. As he tried to lift her in to where Michelle was waiting, she clung to him, muttering incoherently.

'I killed him . . .'

He heard the words, but ignored them, realising she was unaware of what she was saying, so great was her grief.

'Hush, *ma belle*. No, don't hold on to me . . . Tante Michelle is here. Let her take you.'

Disengaging her arms from about his neck, he gave her into the care of the Creole woman, who held her in her arms and began to rock the girl like a little baby. Dominic's hand lingered on Veroníque's loose hair. His lips briefly touched her cheek before he stepped back and ordered Jacob to drive off. He wanted to comfort her, but words were inadequate at such a time.

He watched the rig until it was swallowed up in the darkness, before going back into the house, not to the library where George's body lay shrouded in shadows, but to the drawing-room where he helped himself to a stiff drink and sat down to await the arrival of the sheriff.

Veroníque lay in bed in Moonshadow for three days and three long, sleepless nights, and the sound of her weeping echoed through the house during the hours of darkness. The funeral of her father was held on the fourth day. By that time she had cried herself to the edge of nervous exhaustion. Her eyes were dull and tired, her face ashen, its pallor accentuated by the black mourning dress Michelle helped her into on a bright sunny morning that held no compassion for her sudden loss.

Dominic was waiting for her in the drawing-room. She had not seen him, at her own insistence, since she arrived.

She had wanted to grieve alone and he, surprisingly, had made no attempt to come near her.

As he pressed a cup of coffee into her hands she began to realise she had been troubled with none of the gruesome details which often accompanied death. He had taken care of everything and she falteringly tried to thank him, but he waved aside such trivialities and she knew he had not expected gratitude.

'Are you going to be all right?' he asked at length. Veroníque did not know it, but he had visited her, several times, when she was asleep. He had deliberately had her installed in rooms which adjoined his own. In the early hours, when the sound of her crying died away, he had unlocked the communicating doors and gone into her bedroom. At first it had been to make sure she had suffered no ill effects from the blow he had dealt her . . . to apologise. But she had refused to see him, and so he had chosen this secret way of finding out for himself. It was not until the second night when he visited her, that he was aware of another presence in the room—Michelle's. She had made up a bed for herself on the floor and was awake, watching him. Neither spoke. He did not consider it necessary to explain his actions in his own house. She just watched.

Veroníque turned and looked at him, standing by the window in his black coat and trousers. So tall and strong. How she envied him his strength—despised his ruthlessness.

'I think so, Dominic. When—when it is over, I will go back to Pinewood.'

'You will do no such thing.' He looked at her with a frown.

'But I must. It—it—isn't . . .'

'Decent to remain here?' he answered sharply. 'That will be remedied quick enough, I assure you.'

'You can't mean to have our wedding immediately,' Veroníque gasped. 'So soon! Father isn't even in his grave yet.'

'You have no need to remind me of that. I promised him I would take care of you and I will. Even you must surely see the sense of us being married at once.' He came to her chair, his expression challenging her to argue. She wanted to. He felt it, saw it in the hand which trembled visibly as she put aside her cup.

'Very well, make what arrangements you please,' she said, rising to her feet. 'I thought you had changed, Dominic, but I was wrong, wasn't I? You are just as calculating as ever. The King is dead! Long live the King! Long live Moonshadow now a d'Estainville rules it again! Of course we will be married quickly, so that you don't have to divert any more attention than is necessary away from the place you worship. I understand—and I will never forgive you.'

She ignored the arm he held out to her as they stood by the carriage, accepting instead Jacob's help. Dominic climbed in beside her, his face a granite mask and they did not speak to each other on the journey to Pinewood.

Melissa's honey-sweet words of pity, offered without the accompaniment of genuine feeling while her eyes searched the sea of faces for Dominic, made Veroníque turn away quickly, seeking the comfort of someone who understood her sorrow.

Paul appeared to offer solace and the sturdy support of his one good arm. It was he who helped her to the graveside, stood with her giving whispered support to her flagging courage as she wiped away the tears which rolled silently down her cheeks beneath the long black veil.

When it was over she was still for a while, then straightening her shoulders, she lifted her head and all the defiant pride of generations of de Brissacs blazed out of her face as she lifted the protective veil and turned to look at the people around her.

'Shall we go back to the house? There are things which have to be settled,' she said in a quiet tone. So calm that it was hard to believe that a few minutes before she had been on the verge of breaking down.

Paul squeezed her hand. But there was no response, and he realised she was deliberately forcing herself over the pain of the past few days so that she could cope with whatever lay ahead. She and Dominic were well matched, he thought admiringly.

Veroníque had scarcely taken a dozen paces when a man stepped in front of her, barring her way. She recognised him as one of the senior clerks from her father's bank, and her expression grew cold.

'Miss de Brissac . . .' beneath her contemptuous gaze the man faltered.

She knew why he had come—and the other men behind him. Not to offer their sympathy or their help, but like vultures hovering for the kill, had come to take everything she possessed. At least her father had been spared this final indignity.

'If you wish to speak to me, Monsieur, please do so in the house. I do not converse with merchants and tradesmen in public.' Her voice shook with anger.

'I have to give you this. I'm sorry.'

She stared at the paper thrust out at her, knowing it was the threatened foreclosure on her beloved home . . . and could not take it. Dominic stepped to her side and took it in her stead. He did not even glance at it before slipping it into his pocket.

'This is neither the time nor the place for such business, gentlemen. It will be attended to in the house.' Dominic stared at the silent creditors coldy. 'You will all be dealt with, I promise.'

'And what business is it of yours, d'Estainville?' someone asked brashly. 'We are here to collect what George de Brissac owed us. It has nothing to do with you. Unless, of course, you intend to settle his debts for him.'

'That is my intention, gentlemen,' Dominic returned, and Veroníque drew in a sharp breath. His eyes narrowed slightly as he looked at her and added, 'Some of you are probably well aware by now, that Mademoiselle de Brissac and I are to be married. Naturally I shall assume responsibility for all financial dealings undertaken by her father before his death.'

'And how will you pay us, with Johnston still retreating towards Atlanta and slaves being taken from the plantations, leaving hardly enough to tend the stock, let alone harvest this year's cotton?'

Dominic singled out the man who had spoken, a fat little man who had grown rich almost overnight by the hoarding of desperately needed food and supplies, selling them at exorbitant prices and making a colossal profit. His mouth deepened into an ugly smile which made the other man fidget uncomfortably with the papers in his hands.

'How shall I pay? In gold, my friend—or with a bullet at

the first opportunity, if you use that tone with me again. Anyone who wishes to do business with me can go up to the house. Should anyone remain out here I shall assume he prefers satisfaction to the settlement of his claim. The choice is yours, gentlemen. I am not a patient man. At this moment I am a very angry one.' Ignoring them he turned to the figure at his side. 'Would you prefer to go back to Moonshadow, Veroníque? I promised your father I would do this, and I don't think it will be pleasant for you to watch.'

'I won't accept your money,' Veroníque said, keeping her voice low as people began to drift past them. 'How dare you humiliate me in this fashion, before everyone? You are too cruel, Dominic.'

'Humiliate you? I've given you back the right to look these people in the face knowing you owe them nothing. When I've finished here all debts will have been paid, even the loan from the bank. It will all but cripple me, but it's what I promised George. You are soon to be a d'Estainville, Veroníque, and we take care of our own. I suggest you remember that in future.'

'You talk about me as if I am one of your slaves.'

'Veroníque, don't! He didn't mean it that way. He's doing his best to help,' Paul protested. But she ignored his intervention.

'All Dominic wants is to protect the d'Estainville name, not me, not Father,' Veroníque said scathingly. 'I come with the house, don't I, Dominic? And you don't intend to let me forget how kind and generous you have been. I shall have a roof over my head and your name because it was the only way you could return to Moonshadow. Don't expect gratitude.'

'I expect nothing,' Dominic returned flatly. 'Will you take her home, Paul?'

'This is my home.'

'The minister will be going back with you.' Dominic ignored her comment. 'He'll be staying at the house for a few days. Veroníque and I have both agreed it will be better if we bring forward the date of the wedding. Will you stay and be my best man?'

'Of course. I was afraid I wasn't going to be asked. It's a sensible arrangement. When is it to be exactly?'

'The day after tomorrow.' Dominic glanced at Veronίque as if expecting an argument, but she remained silent.

'That hardly gives you time to organise the ceremony and reception,' Paul said.

'We have decided to keep both as quiet as possible under the circumstances—just family and close friends, like you and Melissa.'

Family, Veronίque thought miserably. What family? Her father was dead and her only sister lived as an outcast, in poverty, miles away. He kept on saying 'we' as if he had consulted her over everything. It both annoyed and hurt her. Annoyed, because she knew she was doomed to a marriage where he would be the master; hurt, because she herself had deliberately destroyed the few minutes of intimacy they had shared back at the house. He had offered her kindness and she had thrown it back in his face.

'Dominic is right, you know. The next few hours could only bring you more grief if you stay,' Paul insisted. 'You know what's in the will. Your Father made it no secret that you would inherit everything.'

'Inherit everything?' Veronίque echoed. 'He has left me nothing, Paul. I am a pauper, dependent on my future husband for everything . . .'

'You have Pinewood,' Dominic interrupted.

'How gracious of you. Remember it is mine then, Dominic.'

His dark eyes mocked her cruelly as he answered, bleakly.

'It is yours only so long as I pay the bank.'

He left her standing with Paul and walked towards the house. She wanted to call after him, apologise for her hasty words, but instead she buried her face in her hands and began to sob bitterly. Not until she was in the carriage and they were halfway back to Moonshadow, was she able to compose herself.

'If I'm to be Dominic's best man I must go back home and fetch a change of clothes. I'll have a bag packed for Melissa while I'm at it. We won't outstay our welcome, Veronίque, believe me. At a time like this you will probably be glad to see the back of us,' Paul said as he helped her from the rig at the end of their journey.

She smiled and leant up on tiptoe to kiss his grey cheeks.

'I shall be glad of the company,' she whispered. 'Dominic and I—we—we don't get along, as you've probably gathered. Well, sometimes we do . . . but lately . . . oh, Paul, I'm so afraid! I say such terrible things to him, and it provokes his temper.'

'You are both living on your nerves at the moment. Don't worry—in a few months you will be such an old married couple, you won't even know why you were worried in the first place. I'll be back tomorrow.'

'Take care. Let Jacob take you in the rig.'

Veroníque watched the rig go down the drive until the tall trees closed in behind it, hiding it from her view. Wearily she turned to go inside. She was tired . . . on the verge of tears . . .

'Mister Dominic has not come back with you, Miss Veroníque?'

Micah stood in the hallway watching her slow progress. She was about to demand what he was doing in the house when she suddenly remembered that this was Dominic's home, not hers. He was master here, and this darkie was a friend, not a slave.

'No,' she said dully, 'he will not be back until later. We shall be having guests for a few days. Extra rooms will have to be made ready.'

'Mister Dominic told me this morning there might be visitors. I have already seen to everything.' Micah stepped back, opened the door of the sitting-room, and beckoned.

'There is someone here to see you.'

Veroníque's mind refused to function. To see her? Who was there to see her? The figure which appeared in the doorway brought a cry of delight from her lips. She ran across the floor and flung herself into the outstretched arms.

'Alice! Oh, dear Alice, thank God you have come.'

It had grown dark in the room, but no lamps had yet been lighted. Veroníque sat on the sofa, her head on her sister's shoulder. She had wept for almost an hour and then slept, like a child, curled up in Alice's arms. It was like being a little girl again, Veroníque thought as she awoke, each comforting the other when in pain or trouble.

Years of pain and loneliness, and bitter disillusionment, had separated them until this moment. Nothing, nothing, Veroníque silently vowed, would ever drive her sister away again.

'You should eat something,' Alice said quietly, and rang the bell-cord by the door. When Micah appeared, she asked for a tray of sandwiches and some tea. He nodded and left them without argument.

Veroníque pulled a face as she sat down again.

'He wouldn't have been so polite if I had rung.'

'Dominic sent him to bring me from Atlanta. From the way he talked on the way here, Micah seems to have assumed duties all over the place, even at Pinewood. He tells me the harvest will be a good one.'

'If we have enough men to gather it in,' Veroníque returned. 'Did you know we are penniless, Alice? Father left nothing—except debts.'

'I never realised it was that bad. And yet you still made me take money from you . . .'

'What could you have done if you had known?' Véronique broke off, twisting her hands together in her lap in such agitation that Alice grew alarmed.

'What is it, Veroníque?'

'I killed him.'

'Nonsense,' her sister returned sharply.

'I know what I'm saying. I've never told you this before, but I've loved Dominic since I was sixteen years old. I used to watch him with Melissa, and wish it was me. I told Father, the same day he killed himself. He was so depressed, I tried to reassure him. I confessed I loved Dominic, that our marriage would be a happy one, with fine grandchildren for him to bounce on his knee. All I wanted was to wait a little, until his health had improved. Don't you understand what that did to him? It released him: he knew he could die secure in the knowledge that I would be looked after. Until then I had been fighting the marriage.'

'Why, if you love Dominic?' Alice asked, puzzled.

'Father gave him Moonshadow on the condition he married me. It was his way of protecting me after he was gone.'

'My poor dear! But you mustn't blame yourself. It

sounds to me as if Father had been laying these plans for some considerable time.'

'How can you say that? He wasn't so—so cold-blooded.'

'To ensure you were looked after? Yes, he would have been. You loved him, Veronique, but I knew him, better than anyone, I think. Once I cared for him too, but he destroyed that feeling a long while ago when he refused to see Michael. I could have borne his anger, his contempt even, but Michael was his grandson. He should have at least seen him, just once. I wonder if he would have turned you out of the house if you had been in my position?'

The bitterness in her sister's tone helped Veronique to push aside her own problems. Alice had suffered deeply over the past few years. It was up to her to try and ease the pain and humiliation she had been forced to endure. 'You say Dominic sent for you?' she asked.

'I suspect he knew I would not have come back simply for father's funeral, but he wrote a letter which Micah delivered. He said you were in a state of shock and needed me. He is a very kind man, Veronique.'

'He can also be very cruel—and ruthless.'

'And you can be stubborn and extremely wilful. What a pair you two will make!'

The tea arrived. Micah left the tray on a table beside the sofa and lighted two of the wall-lights before leaving them. Veronique drew the heavy brocade curtains across the windows and turned to look around the room. It was a warm comfortable room, yet she felt a stranger in it—unwanted.

'Sit down and have something to eat,' Alice ordered, pouring tea for them both. 'You look exhausted.'

'You must stay with us,' Veronique said suddenly. She did not want to be left alone with the man whc was, at times, a frightening stranger.

'A few days perhaps. Michael will love it. The journey tired him, but tomorrow I expect he'll be awake at the crack of dawn wanting to go and see the horses. How that boy loves horses!'

'Then I shall have to buy him one for his next birthday,' Dominic remarked, coming into the room in time to catch the tail-end of the conversation. He glanced across at Veronique and gave a nod of satisfaction.

'Good, there is colour in your cheeks now. Are you feeling better?'

'Yes.'

She saw Alice frown as she sipped her tea, avoiding further conversation with him.

'Will you have some tea, Dominic?' her sister asked. 'It is still hot.'

'Thank you, no. Micah is bringing me some brandy. You had a trouble-free journey then?'

'Thanks to you. I'm very grateful.'

'I think I should warn you, I've invited Paul Loring to be my best man. He should be arriving tomorrow. I hope it won't send you scuttling back to Atlanta too soon.'

Alice went white. Veroníque could have hit him for the cruel way he delivered the news.

'I shall stay as long as my sister needs me—with your permission,' she said at length.

'You can stay here until you choose to make other arrangements,' Dominic returned. Removing his coat, he tossed it aside and relaxed into the high-backed chair before the fire with a sigh. It was like looking at Grandfather Luc, Veroníque thought . . . as if the two men merged into one the moment he stepped over the threshold.

Micah brought a decanter of brandy and Dominic immediately launched into a detailed assessment of how Pinewood was going to affect the running of his own plantation. Alice turned to Veroníque with a smile. 'He's going to be talking for hours. Why don't you come and help me unpack?'

'You—you don't mind about Paul, do you?' Veroníque asked hesitantly. 'I didn't know he was going to be here, any more than I knew you were coming. Don't run away, Alice—not this time.'

'I'm not going to fall into his arms either, if that's what you're hoping for,' came the bitter answer. 'I went to him, Veroníque, and he turned me away. He refused to acknowledge his own child.'

'Because of Melissa,' Veroníque protested. 'He was so ill after his father's death, he was in no condition to face up to what had happened. You know that. I'm not condoning what he did, only trying to tell you. He's changed—the war has made him so different, so withdrawn, so quiet. At times even I can't reach him. He needs you, and his son. Let me tell him the truth?'

'If you do that I shall leave here and never come back. And this time you won't find me,' Alice warned. 'I'll stay, Veroníque, and I'll meet Paul, but Michael will not be the instrument used to bring us together again. I don't want him just for the child's sake. I want his love—as I had it before.'

Veroníque looked into her sister's thin face and marvelled at her determination. She had survived their father's wrath, the birth of a baby in pitifully primitive conditions, years of hard work, marriage and widowhood. Paul needed her strength!

'You have his love,' she whispered. 'Yes, you have his love. How I envy you.'

That night, when the rest of the house was in darkness, Veroníque made her way along the upstairs landing to Dominic's room. It had taken a whole hour to pluck up enough courage to make this move, but she knew she had to. She knocked rather timidly on the door. There was no answer, and she was about to turn away when it opened and Dominic stood framed in the doorway. Without a word he stepped back, motioning her to come inside.

She opened her mouth to protest as he closed the door behind her. He said abruptly, 'If you *will* come to my room in the early hours of the morning, I'm sure you don't want the fact publicised.'

He did not ask her what she wanted, simply went back to the table where he had been sitting, and resumed his seat. Before him was a bottle of Bourbon and a full glass.

'Would you like one?'

'No, I . . . I didn't come for that.'

'What did you come for then?' he demanded ungraciously.

'You aren't making this very easy for me, Dominic.'

'Should I?' He rose and faced her, his eyes narrowed angrily. 'What's happened to change anything between us? This morning you accused me of humiliating you, of being cruel. My God! You don't know just how cruel I can be when the mood takes me.'

'I wanted to talk. To thank you for bringing Alice here,' Veroníque managed to say at last.

'The prospect of Paul being here hasn't frightened her away then?'

'No, she's promised to stay and to be—civil to him. I think you know it is my dearest wish that they get together again.'

'You are too soft-hearted,' Dominic drawled, draining his glass.

'Was it a hard-hearted man who brought my sister to me?' Veroníque asked. 'Although it would have been nice to be consulted.'

'I sent for her the moment I got back to Moonshadow and Michelle told me you were almost out of your mind with grief. Besides, I'm accustomed to making decisions alone. There is very little around here to consult with you about. The house is, of course, your territory, but the last word will always be mine. As it will with any decisions regarding Pinewood.'

'That place is mine. You promised . . .'

'If we are to survive we have to fight together, Veroníque. I've little enough to spend on my own place now, let alone yours. I'll do all I can until things get really tight. Then Moonshadow takes first priority.'

Little money—because he had paid all her father's debts!

'Dominic—I'm sorry. I don't want to quarrel.' She lifted her shoulders in a pathetic little gesture that brought a frown to his face. 'I came to thank you . . . to ask if we . . . could be friends. I'm not making myself very clear, am I? I feel so—so empty. . . .'

'You have lost a father. For some, it's like losing part of yourself,' Dominic answered gently. He came forward, took her hands and held them and she let him, because his touch was comforting. If only she could put her head on his shoulder, curl up beside him and feel safe, as she had done a few hours ago with her sister. 'It's strange at the moment —for both of us. Don't rush things, *ma belle.* We have all the time in the world. Come, it's time you were in bed.'

Still holding one of her hands, he led her across the room into the adjoining bedroom, and turned the key in the double doors at the far end. Veroníque drew a sharp breath as she found herself looking into her own rooms. So close—and she had not known!

'You said our marriage would be in name only.' She

slipped her hand from his and looked at him accusingly.

'And you immediately take offence because I placed you in the best rooms in the house, which happen to be next to my own.' Dominic's tone reproved her foolishness. Tomorrow, if you wish, you can change them. Goodnight, Veroníque.'

He took the key from the lock and held it out to her. She accepted it in silence and locked the door firmly after her. she was not sure, but as she began to undress, she thought she heard the sound of him laughing.

Veroníque de Brissac was married to Dominic d'Estainville at Moonshadow on the last day of May, in the huge drawing-room which had once opened its doors to a hundred guests in the days when the house was used to entertainment. The ceremony was brief and simple. Paul was the best man and Alice held Veroníque's beautiful bouquet of fragrant white magnolia blossoms and the first lilies from the garden which she had picked herself that morning, as Dominic slipped the ring on to the finger of her sister.

It was over, Veroníque thought, staring down at the gold band encircling her finger and the hand which covered hers possessively. She was his wife. How unreal it all seemed. He kissed her on the mouth, gently, but without passion, and she realised as he drew back and she saw the smile on his lips, that it had merely been a gesture for the sake of their guests.

She had awakened early that morning after a good night's rest, thanks to the sleeping potion Michelle had made her drink before she went to bed. It was a lovely day outside her window, bright and sunny. She had lain in bed until Michelle brought her breakfast, ate it in silence, fighting down the panic which rose up in her as she watched the dress in which she was to be married being laid across a chair. It was the most treasured of her ball gowns and she only wore it on very special occasions. She had sat up, said in a cold tone:

'Put that away. I won't wear it.'

'Do you want to go to him in rags?' Michelle returned. 'Have you no pride?'

A special offer for lovers of Mills & Boon

4 BOOKS
FREE
Mills & Boon
Romance
THE MARRIAGE OF CAROLINE LINDSAY
Margaret Rome
Romance
SEEN BY CANDLELIGHT
Anne Mather
Mills & Boon
Romance
THE UNWILLING BRIDE
Violet Winspear
Mills & Boon
Romance
THE IVORY CANE
Janet Dailey
SEE INSIDE FOR DETAILS

Your special introduction to the Mills & Boon Reader Service.

A chance to enjoy 4 spellbindin Romances absolutely FREE.

Four exciting Mills & Boon Romances have been specially selected for you to enjoy FREE and without any obligation. You can meet Carolir her imminent marriage threatened by a misunderstanding . . . Karen, forced to meet the husband she still loves two years after their divorce . . Sabrina, tragically blinded and fighting a little too hard to be independer . . . Ravena, about to marry a forbidding stranger to protect her beloved guardian from a terrible secret.

Intriguing relationships . . . memorable characters . . . exciting locations . . . Our readers tell us that the books we select have them 'hooked' from the very first page. And they're a joy to read to the last loving embrace.

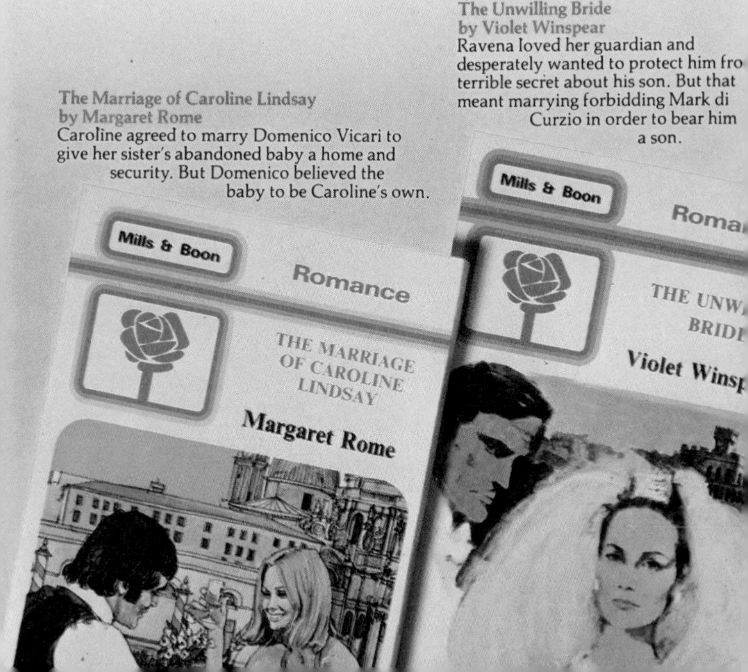

'What does it matter what I wear? He won't be looking at me for long.'

'Then make him look—make him see what's under his nose.'

Veronique wore the dress of white lace over four ruched petticoats and the last two items of jewellery she had baulked at selling—the diamond pendant her mother had worn on her wedding day and a pair of matching earrings which had been an anniversary present. Michelle brushed her hair until it gleamed, swept it high on to her head in a profusion of curls, and nodded in satisfaction at the result.

'I—I am not going to throw myself at him,' Veronique said. She liked what she saw in the mirror: a woman of dignity and breeding, not a frightened child. 'He has to really want me, Michelle . . . do you understand?'

'*Oui, mignonne*. I understand very well.'

But he didn't want her, Veronique thought, watching Dominic as he opened the first of the bottles of champagne.

'You look lovely, my dear,' Alice murmured. 'I swear Dominic could scarcely take his eyes off you when you first came in.'

'It's all right, Alice, you don't have to boost my morale. Tante Michelle has already done that. I'm not going to break down and cry, I'm over that now. I'm resigned to my new life. What about you—and Paul? You were with him when I came down.'

Veronique searched her sister's face expectantly, hoping against hope for good news. Alice had borrowed one of her dresses, the dark burgundy silk went well with her colouring. She looked almost well again.

'It's so silly,' Alice said, 'we met and talked as if the last time we had seen each other was only a day or two ago. I talked of such idiotic things—this place—the weather—Sherman—everything but what I wanted to say. He was the same too. It isn't going to work, Veronique.'

'Did you expect miracles? You could have gone to him when I first told you he had been wounded. He was in hospital in Atlanta, less than two miles from where you lived. Yet you refused to put aside your pride.'

'My pride!' Alice repeated. Pale blue eyes, so like those of George de Brissac, sparkled with sudden fire. 'What is it about us, Veronique? I am too proud to go to Paul, and you will not go to Dominic. When you decide to put your own life in order, perhaps then I'll allow you to decide what is best for me and my son. Now, if you'll excuse me, I have left Michael upstairs, playing. Please make my apologies to Dominic.'

Veroníque was left alone, hugging her bouquet of flowers, knowing she deserved the rebuff. She, who had never known a man and was afraid to offer her love to the only man who had ever interested her, was attempting to give council to an older woman who had known childbirth and the loss of a husband. How inadequate she felt!

'Will you not drink to our life together, *ma belle*?' She looked up at Dominic standing before her, and took the glass of champagne he offered with a forced smile. 'Is it such an ordeal?'

'No—I mean . . .' She drank in an awkward silence, wishing his gaze was not so intense. 'I don't feel—married.'

'It will come in time. Everything does, if you let it,' Dominic murmured. 'Drink up, we don't want others to think we are quarelling, do we? We d'Estainvilles deal with our problems in private.'

A few days ago his words would have irritated her. Now they aroused a strange feeling of pride. It showed in her face, which suddenly brightened. A d'Estainville. Yes, she was one now, and despite their strange relationship, she would try to be a good wife. She could control the plantation as well as any man, efficiently run his home, and in times of trouble she would willingly stand by his side with strength to match his own. Perhaps in these ways she could bring him close to her and break down the barriers separating them.

She went upstairs to find her sister, and when Dominic followed some time later to say that the minister was leaving to go on to Macon, he found Veroníque singing to the sleepy child held in her arms while Alice straightened the stools and chairs which had been erected as a castle. Veroníque was aware of her husband's eyes on her as she handed Michael back to his mother. She found herself wondering if she would ever hold a son of theirs.

The house was suddenly quiet. Michael slept; Paul was browsing through books in the library; Melissa had gone to her room. Veroníque stood watching the remains of her wedding breakfast being cleared away.

'You look tired,' Dominic said unexpectedly. 'Why don't you go upstairs?'

She nodded, grateful for the opportunity to escape before Melissa reappeared, but wishing he had not found it necessary to show her that he preferred his own company, even on this special day.

Michelle was laying out her night things on the bed. Veroníque stared at the gossamer-soft wrap and nightgown which the woman had made herself, and shook her head. She had backed down on the matter of the dress, for all the good it had done, but this was too much.

'Find me something else to wear,' she ordered.

'Don't you want to look your best for him?'

'I've told you before, it isn't going to be that kind of a marriage,' Veroníque returned. 'Help me out of this dress, and then you can go.'

Michelle shrugged her shoulders, sensing her mistress was in no mood for an argument and began to unhook her. She left Veroníque standing by the open window, lost in thought. As she closed the door of the bedroom behind her she heard the sound of the key being turned firmly in the lock.

CHAPTER SEVEN

THE days slipped by quickly for Veroníque. Happy, care-free days spent with her sister and the child she had come to love. There were picnics on the banks of the river near Moonshadow, visits to childhood haunts. Pleasant memories of days gone past. There were also more sombre times, like those when she rode back to Pinewood alone, to stand over the graves of her parents. She was lonely. She tried not to show it in her sister's company and had never confessed about the locked door which separated her from a husband she rarely saw.

She was often still in bed when he left the house in the morning, and asleep when he came back. If she was not, the fact that he and Micah were together downstairs deterred her from joining him. Days turned into weeks; four weeks since she had become his unwanted wife.

Dominic returned unexpectedly to the house one morning. To change his clothes, he told her, before he went to Macon on business. She could not conceal her surprise when he said: 'Do you know what day it is?'

'Yes. We have been married a month today.'

'You say it as if it has been a year. I have been neglecting you, haven't I? Why don't we have dinner tonight, just the two of us? Ask Michelle to do something special. If you want to, that is?'

'It would be nice to see you occasionally, Dominic.'

'I'll be back around nine.' He ignored the jibe. 'Probably starving.'

'I think we shall be able to provide a hearty meal for the master,' Veroníque said, with a smile that wiped the tiny lines of tiredness from the corners of her eyes.

He nodded and she walked with him to the stables and watched him ride off. He did not kiss her goodbye. He never touched her at all now, had not even pecked her cheek since the wedding ceremony when it was expected of him. The only thing he wanted was Moonshadow, she thought. Well, tonight he would discover he had a wife who also liked attention.

Veroníque wore the same gown as on her wedding day. Her mother's diamonds flashed and sparkled at her throat and in her ears. Her hair, worn in a more casual style, was loosely tied back with the last piece of silk ribbon she could find. The dining-table had been laid for hours. Two places set, the candles ready to light, the wine being cooled. Where was Dominic? Nine, he had said; it was now nearer ten.

At eleven o'clock, she knew all her well-laid plans had been for nothing. He had never intended to come back, she thought in a miserable silence; he had been humouring her again. The fried chicken was spoilt, the sauces cold; the hours Michelle had spent cooking, all for nothing. She would not make a scene. She would be very calm and unconcerned. Tomorrow she would suggest to Alice that they went over to Pinewood for a few days. That would put Dominic in his place. If he preferred his own company, then he would have it.

'I am going to bed, Tante Michelle. Tell Jacob and Letty they will not be needed any more,' she said. By the dining-room door she paused and stared bitterly at the table before her. 'Divide the food between you. I don't want any trace of this tomorrow morning.'

She was nearing the top of the stairs when the sound of voices arrested her. She watched Michelle open the front doors, heard the relief in her voice as she said, 'Monsieur Dominic—we were beginning to get worried. It is so late.'

Far too late, Veroníque thought, and her expression grew cold as Micah followed Dominic into the house. They both looked dishevelled. Dominic's coat and shirt were streaked with dirt. He looked up and saw her on the stairs.

'Veroníque—you waited up. I'm glad. I've had one hell of a day. Come down and talk to me.'

She hesitated, and was about to go down when he spun around on Micah and touched his shoulder.

'Come on—we need a couple of stiff drinks. Is there any food, Michelle? You didn't eat without me?'

'No, Monsieur, it is still in the kitchen with the wine.'

'Bring it into the drawing-room. Is there a fire? Good! I can see there is. Would you believe I went swimming this evening—not intentionally, I might add—my clothes are still damp. Veroníque, I thought you were coming down.' He broke off, frowning at the figure slowly making her way upstairs.

'I'm tired, Dominic.' Veroníque did not even look back at him as she answered. Did he expect her to sit in the same room with him, listen to him discussing the plantation with Micah, as if she did not exist? She heard him call her name again, heard the angry undertone and ignored it.

As usual she locked the door of her room as soon as she went in. She undressed and threw the white lace dress into the farthest corner of the room. She would never, never wear it again.

Extinguishing the oil lamp she climbed into bed and lay watching a shaft of bright moonlight slanting across the floor. In the still of the night, the sounds of the river invaded her room, bringing with them a strange kind of peace which always managed to disperse her troubled thoughts. She lay listening, remembering the gleeful smile on Michael's face the last time he had splashed his feet in the crystal-clear water, the contentment on that of her sister. And before long she fell asleep.

The sound of knocking on the communicating doors awoke her.

'Open the door, Veroníque,' Dominic ordered.

She did not answer and he knocked again, louder this time.

'Go away, Dominic. I was asleep.'

'If you had remained downstairs, I could have said what I wanted to then and saved this disturbance. I still want to talk to you. Are you going to open this door, or do I break it down and arouse most of the servants and probably your sister in the process?'

His tone warned her that the threat was not an idle one. Gathering up a wrap, she slipped it about her and turned the key in the lock, stepping quickly back. He stood between the two rooms, waiting while she lighted the lamp. When she turned she saw he was holding the bottle of wine they should have drunk at dinner and two of the glasses Paul had given them as a wedding present.

'We'll have that drink together now, shall we?' She watched him fill the glasses to the brim, stared coldly at the one he offered her, making no move to take it. 'A truce, Veroníque. I know you're angry, but I couldn't help being late. Everything went wrong. Well, almost everything. Take it, please. Let's be civilised.'

Words, only words, Veroníque thought. She drank quickly, emptying the glass before he had half-finished his, and felt, almost at once, its potency. With a surprised smile, Dominic refilled it and then his own.

'What are we celebrating?' she asked tartly. 'Have you bought more slaves for Moonshadow, more land perhaps?'

'No.' He frowned at her manner. 'I told you I had business in Macon, but it had nothing to do with the plantation. I do have some other interests.'

'Apart from Moonshadow, how can you spare the time? You don't even have time to have dinner with your own wife. No, that's wrong isn't it? I'm only something that belongs to you, like the Negroes, your horses, like Micah. You treat him better than you do me.'

'I have reasons for everything I do, Veroníque, but I'm damned if I'll be forced into explaning them just to accommodate your hurt pride,' Dominic snapped, tight-lipped.

'I don't care what you do,' Veroníque returned, her anger increasing. 'Why should I? You're nothing to me.'

'Then why did I come home to find you in that white dress, waiting for me even though I was two hours late? For a woman who doesn't care what a man thinks of her, you made yourself look extremely attractive.'

'I am a d'Estainville, Dominic. You told me to remember that at all times. What a pity you do not set the same high standard for yourself. Will you please go now? I want to go to bed.'

'You'll listen to what I have to say and then you will apologise, damn you, for whatever nasty little thoughts are being harboured in that head. Are you thinking I was with Melissa? Is that it?' Dominic demanded. Veroníque paled, and he knew his assumption had been correct.

'She has more claim on you than I have.'

'No one has any claim on me. I went to Macon with Micah. If you want to know the truth, I was looking for Sarah. I've been trying to find out where she might be ever since I came home. When I went through your father's papers the other day, I found a reference to a man who lived there, who had owned her for a few months.'

Her eyes blazed. 'Time for a Negress, but not me. Are you deliberately humiliating me?'

'Don't be an idiot. She wasn't there anyway and he didn't know where she had gone.' There had been a deep emptiness inside him since he had discovered the trip had been in vain. Returning to Moonshadow, to Veroníque, to try and talk and unload some of his pain had helped to ease the disappointment. Why didn't she try to understand? But then, why should she? What was Sarah to her but another Negress, while to him . . .

'So while I waited here for you, planning the dinner we were going to have together, at your own suggestion, you were chasing after news of your precious Sarah,' Veroníque said and her voice shook.

'I left Macon in enough time to get back here by nine,' Dominic went on, 'then I remembered old Frank Watson who used to raise the finest horses in the county, lived only a few miles out of town. Micah and I stopped there on the way. I saw a colt, a high-spirited young thing, but just right for Michael. It doesn't matter about his birthday; I couldn't resist buying it for the lad. He's a fine boy, Veroníque . . .'

Veroníque stepped back from him. With every word he drove the wedge deeper between them. Sarah came before her, even her own sister's child. Ordinarily she would have thought first of Michael and the pleasure the gift would give him, but at that moment she was by no means in control of her thoughts or her emotions.

'We have no reason to quarrel. Have another drink, Veroníque, then come and see the colt.'

Dominic held out another glass of red wine. Her head was already spinning. To drink more, she knew, would give her a terrible headache in the morning. As she shook her head, his face darkened.

'Take it. I'm tired of being polite. I didn't have to come up here and offer explanations, but I did. Meet me halfway, for God's sake, and drink with me.'

He thrust it towards her. A few spots spilled over the edge of the glass on to Veroníque's nightgown.

'You're drunk,' she accused, and her open palm caught

the side of the glass, sending it flying from his hand against the door.

Dominic's fingers fastened over her shoulders, biting into the soft skin beneath the thin robe, so fiercely she bit her lip in pain.

'Drunk?' he laughed, and the sound made her suddenly afraid. 'I wish to God I was. It would make being married to you a damn' sight easier.'

He shook her, so that her loose hair fell wildly about her face, then pushed it back with one hand, found her mouth with lips that burned like fire, holding her tight against him in an embrace that drove the breath from her body. Veroníque knew she had provoked him too far. She tried to free her wrists, but he had clamped them together behind her back. He seemed oblivious to her struggles, her pleas that he should release her.

'No. No, Dominic!' She twisted her mouth free, threw back her head to appeal to him.

'You are my wife, Veroníque. I'll have what is mine whenever I choose.'

'You're drunk, or you wouldn't talk this way, act like, like an animal,' Veroníque accused. 'You don't want me. You have Moonshadow. Or have you forgotten that is all you have ever wanted in life?'

'Not the only thing . . .' Dominic said and she suddenly stopped fighting against his hold. They had been in her room at Pinewood, she remembered, and grew afraid. 'Yes, you do remember, don't you? I said there was only one other thing I wanted. I was holding you in my arms then, wasn't I, and you weren't so eager to be rid of me then because you knew I wouldn't touch you under your father's roof. Well, you're in my house now, *ma belle*. Shall I tell you what I want? A son—a boy like Michael, bright-eyed and bonny. A son to inherit the biggest, grandest plantation in the whole of Georgia.'

Veroníque gave a cry of horror. He had lied to her. He would use her as her father had used Alice's mother; come to her bed only so that she could conceive his child, and then no doubt he would go back to Melissa's welcoming arms, satisfied that he had done his duty!

His fingers fastened in the front of her wrap, ripping it open. She thought she was going to faint as it was pulled from her shoulders, together with the nightgown beneath, and they fell in a huddle around her bare feet. But his mouth on hers dragged her back to life, threatening to expose her well-kept secret. She resisted, with all her might, his efforts to master her, to reduce her to the level of other women he had made love to over the years, but he was stronger, experienced, cruelly determined. His kisses parted her bruised lips, the confident hands which explored her body slowly, deliberately overcame her attempts to resist him.

She felt him lift her, his lips still against hers and carry her, not to her own bed, but into the other room, his room, to lay her on the huge, canopied double bed surrounded by heavy velvet drapes. The marriage bed of the d'Estainvilles: she had heard him joke about it one day as a little girl. Each new bride spent her first night here!

'This is where you should have been from the beginning,' Dominic said harshly in her ear. He had blocked his mind to the outcome of this moment of wildness. She was his wife and he wanted her in his bed.

It was morning! Veroníque was not aware she had slept after Dominic had turned away from her and gone to sleep, without one word of apology, or comfort. Her whole body ached from his love-making. She lifted her arms and found dark smudges on her wrists and upper arms where she had fought him.

Hot tears scalded down over her cheeks. She wiped them away, but more came, dampening the pillows. She felt Dominic move beside her, turned on to her side and pressed her hands against her mouth so that he would not hear her moment of weakness.

A hand touched her shoulder. When she did not move, she was pulled bodily around to face him. She heard him utter a savage expletive at the sight of her wet eyes. What was it she watched flash across his face? Pity? Regret? Remorse?

'Even now you don't use your tears as a weapon? I'm everything you ever thought me to be, Veroníque—and worse. Curse me, for God's sake! Tell me how I've outraged not only your body, but your dignity. That hurts more than anything, I think, because you know now if I want you again I'll have you, and the next time you won't be so foolish as to try and stop me.' He wanted to shake an answer out of her. She just lay there, looking at him, her eyes swimming with tears which ran down on to his hands and on to the sheets. No reproach—at least delivered with words. It lay in those tears, more eloquent than all the curses she could have rained on his head.

He sprang from the bed, gathered up his clothes and disappeared into the adjoining room which he used as a dressing-room. As the door slammed behind him, Verónique lay back in the huge bed and allowed the tears to drain from her.

The days which followed were unreal. The long sleepless nights spent listening for the sound of Dominic entering his own room. Towards dawn she would fall asleep, not awakening sometimes until noon. Her afternoons were spent with Alice and Michael, her evenings, after they had eaten together, alone in the drawing-room. Pride forbade her to make her peace with Dominic.

As the weeks passed and June slipped into a sweltering July, she at last accepted he was not going to play the heavy-handed husband again. Her cold attitude relaxed slightly, enough to be civil to him in front of her sister, at least. Once she caught him off guard, watching little Michael riding the pony he had bought. Saw his face soften, heard the voice which taunted and abused her lose its brusqueness and grow gentle, and his words came back to her. 'Shall I tell you what I want? A son—a boy like Michael, bright-eyed and bonny. A son to inherit the biggest, grandest plantation in the whole of Georgia.'

A child! Would she become pregnant from the wild night? The thought both frightened and excited her. If she gave him a son, would it draw them together or would he lavish all his love and affection on it, driving yet another wedge between them?

She managed to persuade Alice to stay at Pinewood with her for a few days. Dominic was not in the house when they left, taking Tante Michelle and two of the kitchen staff with them. Jacob drove them over in the rig and then went back to Moonshadow. When they returned five days later, Dominic made no mention of the curt letter she had left him informing him of their departure. He asked after the house and if she thought the harvest would be a good one, but never once did he rebuke her for leaving.

She had to admit, reluctant though she was to do so, that Pinewood was well run under Micah's supervision. He had kept his word, she realised, and given her the freedom she had demanded at the start of their marriage. She was free to come and go as she pleased, to stay at Pinewood or beneath his roof. And yet she was not free. Chains of love, as strong as chains of iron, bound her to his side and could never be broken.

Atlanta was besieged by the army of General Sherman. When the news reached Pinetree County it stunned every man, woman and child, old enough to comprehend its meaning. Yankees about to take Atlanta! Impossible! Following on the heels of rumour came fact. Families on their way to Macon or Augusta told of continuing Confederate defeats and withdrawals from fortified positions they had once held secure. Sherman always followed close on their heels, driving his men through drenching rain and thick mud, across the river to menace Atlanta. The city came under fire for the first time on the twenty-first of July.

Despite the gloom which had descended over the house when the news of the siege first reached Moonshadow, the war still seemed a very long way away during that scorching hot July. Besides, there was so much to do. Veroníque now spent at least two days a week at Pinewood and revelled in the fact that, for this short time at least, she was her own mistress.

She had noticed how easily Alice had settled there again now that their father no longer sat in judgment. With Atlanta a dubious spot to live in, especially with a young child, Veroníque insisted her sister remained with her, and Dominic, somewhat surprisingly she thought, approved the suggestion. She knew he was growing fond of Michael and was reluctant to see the child leave.

It was at the back of Veroníque's mind that she might still be able to reunite Paul and her sister. Dominic had taken away the home she had planned for them, but she had Pinewood, and would gladly give it up if the need arose.

More and more people, friends of hers and Dominic's and of her father's, broke their journey at Moonshadow on their way south. The news did not improve. The Union army was encamped twenty miles from Atlanta. Sherman was rapidly becoming known throughout the South as an advocate of 'total war'. Divide and conquer—and then push on, living off the land.

'Don't worry,' Veroníque said, placing a comforting arm around her sister's shoulders. For days she had watched her grow more and more anxious, and knew that she was concerned for Paul. Less than an hour ago they had heard the railroad had been cut by Yankee troops, ten miles east of the city. 'The cavalry will soon chase them off and take it back. If our men leave Atlanta Paul has more sense than to remain, even to write his book. He has you and Michael to come back to, and I think it will bring him back very soon.'

'You always were so sure he loved me. I'm not. He didn't have to go back to Atlanta again. I know I said it wouldn't work between us, but that doesn't stop me wanting him, Veroníque. What fools we both are . . .'

'I've written to him,' Veroníque blurted out, unable to bear the sadness in Alice's eyes. 'A week ago.'

'Write to him again, Veroníque. Tell him . . . tell him I am going away . . . anything, only make him come back where it is safe.'

'I will. I promise.'

'Are you going to Pinewood again today?'

'Yes, but I won't be long. What are you smiling at?'

'You—my baby sister. How you have grown up. What about Moonshadow?'

'What about it?'

'This is your home now, not Pinewood. When the war is over and you and Dominic have more time to spend together, he's not going to like you running off over there every five minutes. He'll want to install a proper overseer and take things easy. If you ask me, you're both working yourselves to a standstill. He uses this place as an excuse to avoid you, and you do exactly the same with Pinewood.'

'Nonsense,' Veroníque returned. Her face was suddenly pale as she stood up. The room swam out of focus. She reeled backwards grabbing at her sister for support.

'My dear, what is it? You look ghastly. Sit down, I'll ring for Tante Michelle. There now, didn't I say you were working too hard?'

'It isn't that . . .'

'Has it happened before?' Alice knelt at her sister's side, her eyes questioning. Veroníque knew what she was thinking, had considered the possibility herself and dismissed it. 'Well?'

'At least twice this week. No, Alice, it's too soon. It couldn't be . . .'

'I think you should send for a doctor. If only Paul was here . . . he's a qualified doctor, remember?'

The dizziness slowly receded. Ignoring her sister's protests, Veroníque stood up again and drew on her gloves.

'I'm tired, that's all. Promise me you won't discuss this with anyone, Alice. Please.'

'With Dominic? If you're pregnant, Veroníque, then he should know. You must begin to rest. No more riding over to Pinewood.'

'You sound just like Father! I'm not a precious piece of porcelain. I'll be back by twelve, I hope. We can finish putting the furniture into the play-room for Michael if you like.'

It was, in fact, almost three o'clock before Veroníque returned to Moonshadow. She was hot and tired from the ride back and still inwardly fuming at the stroke of ill fortune which threatened to ruin her old home. She had been informed that thirty of the field-hands had been conscripted the previous day and shipped by train to Atlanta, where they were needed to dig trenches and build barricades for the defence of the city.

Atlanta needed them? she had queried. What about Pinewood? Not enough men remained behind to harvest the cotton when it was ready. She pleaded for their return, threatened when that failed, damned the red-faced Confederate captain to the fires of hell when he said there was nothing he could do, and rode back to Moonshadow in a black, despairing mood.

At first she had thought of asking Dominic to transfer some of the Negroes, but as she passed through the fields and saw the cotton beginning to flower in the hot August sun, she knew he would not allow one man to leave. This place came first.

When she first saw a carriage in the driveway she thought Paul had come back in answer to her letter, but the man waiting beside it was a stranger, hard-faced and unfriendly, who stared at her rudely as she went into the house. Alice met her in the hall and she looked worried.

'There is someone to see you.' She took her sister's arm, and drew her into the library. 'My dear, I don't know quite how to break this to you. If only Dominic was here! I don't know whether he would want you to see her.'

'See who, Alice? What are you being so mysterious about?'

'Elizabeth d'Estainville is here—his mother.'

'Why, she must have just heard about the wedding.' Veroníque's pale face brightened. 'They have made up their differences. That's wonderful, isn't it?'

'I don't think so. Veroníque, she hasn't been living in Richmond. She—she isn't the same woman we knew before. Dear heaven, am I doing the right thing in telling you? Perhaps Dominic doesn't want you to know what she has become.'

'Become?' Veroníque echoed.

'For the past two years she has been living in one of the houses in the warehouse quarter, not far from my home. Do I have to tell you about places like that, Veroníque, the women who live there and how they make their living? Mrs d'Estainville, or Madame Elizabeth as she prefers to be known, has earned herself a certain reputation.'

'Go on.' Veroníque visualised the area where Alice had lived. The filth and squalor of the houses, the unkempt men and women who wandered the streets. 'She is living with another man . . .?'

'Who knows how many she has had since her husband died?' Alice returned. 'Poor Dominic! To come home and find his mother is no less than—than a whore. I'm sorry, my dear. I am no longer the genteel young lady who went away. I've learned to stand on my own two feet in some pretty rotten circumstances where polite chit-chat gets you nowhere.'

'Dominic knows about her, then?'

'He was out on the town that night with Paul, if you remember—the night he found me. I suspect he had been to see her. He was in a very strange mood.'

'What shall I do?'

'Let me send her away,' Alice pleaded.

'No. She is Dominic's mother. Whatever she is now, she once was mistress here, Alice. Without knowing what Dominic will do, I shall have to act as I think best. Will you ask Tante Michelle to bring some mint tea and some of those little cakes we had yesterday? I must make her feel welcome.'

Hesitantly Veroníque pushed open the door of the sitting-room and went in, pushing back wisps of stray hair which were brushing untidily around her face.

Elizabeth d'Estainville turned to watch the young woman moving towards her, hand outstretched in welcome, and ignored it. The pointed snub brought Veroníque to an abrupt halt. She had always been a little afraid of Dominic's mother, of her worldliness. Alice's revelation as to what she had become had not shocked her as deeply as it would have done three years ago. She had grown up, become a woman, and even though she coloured slightly, she stood her ground in the face of the other woman's cold reception.

'I am Dominic's wife . . . perhaps you can remember me? Veroníque—Veroníque de Brissac.'

'I am hardly likely to forget you, or the trick your father played on me in order to get this place,' Elizabeth returned, staring hard at Veroníque's dusty riding skirt and wind-blown hair.

'I apologise for my appearance, Mrs d'Estainville. You did not send word you were coming, and I have had a very busy morning over at Pinewood.'

'Are things so bad that Dominic cannot install an overseer to run his plantations?' The woman's voice was tinged with a mockery which immediately aroused Veroníque's temper, but she quickly curbed it.

'I have ordered some tea and something to eat. I am sure you must be hungry. Alice tells me you have come all the way from Atlanta? Is that so?'

'Alice? Oh, yes . . . your sister. I thought the face was familiar. I see so many these days.' Elizabeth relaxed down on to the velvet chaise-longue beneath the window. This is where she had sat and done her sewing, she recalled, the windows thrown open to allow the scent of magnolias and honeysuckle into the room. Dominic had changed nothing, not even Grandfather Luc's old chair before the fireplace.

The sight of it irritated her because it was a reminder she was now no longer the mistress in this house. That right belonged to the chit of a girl standing in front of her, Dominic's wife, and as ignorant of the world as he was knowledgeable, by the looks of her. 'The de Brissacs don't seem to be having much luck lately, do they? She married beneath her, I believe, a seaman or something, after he had made her pregnant.'

'That isn't true.' Veroníque sprang immediately to the defence of her sister and saw by the smile on Elizabeth's face that the reaction was expected. It was as if she had come prepared to dislike her, Veroníque thought.

Michelle brought in the tea and cakes. For a moment Elizabeth's gaze fastened on the face of the quadroon. She watched Michelle leave and then gave a laugh.

'Dominic has inherited his father's weakness, I see.'

'Tante Michell has been in my family since I was a little girl, as you well know. Dominic is nothing like his father. It is his grandfather he resembles. I didn't know he had written to you.'

'He didn't. Oh, he told me you were to marry him. I learned the rest from someone else—a friend of yours. Paul Loring.'

'Paul? Paul came to see you?' Veroníque echoed in surprise. 'For what reason?'

'He believed he had a grievance against a man in my employ. He and Dominic were set upon one night in Atlanta after they visited my establishment. He blamed me for sending men after them. He was right, of course, I did.'

'I'm sorry, I don't understand. You—you sent men after your own son—to beat him up—rob him? Do you know what you are saying?'

Veroníque stopped pouring out the tea and looked across at her visitor. Elizabeth d'Estainville wore a pale brown travelling dress, the sleeves and the hem of the skirt embroidered with a fancy design in beige silk thread. Long gloves covered her hands and on her head was perched a small, feather trimmed hat. She looked elegant, respectable, yet Veroníque was suddenly aware of the hatred burning out of her eyes.

'Why—why have you come, Mrs d'Estainville?'

'I no longer use that name. I am called Madame Elizabeth.'

'By your customers?' Veroníque asked, rising to her feet. 'Am I mistaken in thinking you came to make peace with Dominic?'

'Don't get on your high horse with me, you stupid little fool!' Elizabeth spat the words at her, her face twisting into a sardonic smile. 'You may be his wife, but that only puts you on the same level as me. Are you his wife? Yes, I suppose you must be. Dominic's man enough for that even though I hear the marriage wasn't to your liking. Your friend Loring was most concerned about you both. He has some idea in his head that I might have wanted to upset the apple cart. How right he was.'

'I'm sorry, I don't understand. I know you and Dominic have had some bad feeling between you in the past, but couldn't that be resolved now we are married?' Veroníque asked.

'Resolved?' Elizabeth's bitter laughter echoed in the room. 'Do you know what he did? He took a whip and beat his father senseless, over my husband's mistress—Sarah!'

White-faced, Veroníque nodded.

'He—he has been trying to find her ever since he came home.'

'Has he now? Perhaps he wants to set her up here again, as his father did.'

'He is very concerned over what happened to her, but he has not spoken of bringing her here if he does find her.'

'You had better get used to the idea that he might. After all, as his mother, she has as much right here as you—perhaps more.'

For a full moment Veroníque did not realise the implication behind the quietly spoken words. As she stood stock still, the colour draining from her cheeks, Elizabeth rose to her feet. She was smiling. Veroníque remembered she had seen that smile the day she had come to Pinewood looking for Micah. When she had found him gone she had returned to Moonshadow and burned the cottage where Sarah had lived.

'Did you hear me, Mrs d'Estainville? Do you understand what I am saying? Dominic is not my son.'

'I don't believe you.' Veroníque's reply was barely

audible. She swayed unsteadily, caught at the edge of the table for support and stared with horror-filled eyes at the woman facing her.

'Why do you think he's never been able to find Sarah? Because she's with me—out of his way. Do you think I want to see her installed in this house again—with her son? What a cosy little group you would make! What an inheritance he has given you—and your children. You do plan to have children, I suppose? I doubt if anyone will suspect the bloodline isn't pure—you are both so dark . . .'

'Stop it! Stop it, do you hear! I don't believe a word. My father would never have agreed to the marriage if what you say is true.'

'You don't think Dominic admitted it, do you? My God, what an innocent you are! He wanted Moonshadow back, and as you say, he's like his grandfather—utterly ruthless. He would have done anything to get this place, and the respectability which comes with it. You have given him that. When a baby comes you will be a complete family . . .'

'There won't be any children,' Veroníque blurted out and again Elizabeth's laughter filled the room. 'Get out! You are evil . . . Get out!'

Her composure broke. She began to sob, clinging to the table for support. Elizabeth reached the door and then turned to take a last look at her. The men she had sent after Dominic had failed miserably. One had died and it would be a long time before the other one returned to her favour. She had made up for their mistakes. It was work well done. In her time Moonshadow had been a prison. Now it would be so for Dominic, and for the sobbing girl a few feet away. Her satisfaction would be complete when she returned to Atlanta and told Sarah what she had done. Three people unhappy—a marriage wrecked. . . . Elizabeth felt well pleased with herself as she walked slowly out to where Henri Dolman waited in the carriage.

Alice sent one of the yard-boys into the fields to find Dominic. It was an hour before he dismounted in front of the house, together with another rider, and came running into the house.

'She's in the study,' Alice cried as he turned towards the stairs. 'She won't open the door, Dominic. She's . . . she's

. . . I don't know how to describe her. After your mother had gone . . .'

Dominic stopped short with a savage oath. Paul came through the doors behind him, saw the coldness which settled over his face and wished himself a thousand miles away.

'I didn't think she'd come here. I only wanted to warn her off . . .' he began.

'I could have told you that wouldn't work. The next time I'll deal with her,' Dominic snapped bleakly. 'How long was she here, Alice? What did she say to Veronique?'

'I don't know. She saw her alone. When I heard her leave, I went into the sitting-room. Veronique was just standing there, crying. She looked . . . Dominic, she looked as if someone had just destroyed her world.'

'Oh, my God . . .' Paul breathed.

The hard black eyes which settled on him held murder in them. Alice saw it too and was frightened.

Dominic stepped up to the study door, rapped on it sharply. There was no sound from within. Paul moved closer, put his ear against the oak panels . . . shook his head.

Dominic knocked again, forcing down a moment of panic as he heard a familiar sound from within—the faint, but unmistakable click of a pistol hammer being drawn back.

'Veronique—open the door.'

He did not expect an answer, was surprised, immediately alert to danger, when the door was unlocked, but not opened. Paul started forward, but Dominic blocked his path.

'Stay outside. I think she has a pistol.'

'That's all the more reason for me to go in then,' Paul replied in a fierce whisper. 'It's my fault that woman came here. She's raked up that old lie again about you and Sarah. Nothing else could have provoked this kind of hysteria in someone as sensible as Veronique.'

Again he tried to step forward, but Dominic caught him firmly by his good arm and pushed him back. He swung the door open. A single lamp burned on the desk in front of the french windows. Veronique stood to one side of it. The tears had dried on her cheeks, but her lashes were still wet.

She looked like a ghost. Behind him he heard Alice gasp, heard Paul order her to be quiet.

'Put down the pistol, Veronίque,' Dominic said quietly.

The silver-mounted duelling pistol she held by her side was slowly raised until it was in line with his chest. Behind it, her eyes stared at him blankly. Her free hand was wound into the heavy curtain drapes in order to support herself. A groan broke from Dominic's lips.

'Dear God, what has she done to you?'

The pistol wavered and then became steady again. He stepped forward, ignoring Paul's warning and looked down the barrel aimed at his heart.

'It's not true what she told you. She did tell you I was not her son?' A faint nod, nothing more. 'It's a lie, but you have only my word. She would like to see me dead, Veronίque. She tried to kill me some time ago and failed. You're the instrument she has chosen this time. Do you want to see me dead too? If you believe her, *ma belle*, then you had better use that pistol.'

Veronίque looked down at the weapon in her hand. Dominic measured the distance between them, knew he could throw himself forward and probably succeed in taking it from her, but he did not move. At that moment he cared little if she pulled the trigger or not. Her face tortured him—the grief expressed there—the indecision—the look of a little lost child.

She raised her eyes to his face. They were suddenly clear and rational.

'I loved you.' Her words hit him like an iron fist. 'I've loved you since I was sixteen. I don't feel anything now—just an emptiness. A terrible emptiness . . .'

The gun fell from her fingers on to the carpet. She began to sway unsteadily. Dominic moved forward just in time to catch her as her knees buckled and she folded like a rag doll towards the ground.

CHAPTER EIGHT

VERONÍQUE opened her eyes and turned her aching head slowly towards the window, where the drapes had been pulled to keep out the bright sunlight. One faint yellow ray slipped through across the bed.

'She's awake,' she heard someone say close by.

'Alice . . .' She tried to sit up, but immediately her sister was bending over her, restraining hands pressing her firmly, but gently, back on to the pillows.

'Lie still, my dear. Tante Michelle, open the curtains just a little.'

'How are you feeling, Veroníque?' Paul perched himself on the edge of the bed, his fingers closing purposefully over her pulse.

Veroníque managed a weak smile. She didn't feel like smiling, but the three faces crowding around her looked so anxious.

'I have a terrible headache,' she murmured. Memories came flooding back. Paul felt her grow tense beneath his grasp as she fought to shut out what had happened downstairs.

'It's all right,' he soothed. 'A day or two in bed and you'll be fine again. You've been doing too much, you know. As a doctor, I'm telling you to slow down. Let Micah deal with the problems at Pinewood for a while. As a friend I'm going to make sure you carry out my instructions, even if I have to spend the next week here.'

'I fainted.' Veroníque said slowly. She had never done that in her life before. 'Paul—I didn't hurt my baby, did I?'

She knew something was wrong by the look Michelle exchanged with Alice, and caught at Paul's sleeve with a distressed cry.

'I'm sorry, Veroníque. There was no baby. A number of things could have induced the symptoms—the shock of your father's death, for one . . . your relationship with Dominic. Dominic has told me everything. I wish I could tell you otherwise, but I can't. You are not pregnant.'

Veroníque did not answer. She had not wanted Dominic's child, so why did she not feel glad at the news?

'Dominic is waiting . . .' Paul murmured.

'I don't want to see him.'

'He's almost out of his mind with worry.'

'As you wish.'

The door closed behind him leaving her alone. A moment later she heard it open again and saw Dominic's reflection in the mirror on the opposite wall.

She looked at him as if he was a stranger. That he could bear, painful though it was, but as he watched her lift a hand to her dishevelled hair, a hand that trembled visibly, betraying agitation she refused to acknowledge in his presence, that hurt him far worse than any tirade of abuse.

'We must talk, Veroníque.'

'We have nothing to say to each other,' she returned tonelessly.

'Perhaps you have nothing to say. I must speak, make sure we understand each other before this ugly mess gets any more out of hand than it is.' Dominic walked slowly across to the window and stared down at the horses being exercised below. He had been alone before—he could cope with it again. Deliberately he shut his mind to how difficult it was going to be. 'I don't believe for a moment you accept the story she told you. It's an excuse to erect yet another barrier between us. That's what she wants.'

'Think that if you like,' Veroníque returned.

'When we were first married, I intended things to be exactly as you wanted, a very uncomplicated marriage of convenience. For a while we were beginning to make two separate lives for ourselves and then . . .' Dominic turned and looked at her huddled in the large bed, holding the clothes tightly around her shoulders as if afraid he might suddenly pounce on her and rip them away. 'I spoiled what there was between us, I realise that, but if you're honest with yourself, you must admit that part of the blame was yours. We both have too much pride, are easily angered. You never could back down, even as a young girl. But that's past. Paul tells me you must rest for a few days. I expect you are relieved your fears for a child are unfounded?'

She looked into his face, searching for some sign that would tell her that he too was pleased—or disappointed his dream for a son was not to be realised. No sign, no flicker of expression in those black eyes. Whatever he felt, she was not to share it with him.

'It is inconceivable that you expect me to remain in this house. Your mother will not stop with me, you know. I saw it in her face. She is going to take great pleasure in circulating that story again and again. I—I don't think I could bear the gossip.'

'The only alternative I might consider is for you to live at Pinewood, but until the war is over I consider that unwise, and unsafe, even if Alice was to go with you. No, Veroníque, I must insist that you remain here where I can care for you as I promised your father I would.'

'Care for me?' she echoed. 'You have treated me disgracefully.'

He came very close to the bed and she flinched away from him, afraid he was going to touch her. Dominic's mouth deepened into a grim line. 'You will stay. You remember too well what happened after Alice left home . . . the way people talked. Yes, you will stay. You know it is the only sensible thing to do.'

'And when the war is over?' Veroníque forced the words out through stiff lips. 'Will you set me free? Just let me go?'

'Is that what you want?'

'Yes.'

'Then you shall be free—of this house you hate and a husband whose very presence makes you tremble in fear. Yes, Veroníque, you shall have your freedom. I wish it was as simple for me.'

That August Moonshadow became a halfway house for people who had left Atlanta under the threat of Sherman's determined attacks upon the city and sought refuge with relatives further south or in towns like Macon or Augusta. Southern hospitality being what it was, no one was ever turned away from the door, and Veroníque found her days so occupied with the troubles of others that she had little time to dwell on her own unhappiness. Not until she lay in bed at night, listening to the soft murmur of the river, the call of a night owl and loneliness overcame her, did she give way to her feelings. Often, during those long hours, she cried until she slept from sheer exhaustion.

Sometimes a troop of Confederate cavalry stopped by for food or to water their horses or even replace them with fresh mounts which Dominic allowed them to choose from his personal stock. Veroníque was shocked by the change in these grey-clad soldiers, many of whom were husbands or sons from neighbouring plantations, who she had watched ride off to war proud and confident of victory. The men who now lounged wearily beneath the shade of the trees on the lawn were hollow-eyed, unshaven, their clothes uncared for. Atlanta was about to be abandoned. If it fell, the South would be open to Sherman and his inhuman policy of 'total war'. War on helpless old men and women, children who played at soldiers while their fathers and brothers died in some far off place in another State.

Since she had collapsed Paul had visited her every day. Whether it was to see her or Alice, Veroníque was not sure, and did not mind if it was the latter. When Michelle brought him to her room, she was already up and dressed and the sight of her in riding attire brought an immediate frown to his his face.

'And where do you think you are going?'

'To Pinewood. Don't look at me like that. I have to. Five more of the field-hands ran off last night—and six from here. If this goes on neither Dominic nor I will have the cotton harvested this year.'

'Does he know you're going out?' Paul perched himself on the edge of a chair, watching her as she pulled on high leather riding boots.

'I'm not a prisoner here. Until this beastly war is over and we can go our separate ways, I have to make the best of this marriage,' Veroníque returned. 'I regard Pinewood as my home more than this place. Dominic understands this and has said I may do as I please.'

'You would anyway,' Paul said dryly.

'Yes. I would.' Veroníque's eyes were shadowed with sudden pain. 'I haven't seen him for days? Where is he?'

'Yesterday he stayed with us. He rode back with Melissa and me this morning. Do you know anything about this idea of his to band the plantation owners together and pool the labour? It's a damn' good idea, but I wonder how many of them will stick to it when the going gets harder. Bart Richardson and his family moved out of their place a week ago.'

'But—but they're only three miles from you,' Veroníque gasped. 'Why? Our soldiers still control the area. Sherman may be ready to take Atlanta, but he can't come any further. Can he?'

'I think we are both prepared for the fact he could,' Paul returned gravely. 'But there are other things to be considered besides the bluecoats. Deserters, for instance. We've had four cases of murder in the past month. There's even talk of an armed band operating in the county, raiding unprotected places, robbing women left behind in lonely plantation houses with no protection except a couple of black servants, and I'm sure they are no longer trustworthy.'

'We have always treated our servants well,' Veroníque said. 'Michelle and Jacob—they are more to us than just employees.' Once she had wondered what would happen if the opportunity arose for Michelle to leave. That day seemed almost upon them.

The door was flung noisily open. Michael appeared, banging a toy drum which Dominic had found for him in the attic and proudly announced he had used as a child. Veroníque saw Paul's face grow pale as the boy paraded around the room, banging noisily and trying to sing *The Bonnie Blue Flag*, which Alice had been attempting to teach him for several days. Usually he was not allowed to appear when Paul was in the house, and Veroníque wondered how he had managed to slip unnoticed from her sister's watchful gaze.

'Mr Paul Loring, sir, may I present General Michael . . .' she hesitated, catching the tightening of Paul's lips, 'Tanner. Staunch defender of our gracious home against the Yankees.'

'I'm honoured, General.' Paul rose to his feet, bowed slightly. Michael beamed at him. Soldiers! His favourite game. He gave a loud imitation of the rebel yell which he had heard the other soldiers do who came so often to the house, wheeled excitedly around towards Veroníque—and bumped heavily into a table. Paul caught him around the waist with his one arm and landed him safely on two feet. 'Easy, General. We don't want you hospitalised for the duration of the war. Good men are hard to find.'

'Who are you?' Michael was gazing, with all the wide-eyed innocent fascination of a child, at Paul's empty sleeve.

Veroníque caught her breath as Paul reached out with a smile and ruffled the boy's hair. Did he see the resemblance in the smile—those large eyes? Surely he could not ignore what she knew to be in his heart. She watched Paul stiffen. He stepped forward and found he was looking at the birthmark beneath Michael's hair.

'Oh, my God,' he ejaculated softly. 'Why didn't she show me this? Why didn't you tell me?'

'Would you have been able to accept it? I've never lied to you, Paul—no more has Alice. You chose to believe Melissa.'

'She is my sister. Why should she want to destroy me, Veroníque, and deprive this child of its rightful father?' Paul looked across at Veroníque as if expecting her to supply all the right answers.

She shook her head. Melissa's dislike of her gentle brother was beyond her comprehension. 'What can I say? Only what I have already told you, Paul. Michael is your son—you can see that for yourself. Alice could have shown you the birthmark in the beginning, given the proof you so unfairly demanded. But she chose otherwise. You had no reason to doubt her. She had never loved any other man in her life. You were very drunk the night she comforted you. When she needed you . . .'

'I ran away. I listened to my vile-tongued sister because I couldn't face the responsibility of what I had done—or your father, to confess I couldn't remember a single moment of the time Alice and I spent together. I chose the coward's way out, didn't I? The easy way.'

'By enlisting?' Veroníque asked quietly. 'You have suffered as deeply as my sister.'

'Is that why she kept the boy out of my way? If I had seen this before . . .'

'You would have offered to marry me . . . as you would have done three years ago if I had remained at home and given Father your name as he ordered.' Alice stood in the doorway, pale but composed. She held out her arms towards Michael, but he had found a new friend. Ignoring his mother, he offered Paul his drum and it was taken with a slow smile.

'Veroníque, will you take care of the child for a few moments? Alice and I have things to discuss which are long overdue.'

'Of course. He can come downstairs with me while I have coffee.' Taking Michael's hand she led him to the door, to where her sister stood, silent and grave-faced. 'It took two of you to make a baby in the first place. Now it's going to take two to patch up this stupid separation.'

Her sister's lips quivered. Veroníque saw she was close to tears. She led Michael out of the bedroom and closed the door behind her, and took him downstairs to the dining-room where she found Melissa seated at the table, drinking coffee.

'Go and find Belinda,' Veroníque murmured, pushing Michael towards the kitchen. 'Tell her I said you can have chocolate cookies and milk until Mummy comes down-stairs.'

Melissa's eyes followed the boy as he scampered eagerly away and then fastened questioningly on Veroníque as she poured herself a cup of black coffee.

'Alice is still here, then?'

'Of course.' A smile touched Veroníque's mouth and the other woman looked at her with a frown.

'You look like a cat who has just had the fresh cream,' she said acidly. 'What's so funny?'

'Thoughts—private thoughts.' Veroníque drank her coffee. Dominic joined them as she replenished the cup.

'Did Paul come to see you?' her husband asked.

'Yes. He is with Alice now. I—I think they have resolved their differences.'

'How cosy.' Dominic's sardonic smile mocked her. 'And where do you think you're going?'

'To Pinewood. The place might be needed soon.'

His eyes narrowed sharply and she realised he had mis-taken her meaning. He thought she meant to live there, against his wishes.

'There are reports of armed deserters only a few miles from there. You're not going alone. Micah will accompany you and if you give me any trouble over it, I'll lock you in your room until I get back. It's too dangerous to ride alone.'

'Very well, if you insist.' She was not going to argue with him in such an awkward mood. He looked tired, she thought, but then remembering Paul had told her he had stayed at the Folly the previous night, she hardened her heart against feeling sorry for him. He had Melissa still—that was enough.

'Has Paul mentioned the plan I have to pool our labour resources?'

'It sounds a good idea—if it works.'

'It means I'll have to use the Negroes from Pinewood too,' he warned. 'If there are no more runaways, the work force there should still be quite high. Give Micah a list of capable men—and the house staff, we may need them to double up on other work.' Dominic looked at Veroníque for a long moment and then, with great hesitation, he asked: 'Will—will you be here when I get back tonight?'

Of course, she almost answered, but the words died in her throat. After the meeting, he would go to Melissa again. Then let him go—and let him wonder if he would come back to an empty house. For all it mattered to him! She shrugged non-committally and heard him swear under his breath.

'Damn you! Please yourself.'

Veroníque threw open the french windows and gazed out at the tall pine trees which lined the driveway up to the house. For more than an hour and a half, she had toured the fields with Micah, secretly hoping to find some fault with the way he had looked after the place during her absence, but at the end of the inspection, she was forced to admit he had done his work well. She turned and looked at the silent figure standing by the door and said quietly, 'Come in and sit down.'

He came into the room, but stood by a chair, obviously waiting for her comments on what she had seen. Crossing to the decanter of sherry on the sideboard, Veroníque poured two drinks and held one out towards him.

'You drink with my husband, will you drink with me?'

Micah's eyes scrutinised her face. For a moment she

thought he was going to refuse, then he took the glass and sat down. She seated herself on the couch, wondering if she had taken leave of her senses to offer not only a drink, but polite conversation to this man who had made it abundantly clear he disliked her.

'I hope you are satisfied with what has been done here?' Micah said at length when she made no attempt to open a conversation.

'I think you know I would have expected to find things not to my liking,' she returned honestly. 'However, I can find no fault with your management of my home, Micah. I shall give a good report of you to my husband.'

The smile on the Negro's face told her how ludicrous her words must sound to him. He acted the slave, but he was more free than she was. He had Dominic's friendship—his loyalty—spent more time with him than she did, talked more easily—shared confidences.

'Tell me about Sarah,' she ordered suddenly. 'I want to know all about her.'

'Why should my mother interest you?'

'Mrs d'Estainville made a special journey from Atlanta to tell me that Dominic was not her son but Sarah's. Did Sarah ever tell you she was Dominic's mother? Please—be truthful with me.'

'It was Elizabeth d'Estainville who first spread the lie about his birth,' Micah said. 'You have met her . . . have surely seen the hatred she has for Mister Dominic. She was a jealous woman possessed with the idea of revenging herself on her husband and the son she did not want. If my mother was here, she would confirm my words.'

'Dominic has been trying to find her . . .'

'I know. Perhaps it will be better if he never does. He has been hurt too much already. For her he almost killed his father, and was forced to leave the home which meant everything to him. During the years he was away, I watched the bitterness and loneliness eating at his heart until he became a different man. More ruthless than his grand-père—dedicated to retrieving Moonshadow no matter what it cost him—and regardless what it might cost others. Since he has returned, only you have ever made him stop and question whether he has been right or wrong in his methods. There was a time when I saw you both together and it was like the old days. I was an illiterate field-hand then, but I would gladly have given up my education and the high position he has granted me to see him happy again. He smiles, but it does not come from within him. There is no warmth, no satisfaction in anything he does.'

'I cannot help him,' Veroníque said, turning away so that he would not see the bright tears which flooded into her eyes.

'If you love him still, then stay with him—help him. God knows he has need of allies . . .'

'Yes.' Veroníque looked out on to the gravel drive and in her mind's eye saw herself as a little girl again, swinging on the padded seat Dominic had just erected beneath the trees. She had decided. A child no longer, but a grown woman, who must say goodbye to girlish dreams and face reality . . . the reality that she would always love Dominic, but he would never love her. Such marriages had worked before. This one would, too. She would make it work. He needed her by his side in these troubled times. Afterwards—well, she would not think of that until the war was over . . .

'If the horses are ready I think we should be going back home,' she said bravely.

It was dark before Dominic returned to Moonshadow. Veroníque heard his voice as she sat in the study, a pile of ledgers open before her. She fully expected him to go into the drawing-room or directly upstairs and was surprised when the door opened and he stood there, looking across to where she sat in front of the escritoire.

'What are you doing at this time of night? Do you know it's almost ten-thirty?'

Closing the door behind him, he paused to light another lamp, for the one on the desk was the only one Veroníque had bothered with, and then went to the tantalus on the table. She heard the chink of the cut-glass decanter as he poured himself the customary drink and bent lower over her work, unable to find any words of conversation.

'What are you doing?'

'These are the ledgers from Pinewood . . .'

'Oh! You've taken them over again, have you? Aren't you satisfied with Micah's handling of the place?'

Veroníque turned and looked at him, standing with his

back to the other lamp. The flickering light outlined his tall frame, but his face remained shadowed. He sounded irritable. She was too tired to get involved in a squabble.

'From what I saw this morning, I'm more than satisfied with the work he has done—and I told him so,' she returned and saw him stiffen.

'Did you now? Did he persuade you to come back? It was your intention to stay at Pinewood, wasn't it? Against my wishes?'

'No. I went there because I might be giving the place away—to Paul and Alice. Well, not giving it away exactly—loaning it to them. Alice told me this afternoon they are going to be married as soon as possible.'

'So at last the pair of them find happiness. I suppose it does happen for some people.'

The barb stung her. She closed the books in front of her with a loud noise which brought him striding across to her side. In the light of the oil lamp he saw she was pale and her eyes were tired. She had not even bothered to change out of her riding clothes after returning home, but had at once set about trying to find some way out of the dilemma which she found facing her in the ledgers.

'Have you eaten?' Dominic demanded. She shook her head. 'I didn't want you bothering your head about those books until things improved.'

'How can they when half of the field-hands have been taken by the Confederacy and another ten per cent have run away? Without help I can't go on, Dominic. Oh, don't worry, I know things are getting just as bad for you. I won't ask you to send men from here to my fields. I'll manage somehow.'

'*We* will manage—together,' Dominic said.

'Your meeting went well?' she asked, her hopes rising. 'Will our neighbours agree to pooling the labour?'

'Paul and Melissa agreed.'

'No one else? But why? Can't they see all have to help each other?'

'My dear girl, when will you learn the only responsibility a man has is to himself and his family? They come first.'

'Not in the eyes of God,' Veroníque answered defensively.

'God seems to be looking in the other direction at the

moment. Don't talk to me of God, *ma belle* . . .' his voice trailed off into an angry silence. 'We will manage—together,' he had said. At least he had not put Moonshadow first, Veroníque thought.

For two months the inhabitants of Atlanta had been subjected to the noise and destruction of shells bursting in the city. Evacuation of women and children, the old and the wounded began in the first week of September. Carts crammed the only road open to safety. The sky at night was alight for miles as the retreating soldiers put the torch to warehouses and supply depots. During the day, the air was thick with smoke and the stench of cordite and smouldering wood. The following day, the first of General Sherman's troops occupied the outskirts of Atlanta.

At Moonshadow, Dominic looked across the table to where Veroníque was finishing her dinner. The disastrous news had reached them an hour before, but she had received it calmly. So calmly, he was not sure she had understood what it really meant. They often ate their meals together nowadays, often with Michael and Alice, but sometimes, like tonight, they sat alone and found each other's company quietly satisfying.

'I have some close friends in Macon—a cousin too,' he said quietly. 'It might be better if you left here until we know what Sherman's intentions are.'

'If, as you believe, he intends to come through Georgia to the sea, then I should be no more safe at Macon than I would here,' Veroníque returned, motioning Michelle to come and clear away. She rose to her feet with a half-smile that mocked his attempt to be kind. 'No, Dominic. You kept me here when I wanted to leave—well, here I shall stay.'

Dominic's eyes narrowed to angry pinpoints. Damn her! Why did she have to throw every tiny gesture back in his face?

'You are a fool,' he snapped and left her to finish her coffee alone.

CHAPTER NINE

As she watched Paul place the thin band of gold on her sister's finger, Veroníque's thoughts went back to her own wedding day and her heart ached. The same small, intimate ceremony, the same minister from Macon, Micah and Michelle standing in the background, nodding approval. The only difference was in the way Alice and Paul looked at each other—in love, and proud to acknowledge it openly. Veroníque stole a glance at the face of the silent man at whose side she stood, and quickly looked away again. Dominic's black eyes were looking directly at her and their intentness was unnerving.

'This is the most wonderful moment of my life,' Alice breathed, her face radiant with happiness, as she allowed Veroníque to press another glass of champagne into her hand. 'Goodness! Another one of these and I shall have to sit down. Thank you for letting us be married here, Veroníque, and for the loan of Pinewood for a few days. Paul and I need to be alone for a while—to talk—sort ourselves out.'

'It's as much your home as mine,' Veroníque returned smilingly. 'I only wish you would stay there all the time. You need a proper home.'

'Paul and I did talk about it. It would be so nice to have a real home of my own, but then Dominic convinced him he was needed more here at Moonshadow.'

'He had no right,' Veroníque retorted indignantly. 'What about the plans Paul had to harvest the cotton there when it's ready?'

'Dominic says—and I must agree with him—that it's more important to ensure we have enough food for the winter. He is certain the South has lost the war. If he's right, we shall need to hoard all the foodstuff we can, won't we? It's a shame you didn't put more of your fields to corn, like Dominic has. We can't eat cotton.'

'But it would have solved all Father's problems when the war was over and we sold it,' her sister answered bitterly. 'None of us thought it could go on for so long—or come this close to us. I wanted Pinewood to be as it once was . . .'

'Nothing is ever going to be as it was,' Alice said with a faint frown, 'General Sherman is going to see to that. That awful man—how inhuman he is to turn those poor people in Atlanta out of their homes! I wonder what would have happened to me if Dominic had not brought me here. I'd be homeless now, no money, alone with Michael! Will they come this way, Veroníque? Burn our homes over our heads? Destroy our land?'

'Hush! It will never happen. We have faithful servants here who would not dream of running off and leaving us to the mercy of monsters like Sherman, and Dominic has helped to organise armed protection for isolated plantation houses. Half the remaining men in the county have volunteered their services.' Veroníque shut her mind to the possibility of Pinetree County being invaded by the Yankees, and quickly looked around for Paul. 'Come and take your wife away, Paul, or are you still waiting for Melissa?'

She had thought it strange that Melissa had not been at the ceremony, and had expected her to turn up before the newly-weds left for Pinewood. Paul's frown told her there had been an unpleasant scene.

'Isn't she coming?' she ventured to ask.

'I doubt it. We had an argument. That's partly why I agreed to Dominic's suggestion to stay on here. Melissa has made it impossible for me to take Alice back to the Folly. I never want to set foot in it again. I only hope we don't get in the way of you and Dominic too much.'

'I think you know there's little chance of that.'

'Things are no better between you?' Paul asked concernedly.

He wore his best dress uniform. For the first time ever she noticed threads of grey just visible at his temples. Alice was right. Nothing would ever be the same again. A way of life was being slowly and ruthlessly destroyed, a people disheartened and broken by the loss of their homes and the ones they loved most.

'At least we're civil to each other these days and there are times . . .' Veroníque paused, a smile touching her lips. 'There are times when I begin to like this house. I don't want to, because I know I will never belong here.'

'The house—the war. How can you say they keep you here when you know it's Dominic?' Alice reproved. 'You stay for him. I won't believe the love you had for him is dead.'

Veroníque looked across the room to where Dominic stood by the open windows, talking to Michael. One arm lay affectionately around the boy's shoulders. No, her love was not dead. Sometimes she felt him watching her, aware of the question in his eyes. At first they had reproved her; now they were often full of sadness, as if he had come to accept that part of his dream at least would never materialise. There would be no son—no heir.

Paul and his bride were about to leave when another rig came careering into the driveway and was pulled to a halt amid a shower of gravel. Melissa sat staring at the astonished faces. Her hair was dishevelled, her face red with exertion. The sweating horses told of the speed with which she had driven from Folly.

'So—you married her!' Her voice was like a whiplash and Alice leaned closer to Paul, seeking comfort from the arm he slipped round her shoulders.

Veroníque moved forward to the edge of the steps, masking the anger which rose up inside her at this unwarranted intrusion on her sister's happy day. 'Have you come to offer your congratulations, Melissa? We were all so sorry you did not arrive earlier. As you can see, Paul and Alice are about to leave, but you're welcome to stay and have supper with us, and drink their health.'

For a long moment Melissa considered the slender figure in saffron silk whose poise and dignity did not falter beneath her own contemptuous gaze, and then she turned and looked again at her brother and her mouth curved into a malicious smile.

'Congratulations? Yes, why not? Congratulations, my dear brother, on the acquisition of your new family. You didn't really believe what I said last night, did you? Well, I warned you what would happen if you married that little whore. Look!' She swung round, pointing into the back of the rig, to the books and papers and ornaments scattered in confusion over the seats and floor. Books with torn pages and defaced covers, manuscripts which had been deliberately torn in half, ornaments cracked and broken . . .

'Your books,' Veroníque whispered horrified. 'Paul . . .'

'Yes, his precious books. I want nothing of him in my house.'

'Your house?' Alice asked, tightening her hold on Paul's arm.

She had known of the argument between them when he had told his sister of his intended marriage and of her threats to keep him from returning to the Folly with his bride by any means in her power. And when he had said he would never be back, she had picked up a piece of crystal which she knew he treasured and smashed it in front of his eyes. He had ridden away from the house with her laughter ringing in his ears, her threats to burn his books, rid the house of everything he possessed. She had been like a madwoman!

Paul stared at his treasured books, many of them first editions, and the manuscript he had been working on until the previous evening.

'I pity anyone who has to destroy beauty because they cannot understand or share it,' he said. 'You always had to have your own way, even as a child. Toys—friends—lovers—even your husband—you used them all and then discarded them because they failed to give you any real satisfaction.' He smiled down into Alice's white face, close to his, at Michael, silently questioning what he could not understand. 'Each malicious act you perform helps to destroy part of you. I don't think you have ever realised that. You can't take what I have from me, nor spoil this moment with your senseless act of butchery. I can buy more books. Alice and I will read them together, teach our child to read them, and the children that are to come in the years ahead. What was in my manuscript can be rewritten too, because it is still in my head. I will rewrite it with the help of my wife, and friends like Veroníque and Dominic. Go home, Melissa, back to your Folly—I want no part of it any more. It's all yours, to live in all alone, with only the occasional comfort of some poor unfortunate man you can bribe into your bed with promises you can't fulfil. Sometimes I wonder if we were sired by the same gentle father.'

'I think this has gone quite far enough,' Dominic remarked tersely from the doorway.

'Thank you for your hospitality, Dominic,' Paul said, 'and you too, Veroníque. Alice and I both appreciate it, and the understanding you have given to us, especially when I didn't deserve half of it. We'll see you at the end of the week.'

'Goodbye, Veroníque, Dominic.' Alice's voice was noticeably unsteady. She wanted to get away from this place to the peace and quiet of Pinewood, to love and be loved in return, to share Michael with his father and watch the joy on the little boy's face as his every whim was indulged.

'Bless you both,' Veroníque murmured. 'I wish you all the happiness in the world.'

'We both do.'

Dominic added his good wishes to hers. She was so close to him that he could smell the light perfume she always wore. He thought how nice it would be to reach out and put his arms round her shoulders. Paul escorted Alice to the waiting buggy, helped her in and placed Michael on her lap. Veroníque ran quickly down the steps and into the drive, waving her hand until they had disappeared from view.

Taking a deep breath, she turned and looked at the two people who remained. Dominic, on the verandah; Melissa, smiling hatefully at her from the rig.

'I'm invited to supper, I believe. Good. Dominic, have one of your boys unload this thing. This rubbish can stay here until Paul comes back.'

Veroníque moved back towards the house, in front of Melissa as she climbed to the ground and put one foot on the steps. 'You are not welcome here,' she said coldly.

Melissa's eyes flickered past her to the figure of Dominic. Slowly she removed her gloves and dusted the dirt from her calico skirt, ignoring the words. 'Have you any champagne, Dominic? I'm dying of thirst,' she said meaningly.

'There is plenty inside, but under the circumstances I think it best if we call a halt to the festivities here and now,' Dominic returned. Leaning against the post, he selected a cigar from an inside pocket and lighted it, and his gaze considered each of the women before him in turn, daring either to defy the authority in his tone.

'Do you think I have behaved disgracefully, my dear?' Melissa asked, her tone softening. Veroníque stiffened as she laid a hand on his arm and looked towards the room behind them, where Michelle was clearing away glasses and wafer-thin bone china. 'Very well, I admit it. But that fool brother of mine should have known better than to defy me. Don't I always mean what I say? You know that better than anyone.'

The look she directed at Veroníque implied that she knew him better than his own wife. How right she was, Veroníque thought, but she was too angry to back down and allow this creature, who for so long had been a thorn in her side, to enter the house as if she owned it.

Her hands clenched into tight fists at her side as her eyes sought Dominic's. 'I won't have her set foot inside my home again,' she snapped. The instant narrowing of his eyes, the momentary shock registered there, made her realise what she had said. *Her* home! As if she was really mistress here. She had never called it that before.

Without a word he disengaged Melissa's hand, looked back into the dining-room and ordered, 'Michelle, are you still there? Mrs Beauville is hot after her long ride. Bring out some champagne, and some wedding-cake too, and then you can fetch Preacher Meridan's horse. He looks as if he's about to wake up.'

He heard Melissa's sharp intake of breath at the snub, turned in time to see her running towards the rig. Moments later she was throwing everything from it on to the ground. The air was filled with the sound of crashing china and glass as she hurled objects from her, swearing with a proficiency which made even Dominic wince.

'Stop her,' Veroníque pleaded, and when he did not move, wheeled towards the door, intending to call Micah. He caught her arm, pulling her to his side, shaking her slightly as she tried to free herself from his restraining grip.

'Leave her. It's the best way. I've seen her in these rages before. In a moment she'll be calm again.'

'She's—she's mad!'

'With rage—frustration, perhaps. This isn't quite the outcome she expected. She wanted to ruin the day for Paul and Alice. Thanks to you, that hasn't happened. Don't let her spoil it for you either—she'd enjoy that just as much.

Be still. Let her vent her anger on things which can't hurt any of us.'

At last Veroníque became still. Dominic released her and stood silently puffing at his cheroot until the last scrap of paper, the last book, the final piece of china had been thrown from the rig. Breathless, her breasts heaving beneath the tight blouse she wore, Melissa climbed back on to the driving seat. There was no wildness in her any more. The bright colour which had stained her cheeks slowly began to recede, and Veroníque was inexplicably alarmed by the change in her. One moment a madwoman—the next a smiling angel. She looked around at the chaos she had left behind her and laughed softly.

'There you are, Veroníque—a chance to use some of the authority you have acquired lately. Call your servants, have it cleared away. I'd like to stay and watch it all burn, but it's almost dusk and I have to get home and change. I have a guest for supper this evening.'

She was looking at Dominic as she spoke, Veroníque noticed, but he gave no sign to indicate they had a clandestine meeting. Picking up her skirts, she went back into the house, realising she was beginning to shake from the scene she had witnessed.

'Shall I clear away?' Michelle stood, holding a tray which she had been about to bring out.

'Mrs Beauville has left.'

'Good riddance too,' the Creole woman muttered fiercely. 'You did right to stand up to her, *mignonne*. One day she will be brought to account for the terrible things she does, you mark my words.'

'I shall be in the sitting-room,' Veroníque answered. 'Bring me some mint tea.'

'Nonsense! What you need is more of this.' Dominic came in behind her, took the tray from Michelle and followed Veroníque into the long room where the fire had just been lighted. 'This is the last bottle of champagne. It went off quite well, don't you think?'

She could not make up her mind whether he was pleased or relieved.

She sipped her champagne in silence. Apart from the servants, they were totally alone in the house for the first time since he had brought Alice from Atlanta. They had been married for almost four months and there had always been someone else present to ease the strain of their relationship. Tonight it was different, and that began to make her feel uneasy.

She watched one of the boys gathering up pieces of broken glass and scraps of paper. Probably part of the manuscript on which Paul had hoped for a bright new future as a writer.

'She was like that even as a child,' Veroníque remembered. 'Spiteful and vindictive.'

'Someone should have taken a firm hand with her long ago. But she could be an angel when she chose, and she could twist her father around her little finger.'

And yet you still find her attractive! It was on the tip of Veroníque's tongue. His eyes searched her face and must have instinctively recognised some betraying sign, for he said:

'You are wondering why I still go to her? Yes, you are right—we did have a supper engagement this evening. But her show of temper has rather dampened my enthusiasm. Shall I tell you why I haven't given her up? Because she's warm and willing in my arms, and there are no locked doors between us.'

Veroníque flinched as if he had struck her, and set down her glass rather unsteadily on the table, as memory of that wild night flooded back.

'How dare you compare me with her?' she said fiercely. It was the first time either of them had mentioned the incident since it happened, but it had lain dormant between them, as a solid wall of misunderstanding and mistrust.

'Compare you?' Dominic smiled sardonically. 'How can I do that? There is no comparison. My mistress welcomes me. My wife refuses me her bed, often her company, and whenever possible her conversation.'

'And whose fault is that? You tricked me. I was lied to and cheated. A marriage of convenience, you promised. We would each live our own lives, and, fool that I am, I believed you. I thought you only wanted Moonshadow back . . . I never thought . . .' She broke off, feeling her cheeks begin to burn with embarrassment.

'We could still be happy.' He put down his glass and moved across to where she stood, deliberately blocking her path to the door. 'Moderately so, at least. You and I are well suited to each other.'

'I—I don't know.' What was he trying to make her say? What might have been, was in the past and no longer possible.

'You said you loved me. You will forgive me if I say I find that a startling admission—and hard to swallow.'

He stood so close it was impossible not to look directly at him. His gaze was merciless and Veroníque felt herself begin to tremble. Why had he chosen this moment to bring it all out into the open?

'It was true once, but you destroyed what I felt when you took me like—like an animal.'

'I have killed men for less insulting words than those you hurled in my face that night,' Dominic returned and his voice was suddenly harsh. 'Any man worth his salt would have acted the way I did.'

'What are you trying to say?'

'What you felt for me, if anything, was not love. The infatuation of a young girl, perhaps, which became blown up out of all proportion when I went away.'

'Is that how you intend to justify what you did to me?' Veroníque cried. 'By attacking my own feelings?'

'I see no reason why I should offer any defence. I expected no more from you than any other husband would his wife. A pretence of love to make me feel a heel just wasn't necessary. If you loved me—if, I say—then I could take you in my arms and you would welcome my touch, not shrink from it.'

Without warning he caught her by the shoulders and instantly felt the tremors which were racking her body. Veroníque braced her hands against his chest, holding her face back from his.

'I once told you I would love the man I married—willingly share his bed and bear his children. You offered me a marriage without love, a cold, humiliating contract which should never have existed between a man and a woman. I could have given you my love even then, but you didn't want it, did you? You had Moonshadow and Melissa, and I was a burden you could have done without. I was the price you had to pay to get this place back, and you made sure I knew it, and how much you despised my being in your precious house.'

'Perhaps in the beginning . . .'

'Don't lie to me now, Dominic. There was always honesty between us, you used to say. Alice is not here to stop us arguing, and Michelle is safely in the kitchen.' She blinked back bright tears which pricked the corners of her eyes. She felt the warmth of his hands as they slid over the smoothness of her bare shoulders, and firmly resisted his attempts to draw her closer. 'Don't, Dominic. I know if I allowed it, you would come to me whenever the fancy took you—saddle me with a family to ensure the continuance of the d'Estainville name and then isolate me in this old house, while you went off to be welcomed by your so willing mistress.'

She forced the hateful words out through stiff lips, not meaning most of them, but knowing that her only defence against his nearness, and the growing weakness in her limbs which it caused, was to injure his pride and drive him from her.

'*This old house* has known great love,' Dominic replied. He bent his head until his lips touched, in turn, the tears at the corners of her eyes, then moved slowly down over her cheeks to her mouth. He never knew the effort it cost Veroníque to remain immobile, seemingly unaroused.

'For pity's sake let me go,' she cried.

'I am what I am,' he answered. 'A person with feelings that I refuse to ignore any longer. You are just going to have to face up to the fact your husband is human after all.'

Since the night they had spent together he had wanted her time and time again, day after day, night after sleepless night, but baulked at taking her that way a second time.

He did not know what methods he might employ now to keep her if she tried to leave again; only that he would use any means in his power to keep her at Moonshadow. He hated the filthy rumour which had ruined their chance of a reasonable life together, despised his own inability to tell her what he had come to feel for her since their wedding day. Then he looked into her disdainful expression and lost the desire to even try.

'I won't be used,' Veroníque said, in a hollow tone. 'If you ever try to touch me that way again . . .'

'Try?'

Dominic's voice told her she would have no choice in the matter.

'Very well, you've already proved how strong you are, but I swear, if you ever treat me like—like a girl you would pick up in Madame Elizabeth's, to be used and discarded like an unwanted piece of clothing when its usefulness has run out, I'll leave this house and never come back, and even your threats to bring me back by force will not stop me. I will divorce you, Dominic, and when I do, I'll tell everyone the true reason why you married me.'

An ugly smile flitted across Dominic's face. 'I don't take kindly to threats, Veroníque. If I thought you meant those words . . .'

'What would you do?' she challenged. 'Whip me like a disobedient slave? Lock me in my room? I've been a prisoner since the first day I came here. Kill me perhaps?'

Releasing her, Dominic stepped back and selected a long cigar from the box of hammered silver on the table. Over the brief flame of the match as he lighted it, his eyes were chillingly cold.

'Never put me to the test—for both our sakes.'

Picking up her skirts Veroníque spun around towards the door, desperate for the sanctuary of her room and the additional protection of locked doors. She heard a fierce expletive behind her and then Dominic's tall frame was blocking her way again.

'At first I thought you hated me because of what Elizabeth had told you,' he said heavily, and she came to an abrupt halt, her cheeks growing pale at the dangerous glint in his eyes. He had looked this same way on that night too—and they were alone in the house! 'That isn't true, is it? Neither your distress nor the indignation was genuine. You could have made our marriage work, do you realise that?'

'No, we both know it would never work. We want different things from life,' Veroníque flashed, determinedly standing her ground despite the apprehension she was feeling.

'I don't mean just by sharing my bed, but by being part of this place—trying to understand how I feel about it. I thought you did once. I was wrong. You're out to revenge yourself on me, not only for marrying you, but for making you into a real woman, something you have never experienced before. I think I awakened you and you liked it. But *la belle princesse* has been brought up never to admit such intimate facts, even to her own husband, hasn't she? And so you vent your frustration on me and pretend, very convincingly sometimes, that I've wronged you.'

Veroníque could hardly believe her ears. At first she could find no words to answer the incredible accusations. And then, afraid of the devil which she had somehow unwittingly aroused in him, she heard herself begin to speak wildly, shrilly.

'You have taken leave of your senses. Stop it! Or are you drunk? Let me pass, Dominic! If you don't, I—I will call for Michelle. Let me pass . . . please . . .'

'I was drunk the last time. Not tonight.' She did not even struggle as he reached out and caught hold of her, pulling her against him until her face was almost touching his. He was not drunk, she realised, but angry, and that made him just as dangerous. 'After Elizabeth's visit I would have done anything to keep you here, to make up for the unhappiness I thought I'd caused. But I don't think you care what I am, do you? If you did you wouldn't even consider divorce—revealing all. The mud would stick to you as well as me. It would be far worse. A divorced woman! You'd be fair game for any man, and yet that doesn't seem to worry you. You want me broken, don't you, Veroníque, like Elizabeth does? Go ahead—try it. If I don't kill you before you succeed, I'll have the pleasure of seeing you wallowing in the mud alongside me.'

'Don't . . . please, don't,' Veroníque pleaded. Her words had brought back to her the nightmare of Elizabeth d'Estainville's visit. 'You sound just like her . . .'

'A pity she can't be here to see how well her efforts to get to me are succeeding. My God, I never thought she could do it, but she has!'

'Don't let her destroy you too. She's taken so much from you. Fight her, Dominic! You must—for Sarah's sake . . .'

'Sarah?' Dominic echoed, and his face was suddenly that of a stranger.

'I—I think I remember something . . . from the day she came here. Elizabeth, I mean.' At first Veroníque could not recall why Sarah's name had come so readily to her lips, but then, as she searched her memory, it was as if a curtain lifted from her mind and she could see Elizabeth sitting in the room, hear her talking, remember every word which had been said.

'I don't think I am interested in what she had to say,' Dominic returned curtly. 'Nor any fabrication on your part.'

'She spoke of Sarah . . .'

'Why should she? She hated her.'

'That day was so terrible I must unconsciously have put it out of my mind. It wasn't my intention to deceive you, Dominic, to keep this from you . . .'

'How convenient you shouldn't remember until this moment. To keep what from me, Veroníque? Twist the knife—if you dare!'

'I'm not trying to hurt you. Not now,' Veroníque cried. 'Believe me, it's something she said about Sarah's whereabouts.'

'You told her I'd been looking?' He sounded startled.

'Yes—before . . . before she told me you were Sarah's son. She said you wanted to bring her here to live—as before. She laughed at that and said she had made sure you could never do that because she was keeping Sarah with her . . .'

'In Atlanta?' Dominic's voice was barely audible. No wonder she had disappeared without trace. So near, but the one place he had not looked. He had a vision of Yankee troops occupying the houses, turning the people out into the streets, using women like those at Madame Elizabeth's. Sarah had always been an attractive woman. She could have changed over the years. He prayed she had, for her sake.

Atlanta! He would go there—find her! No, it was impossible. He would willingly undertake the journey knowing he would find her, but it was unlikely she would be at the house now, and if he were caught sneaking into the occupied city he could be arrested and tried as a spy—or shot out of hand.

Veroníque did not move for a long time after he had stepped away from her, wishing that in some way she could ease the pain she had inflicted. Once she knew she might have felt great satisfaction at hurting him, but now it was different. Everything had gone wrong. They were further apart now than ever before, and the coldness in his expression indicated he neither wanted, nor expected, any sympathy from her. Love had destroyed them both, she thought as she closed the door against his lonely figure. Her love for him—his love for Moonshadow.

Veronique sat at the huge walnut escritoire in Dominic's study, the ledgers from Pinewood open before her. For days she had been seeking a solution to the problem she found there, but came to the conclusion there was no way around the situation. What answer was there for lack of funds? The day before, after a violent thunderstorm had brought torrential rain down on the countryside, she had gone over there to visit Paul and Alice and inspect the progress of the cotton. It was ready to be picked. She found that fierce winds had blown the roofs off two of the barns and Paul had men hastily trying to repair them before the valuable stock of vegetables were ruined by the sudden change in the weather. They needed much more than just patching up, Veronique realised, and had spent hours on her return poring over the books, but always the answer which presented itself was the same. She had no money to spend on her old home.

Her eyes flickered across to Dominic's huge oak desk in front of the opposite wall. She hesitated, then took her ledgers across to it and sat down in the high backed leather chair. The drawers before her were not locked. She opened each one in turn until she found what she wanted . . . the ledgers relating to Moonshadow. She found other things too, letters and papers which brought a sudden pallor to her cheeks. For the first time she saw what Dominic had kept from her since her father's death: the mortgage demands from the bank in Atlanta, the threatening letters from livestock dealers in the county, tradesmen, friends . . .

'Have you found what you're looking for?' Dominic asked coldly from the doorway. Veronique sat frozen at the desk as he advanced into the room and stared down at the mass of papers and books before her. 'If you had told me you were interested in the running of this place I would have let you have the management of it long ago. I hate paperwork.'

'Would you have let me see these?' Veroníque asked, gathering up a sheaf of bills.

'It was the bargain I made with your father. Not with words: we understood each other too well for that. He knew if I had Moonshadow back, I would pay his debts. He omitted to tell me how bad they were, however.'

'But you still paid them,' Veroníque said quietly. They had hardly spoken to each other since the day of the wedding. He looked tired, and she noticed a scratch of blood along one cheek as if he had been caught by a thorn branch—or been in a fight. 'I was part of your bargain too, wasn't I? The way it's turned out I should say you've got the worst of the deal.'

'I'm in no mood for an argument, Veroníque. Is there any Bourbon in here? I've just half-killed a man and I don't feel very good about it.'

'I'll fetch some from the other room.'

He followed her into the sitting-room, took the full glass she offered and tossed it back without appreciation.

'No—no more,' he said as she went to take the glass. 'I have to go out again.'

'What's happened? Who were you fighting with?' she asked in alarm.

'Some fool trying to spread his abolitionist ideas among the stable-boys. He's been coming here for the last three days, so one of them told me, inciting them to run away. God, I'm tired.'

'Sit down, for a few minutes at least,' Veroníque urged. She refilled his empty glass and stood beside the chair into which he slumped. He looked at her with a frown, then took the glass, commenting sarcastically: 'Isn't it a little late to be playing the concerned wife? There's no one around we have to fool, is there? Except ourselves.'

'I deserve that . . . and more. Why—why didn't you tell me how difficult things had become for you because of what you did for Father?'

'I may not be the kind of gentleman you would like,' Dominic returned dryly, 'but I do have my own code of rules—and I never break them. George dared to push me further than most men who know me, but he knew I'd stick to our agreement. I got Moonshadow—and you—and the possibility of going broke very shortly. As you say, I got the worst of the bargain.'

'The bank would lend you money on this place.'

'Money I may never be able to pay back. It's too big a risk.'

'On Pinewood, then,' Veroníque said and then realised what she had offered him. Her sanctuary, the refuge she had planned to use as soon as it became possible to leave him.

'Out of the question.'

'Why? Isn't it better to keep one plantation going, than having two slowly decaying?' Beneath his questioning gaze she faltered, and then, from somewhere, found a strange sense of equality with him. 'I know you love this place, but I don't understand the force that drives you. I never have. This house has never made me welcome. I'm a stranger in it. I always will be, and so you can't blame me for loving the home where I was born and raised. I hate the way you are, Dominic; your ruthlessness, your ability to bend and shape people for your own ends. But part of me admires you too, because in the end you always get your own way. I'll make a bargain with you—as Father did. Pinewood is yours to do with as you wish. Not to sell; I promised Alice that if she wanted it after the war, she could have it. But to mortgage, raise money on it any way you can. And afterwards you must return it to me intact, with me to work the fields, staff for the house, enough money to repay any loans and set me on my feet again.'

Dominic's eyes were blazing with a strange light as he stared at her. She could have asked for so many more things: her freedom, for one.

'Is it a bargain?' Veroníque asked. She had expected him to jump at the offer and could not understand his reluctance.

'You know it is . . . because you know I'll do anything to keep this place. The d'Estainvilles built it, a d'Estainville will always live in it. If it becomes necessary, a d'Estainville will destroy it,' he answered, tight-lipped.

'What are you saying?'

'You didn't think I'd let the bluecoats run riot over it, did you?'

'What would you do?'

'You say you love Pinewood. How much? Could you destroy it, put it to the torch rather than let enemy soldiers take possession of it?'

'No,' Veroníque whispered faintly, 'I couldn't.'

'Then you feel nothing for it, not deep down, the way I feel for Moonshadow. No one . . . no one ever again is going to take this place from me, do you hear? I'll burn it to the ground first.'

'And what will you have then?' He had fought so hard to regain his inheritance, she could not believe he would willingly destroy the most important thing in his life.

A smile curved around the corners of his lean mouth. Mocking, yet somehow sad. 'I came into this world with nothing. Why shouldn't I leave the same way.'

Micah appeared in the doorway, and at once Dominic drained his glass and stood up.

'Soldiers are outside, Mister Dominic,' the Negro said. 'Some of them in a pretty bad way. Going to Richmond, their capt'n says. They've pulled out of Atlanta. The Yankees are in full control of the countryside as far as Nelson.'

'But that's fifteen miles from Atlanta,' Veroníque gasped. 'Where are the cavalry patrols that were guarding the railroad and the men from the city?'

'Mostly on their way to Richmond, I guess, Miss Veroníque.'

She ran to the window and looked outside. Dusty, grey-clad men were sprawled on the grass. They looked desperately tired, unshaven, dishevelled; worst of all, broken. A young officer was wandering among them, stopping to kneel by the side of a wounded man, or issue orders to the soldiers around him, most of whom had at least one bandaged limb.

'We cannot turn them away,' she said quickly. 'They must stay here, Dominic. We can put any wounded in the overseer's house and Micah can move up here. There's room for the officer here too, and the rest of the men can make themselves as comfortable as possible in the stables and barns. It's the least we can do.'

She followed him outside and found Michelle was already distributing hot soup among the soldiers, who almost knocked her over in their haste to grab a bowl of nourishment. Her heart sank at the sight of them jostling each other. At last she came to accept what Dominic had said was true . . . the South was beaten. At least these men were. There was no fight left in them.

'Don't judge them too harshly.' Dominic looked down at her, sensing her discomfort and disappointment. 'From what I've heard, most of them are damned lucky to be alive. Are you sure you can cope? They look a pretty rough lot; only one Southern gentleman that I can see.' He was looking at the young man advancing towards them as he spoke.

Veronique ignored the jibe and hurried down the steps, holding out her hands to the officer.

'I am Veroníque d'Estainville.' She shook his hand, and drew him back to where Dominic stood. 'This is my husband, Dominic d'Estainville. We want you to stay until you and your men have rested. You all look exhausted. Was it bad in Atlanta? We hardly get any news down here. Where are the Yankees?'

'One question at a time, please. Mr d'Estainville, sir, I am honoured to make your acquaintance. My name is Captain Anderson.'

'I shall die if you don't tell me what is happening,' Veroníque said impatiently.

'I don't mean to be rude, ma'am, but first I would like to settle my men comfortably. We've been travelling for three days without a break hardly, and as you can see, they're out on their feet. We've not had a good meal for the best part of a week . . . not since we pulled back.'

'Pulled back?'

'Let the Captain see to his men, Veroníque,' Dominic interrupted. 'Then he can answer all your questions—and a few of mine—over dinner. You will dine with us, I hope, Captain Anderson. We are lucky enough to still be able to set a good table. Your men too, I promise, will eat well tonight.'

'You are extremely generous, sir. I accept your invitation with pleasure.'

'You will forgive me then if I leave you. I have been having trouble with an abolitionist troublemaker, and I want to get him off my property before he incites the rest of my slaves to riot. I will see you at dinner tonight. Please, feel free to make my home your own. My wife, I'm sure, will make you comfortable until I return.'

Veroníque watched Dominic stride down the steps to where Micah waited with their horses. He rode off without looking back at her. For the first time since she had become his wife he had made her feel, unintentionally she suspected, mistress of Moonshadow. Turning on her heel, she smiled at Captain Anderson. Mistress of Moonshadow she was. She suddenly felt very proud—and very capable.

'Come with me. You must refresh yourself while your men are eating. Don't worry about them, the house servants will see they're well fed and comfortably housed for the night. You shall have the best room in the house, and tonight you will be served with chicken in a superb sauce, to remind you of the old days. There might be a war going on, but Southern hospitality has not altered, and Moonshadow offers the best of everything.'

CHAPTER TEN

How well I look, Veroníque thought to herself. Her cheeks were softly tanned from all the hours she spent out of doors, mostly riding, and her figure had filled out again. The dark jade brocade dress she had chosen to wear enhanced her fair skin and the raven hair curled to her bare shoulders. Around her neck she fastened her mother's diamond pendant. She had not taken so much care with her appearance since the night she had waited for Dominic to return from Macon. Waited in vain, with the dinner spoiling and her disappointment growing with each passing minute. 'Is everything prepared downstairs? The wine—have you used the best silver?'

'I think you will find everything to your satisfaction,' said Michelle. 'Such a time I had sorting through the store-cupboards. Why, half of it hasn't been used for years. Piles of the most beautiful lace and linen I've ever come across, and engraved silver goblets, fit for royalty. The table is laid to receive a king, *mignonne*—and a queen. You outshine anything I've done downstairs.'

'I have never taken inventory here,' Veroníque said, ashamedly. The Creole woman ran the house, often without consulting her for days at a time. She did it knowing her mistress's troubled state of mind, the reluctance to submit to the new role which had been forced on her. 'Captain Anderson has been made comfortable, I hope?'

'A real Southern gentleman, that one. But so young to command fighting men! Married, he tells me, with a baby not four months old. The poor lad is homesick, and afraid he'll never see his wife and daughter again.'

'Then we must make tonight a memorable occasion for him, so that he can forget the war. We shall have to depend on men like him in the months to come. And those we have housed outside, rough as they may look. Have they been fed too and given blankets?'

'Micah has seen to that.'

'Are you his mistress, Michelle?' Veroníque asked without warning.

'I am his woman.' Michelle returned proudly. 'I carry his child inside me.'

'I thought so. You must stay with him, whatever he decides to do when the Yankees come. Think only of the child—not me.'

Michelle looked at her with a smile. 'I have been very lucky. I wish you could also find it, *mignonne*. Why do you not let me help you? I could mix such a powerful love potion that not even Monsieur Dominic could remain immune. It's what you both want after all. You look at him with hunger in your eyes—and he looks at you the same way.'

'Hunger of the body has nothing to do with love,' Veroníque returned.

'No? One night in Monsieur Dominic's arms has made you an expert on the subject, *n'est-ce pas*?'

'It is not something I intend to discuss with you,' Veroníque interrupted quickly.

At the top of the staircase, Veroníque met Dominic just coming up to his room to wash and change. He inspected her appearance for a long moment, and she found herself looking into his eyes as he raised his head, searching for that hunger Michelle had mentioned.

'Is this for my benefit or that of Captain Anderson?' he asked, his voice tinged with soft mockery.

'For whoever appreciates it,' she returned boldly. 'Dinner is almost ready. How long will you be?'

'Half an hour. Console yourself with our guest's company until I come down.' He met challenge with challenge, as if knowing she had no intention of carrying it further. 'Oh, there is just one thing Veroníque. Would you consider giving Michelle her freedom? She's pregnant, you know, Micah's child. I promised him I'd ask you to free her, but I said you probably wouldn't agree. I know how much you depend on her.'

'He wants his child to be born free—I can't blame him for that. She told me tonight how it is between them. Have you considered the possibility that Micah might be persuaded to leave, to go North? Would you stop him?'

'I don't have that right. The days when one person can

own another are coming to an end, Veroníque. I, for one, am glad.'

After a moment she nodded.

'I owe her that . . . and much more. What happened to the man who has been making trouble, the abolitionist?'

'He'll cause no more trouble here. But even the beating I gave him won't keep him away from other plantations. He's one of the dedicated type.'

'Dedicated to making trouble and inciting our slaves to revolt,' Veroníque said indignantly. 'What do these Northerners know about us?'

'He was born and raised on the Wilkins Plantation, not fifteen miles from here,' Dominic returned gravely. 'And when a Southerner starts to spread dissent, the way he has, people react one of two ways. They hate him, or they rally to his cause. The freedom of the individual, that's what he's asking them to fight for. It's a cause most of them have been fighting for since the day they were brought into the world. The old days are gone, Veroníque, and sooner or later the South is going to have to face that fact. I only hope something equally good takes the place of what we're about to lose.'

The fire had been lighted in the dining-room and the huge table pulled into the middle of the room. A spotless white damask cloth covered it, and on top of that the polished silver goblets and silver cutlery, engraved, Veroníque noticed, with the initials of Grandfather Luc d'Estainville. She fingered the delicately engraved initials and her gaze fell to the emerald and diamond ring she wore, and the initials there which were the same. Here she was sitting at the same table as the old tyrant who had ruled the d'Estainville family for countless years. At the head of the table, opposite her, sat Dominic, the swarthiness of his complexion accentuated in the candlelight by the brilliant white silk cravat at his throat. So like Gran'père Luc—even his mannerisms and the smile he directed at their companion who was complimenting him on the excellent meal they had just eaten. How wonderful it was to be able to shut out the outside world, to ignore the war going on beyond the walls of the house, to enjoy the warmth and friendliness which existed in the softly lighted room.

She felt content—was that the beginning of happiness?

Aware of Dominic's eyes watching her, she drank her wine and then excused herself, leaving the men to enjoy their cigars and port alone.

She went into the drawing-room. In a while, Dominic would come in and sit near her. He would stretch his long legs out in front of the fire and light another long cheroot, and Micah would bring in the decanter of bourbon as he did every night. It was then she usually retired to her room. Tonight she would remain, because they had a guest. Tonight she did not want to rush away.

October was one of the busiest months for the plantation workers. There was the autumn harvest of vegetables to be collected and stored ready for winter, and fields full of white cotton bolls waited to be picked and stored away in the long row of sheds which adjoined the slave quarters. Endless meals at irregular times, and tired men who could scarcely contain their frustrations at the end of each tiring day. Considering the lack of manpower coupled with the disturbing news which continued to filter through from the captured town of Atlanta, Veronique marvelled at Dominic's energy, and the fierce determination which would not let him give up. Paul sent word that he and Alice would not be returning for at least another week. She smiled at the message, believing he intended to make the most of his newly-found happiness.

After the soldiers departed, she made Michelle take her on a tour of all the rooms in the house. Every cupboard in every room was thrown open for her to inspect the contents. The notebook she carried with her was soon full of scribbled notes. And the silver! She discovered Michelle had not exaggerated. In a heavy box in a small store-room next to the cellars, she discovered candlesticks, cutlery, silver plate and delicate ornaments, all carefully wrapped and laid to rest. Almost every piece bore the crest of Luc d'Estainville. A few pieces even bore his wife's initials—V d'E . . . Veronique's own crest, now!

She had the box taken up to the dining-room and the contents spread across the table there, and she was meticulously examining every piece when Dominic came back for lunch. For a moment he stood and stared at her and then at the items on the table, and she caught her breath, expecting to be ordered to replace them downstairs.

'I wondered if you would ever care enough to find them,' he said quietly, and she looked at him in open-mouthed surprise.

She wore a pale-coloured cotton blouse and grey calico skirt, and her hair was hidden beneath a scarf. Gone was the elegant lady who had sat at the table the night before and charmed their guest with smiles and reminiscences of the old days. He was laughing at her, she decided, but could find no trace of mockery in his expression.

He picked up a silver-backed hairbrush bearing her initials and studied it for a moment. 'Will you put these things to use?'

'If you have no objection.'

'Why should I? Enjoy them while you can. They became yours the day we married. I should have given them to you then, I suppose, but somehow . . .' he paused and shrugged his shoulders. 'We never did get round to such trivialities, did we?'

'Perhaps I should have it all repacked and sent to the bank in Macon?' Veroníque suggested. 'It would be safe there, wouldn't it? Until we need it again . . . after the war is over?'

'The South may be losing this damned war,' Dominic said curtly, 'but I, for one, am not going to change my way of life one iota. I'll go out in a blaze of glory, cursing the Union to hell and damnation for its ignorance. Besides it's food we shall be wanting if the worst happens, not silver and trinkets.'

'But they could be sold,' Veroníque protested.

'And who would have the money to buy them? Yankee soldiers? . . . Speculators looking for an easy mark?'

'If it meant food in our stomachs . . . a way of keeping this place in one piece, I'd sell to the devil himself.'

'Why, *ma belle*, you are beginning to sound just like me. Shame on you!'

Now he was laughing at her and she turned away in confusion. He hadn't called her that in months.

'I have to get over to the Folly,' he continued, and immediately there was tension between them again. She looked back at him and her eyes held an unspoken accusation.

'My visit is simply to ensure that our abolitionist friend hasn't gone there stirring up trouble. Melissa is only one woman against fifty or more restless Negroes, most of whom are just waiting their opportunity to pay her back for all the whippings she has forced on them. Now Paul has left, her overseer is the only man she can rely on. She needs to be warned . . . and to be protected against herself.'

Veronίque knew he was right, but it didn't make the knowledge that he was going to see her any easier to bear.

With the soldiers gone, a strange silence settled over the plantation. It seemed to be waiting . . . Veronίque even noticed a difference in some of the Negroes working about the lawn and yards. Expressionless faces—but fire in their eyes.

A noise outside in the courtyard drew Veronίque to an upstairs window, less than an hour after she had sent Jacob to Pinewood to tell her sister and Paul the alarming news Captain Anderson had given her before leaving. Sherman and his army had left Atlanta! The servant returned, bringing with him not only Paul and Alice, who was clutching Michael asleep in her arms, but a cartload of Negro slaves.

'What on earth . . .?' She hurried downstairs and met them in the hall. Close to, she saw what she had not been able to see before, the pallor of her sister's cheeks, her uncombed hair and the long rent in her skirt. Paul carried a pistol. She glimpsed another in his belt.

'It's all right, Veronίque. None of us is hurt.' Paul sought to reassure her as she stood staring at them incredulously. 'There's been some trouble.'

'What kind of trouble?'

'It was awful—beyond words,' Alice said in a hollow tone. She sounded dazed. Little Michael whimpered in his sleep and she clutched him more tightly against her breast. 'God knows what scar it will leave on this child . . . to have seen what he saw. Oh, dear God. The whole world has gone mad.'

'Alice.' Paul started towards her, but she seemed not to hear him. Slowly she turned on her heel and began to go upstairs.

'Go after her, Michelle. Stay with her until I come,' Veronίque ordered the Creole woman standing silently at her side. 'Paul, for heaven's sake! What has happened?'

'Last night we took in a family refugeeing to Macon,' Paul replied gravely. 'Mother, father and a child of ten, and some old Negress they had taken pity on some miles back and brought with them. We shared our supper with them and offered them the comfort of the house, but they refused that. Alice said they felt out of place in such grand surroundings. I wish to God they had stayed with us—they would be alive now.'

'They—are—dead?' Veroníque asked, with a horrified cry. 'At Pinewood? Paul—how?'

'Deserters . . . and our own men at that. Two of them came just before ten last night. We gave them food, allowed them to water their horses and sleep in the barn if they wished. They told us of Sherman's intention to march South and how they had been ordered to Richmond. I believed them. I had no reason not to—not our own soldiers. One of them was only a lad—bright-eyed and cheeky, talking about his mother's cooking and the sister he had left behind him in Tennessee. We laughed and joked together before I left them and went into the house.

'Around two o'clock, the barking of the dogs awoke us. I grabbed my pistol and ran downstairs . . .' he broke off, his lips tightening into a bleak line. 'Alice had persuaded the family to have the overseer's cottage. From the window I could see a crowd of Negroes in front of the door. They were shouting wildly. Some were laughing. There was a white man there, inciting them to rise up—giving them corn whisky to drink. When I saw a couple of them go inside, I went out . . . but against so many. One arm! I shot the nearest one to me, but then when they all started towards the house I ran back inside—bolted every door—shuttered the windows. They tried to get in, shouting, threatening . . . I took Alice and Michael upstairs to one of the attic rooms. We locked ourselves in and barricaded the doors.

'My God, Veroníque, you can't imagine what it was like, listening to those shouts. The doors held, or they grew too drunk to bother about us any more. I don't know what happened, only that towards morning it became quiet. I waited. I was afraid to go down, do you know that? I've been in battle. I've killed men who were trying to kill me. Old men, young boys, but that was war. This was cold-blooded murder. A man and his wife . . . and the child.

Such a pretty thing she was, too. The more I see of this war—the senseless killings . . . Dear God, it's all so senseless. One day I'll make sure everyone is made to realise how much.'

His voice failed again. With a groan he reeled away from her, stumbling towards the drawing-room. Veroníque followed, took him by the arm and led him to a chair.

'Drink this.'

She poured a large brandy and pressed it into his hand. He gulped it back, coughed violently and then a long, drawn-out sigh escaped his lips. The eyes which looked up at her were filled with pain.

'There's more . . .'

'Not now, Paul. Come and rest. I'll send Jacob to fetch Dominic. Please, you've been through enough torture for now.'

'Yes, perhaps you had better bring Dominic here. This concerns him.' Paul caught Veroníque's sleeve and drew her closer to his side. 'The Negro woman survived. God knows how. She tried to shield the child with her own body. She's badly injured . . . I doubt if she will live out the night, but I had to bring her here. You see it's Sarah, my dear. She was on her way back to Moonshadow again.'

The room in which Sarah lay was dark with long shadows of evening. As the last daylight faded from the sky outside, Veroníque rose from the chair where she had been sitting all afternoon, outwardly watchful and vigilant, inwardly stunned, afraid to contemplate what the future held for any of them.

The Negro woman had changed almost beyond recognition since the last time Veroníque had seen her. Older, thinner, the softly tanned features now heavily lined and in places scarred, as was the hand which lay on the rose-coloured counterpane.

Veroníque realised she would never know what indignities, what shame she had endured since the day she had been wrenched from this very same house, sold to a stranger, separated from Phillipe d'Estainville, the man she loved, and from Micah, her son.

'How is she?' Paul came into the room for the second time in less than half an hour.

'She seemed to stir a while ago—at least I thought she did.'

'How is Alice?'

'Sleeping, thank God. Tante Michelle mixed her a heavy potion.'

'And Michael?'

'Believe it or not, he's in the kitchen enjoying a glass of warm milk and a plate of chocolate cookies. I don't think he realised what was happening last night . . . I've tried to persuade him it was all a huge game. We were playing hide-and-seek with the soldiers. Luckily you've played the same game with him many times.'

'Provided it doesn't happen again,' Veroníque said, her voice almost a whisper. 'You must take him away from here as soon as possible, with Alice. There were soldiers here. . . . The Captain said Macon is safe and protected by the Militia.'

'Will you come with us?'

'No, I shall stay here.'

An odd smile flitted across Paul's face as he carefully shaded the table lamp nearest the bed to avoid it shining directly on to Sarah's face.

'That's a very brave decision.'

'He would expect it of me. After all, I am a d'Estainville,' Veroníque returned and she, too, smiled. 'The other day, when I sat at the same table as his grandfather, I had a feeling of belonging for the first time ever. I want to know that feeling again, Paul. I want to share it with Dominic. If I have to stay here and help this house against the Yankees, then I'll do exactly that—and damn the consequences.'

'Now you sound like Dominic.'

'He said something like that. He was laughing at me, but I mean it. Is that a horse?' She sprang to her feet and ran to the window. 'It's him! Let me go to him first—prepare him . . .'

'Quickly, then. Her breathing has grown worse,' Paul urged.

Dominic came up the stairs two at a time. He met Veroníque on the landing. Before she could speak, he blurted out: 'Paul—Alice? Where are they? Are they safe? What the devil happened at Pinewood?'

'You were there?' she asked faintly. She thought he had

been with Melissa all these hours, uncaring of her need for him.

'I wanted to see how Paul was getting on. The overseer's cottage is a smouldering ruin. Who did it? Where are they? Animals have been slaughtered—the fields burned . . .'

'Safe—they are safe. Oh, Dominic! I don't know how to tell you.' She stepped forward, leaned her head against his shoulder and felt his arms slip, somewhat hesitantly, around her.

'What is it . . . not Michael?'

She felt him stiffen, and drew back slightly so that she could look into his face. 'No, it's Sarah . . . She's here, with us. She's hurt, Dominic . . . Paul doesn't think she can live through the night.'

Dominic's eyes registered amazement first, then deep pain as he realised what she had told him; then disbelief. 'Where?' was all he said.

'Come.' To her surprise he did not resist as she took his arm and led him back into the room where Paul stood beside the bed.

After a moment he disengaged himself from Veroníque's grasp and approached the motionless figure. She had never before seen him so near to losing control. Slowly he went down on one knee beside the bed, his hand covering Sarah's. Paul stepped away, took Veroníque gently but firmly by the hand, and motioned they should leave. She wanted to stay, to watch them together, to see this side of Dominic's nature which had always been hidden from her. There was more than just kindness in his face as he gazed down at the lined face of the woman who had nursed him as a child—there was love.

Dominic raised his head and looked into the faces of Micah and Michelle on the other side of the bed. For the past hour, they had silently shared his grief without the necessity of words passing between them. Paul came and went at intervals, never intruding on their vigil, but his expression told them all there was no change and was not likely to be.

Michelle said in a low whisper, 'Must I watch her die when perhaps I could save her?'

'Didn't you hear the doctor? She is bleeding inside,' Micah returned curtly.

'It was not necessary to be so sharp with her,' Dominic reproved gently. 'We can do nothing for her—except be here if she needs us. Where is my wife?'

'Downstairs. She would not go to bed.'

'Look!' Micah started forward as Sarah gave a moan and her eyes flickered slowly open.

'Fetch the doctor,' Dominic ordered Michelle, and bent over the bed, clutching more tightly the gnarled hand which lay passively in his. 'Sarah—Sarah, can you hear me? It's Dominic . . . Micah is here too.'

'Dominic . . .' The woman's voice was barely audible. She laboured painfully for breath, her eyes widening as she stared up into the two anxious faces above her. 'Thank the Lord . . . I have been brought home.'

'Yes, home. Don't try to talk . . . the doctor will be here in a moment.'

'Micah?' Sarah's eyes centred on the black face on her left. 'My son, it is good to see you here . . . God has granted all my wishes . . . to see you again . . . to be free of that woman . . .'

Dominic drew back slightly, frowning. He had almost forgotten. 'Elizabeth?—She let you go when the soldiers reached Atlanta?'

'I freed myself . . . she is dead . . . she was evil. She threatened to tell everyone in Atlanta you were of my blood and so I had to kill her . . .'

'It doesn't matter,' Dominic insisted. 'You are safe here. No one will take you from us again. Hush now . . . save your strength. Damn it, where the devil is Paul?'

'Here! I was snatching a few minutes rest.'

Dominic moved back, allowing Paul to examine his patient, but Sarah seemed to grow agitated at his presence, pushing away the hand when he reached out to move the thick bandages placed against the wound in her side. Dominic whitened as he saw the fresh blood which had stained the clean cloth.

'Go away!' she stretched out a trembling hand towards Micah, who caught and held it and tried to reassure her that she was no longer in danger.

Sarah's eyes followed Dominic as he closed the door after Paul's departing figure. The fierce pain raging through her body faded as she stared into his strong, dark face and remembered the pride and happiness he had brought her since his birth.

She hardly hurt at all now. She felt peaceful and very content. Dominic came back to the bed and took her other hand. How strong he was! He and Micah both. She had taken Elizabeth's life, and God had chosen to take hers. But He had been merciful too, allowing her to spend her last moments in the house where she had once been supreme mistress. Phillipe was in the room too; she could sense his unseen presence. She had forgiven him long ago for allowing her to be sold. He had paid a thousand times over in the years which followed, lonely, drink-sodden years which brought him no pleasure, for he had been deprived of the only woman he had ever loved and the son for whom he had made so many great plans.

'You have a woman?' she asked Micah.

'Yes. Already she carries a fine, strong boy in her. I will bring her to you when you have rested.'

'And *you* have a wife—but no children?' She was looking at Dominic now, and he felt her fingers curl more tightly around his as she fought to stay in control of her senses.

'They will come—in time.'

He grew very pale beneath his tan, tried to draw back from Sarah's grip, but she grew visibly agitated and clung to him.

'I have thought of you as my son since the day your father placed you in my arms. We thought of you as belonging to us because we gave you the love she denied you, but you are not of my flesh—not of my blood. The d'Estainville line is as pure as it ever was. . . . Tell your wife that . . .' Her voice faded. She fell back on the pillows, coughing blood. Michelle came running into the room in answer to Micah's frantic bellowing and ushered both men away from the bed.

'She must rest . . . you have exhausted her.' She turned on them, her eyes glaring like coals of fire. 'Do you want to kill her?'

Dominic caught the hand Micah raised in her direction, held it until he felt the tension slowly fade from the other man's body. 'We need food and something strong to drink,' he said firmly. 'Call us if she recovers consciousness again, Michelle, or if the doctor needs us.'

'I will stay.' Micah slumped down into a chair, staring fixedly at his mother.

'That is your right,' Dominic returned. 'I'll have something sent up to you.'

Michelle followed him as he went downstairs and turned in the direction of the drawing-room, where a single light still burned. The grandfather clock in the hall struck three times. He had not realised it was so late.

'Good lord, Veroníque is still down here!'

From the doorway they could both see Veroníque curled up in a chair beside the dying embers of the fire. Quietly Dominic approached and looked down at his wife. Michelle stared at his expressionless face, sensing the hunger which dogged him night and day which he would neither acknowledge to himself or Veroníque.

'She loves you.' In the shadowy half-light, she saw Dominic's mouth tighten.

'Then she will come to me of her own free will.'

'You are too hard on her. If only you would bend . . .'

'She said the same thing once—that she loved me. I chose not to believe her. I've known many women, Michelle, and countless numbers of them have whispered that they loved me, and lied in their teeth. Although I have to admit the circumstances in which Veroníque chose to tell me were rather different. What happened between us—and don't bother to deny you haven't been told—such a thing will not happen again. The next time she must come to me.'

'Like an obedient slave.'

Dominic's eyes burned with sudden anger, but he controlled it.

'I don't want a slave, I want a wife, willing to share my bed, my life such as it is. I want sons and daughters—lots of them. What a combination that would be, eh, Michelle? Fire and ice . . .' he broke off, aware of the growing interest in the woman's expression. What had she deduced from those words, hidden for so long inside him? 'Let her sleep.'

Michelle nodded, pulling forward a chair and positioning it a few feet away from the couch.

'*Oui*, Monsieur Dominic.'

Sarah died in the early hours of the morning, without regaining consciousness again, without seeing the two people who waited in her room during those long, empty hours. Micah at the foot of the bed, Dominic leaning against the window frame, listening to the rain hammering ceaselessly on the panes, watching the first streaks of grey coming into the dawn sky.

The house was very quiet when Veronique awoke at nine-thirty. She found her sister in the kitchen, seated at the table, a cup of coffee in one hand.

'What are you doing up already?' she asked in surprise. 'When Tante Michelle gives someone a sleeping potion they don't usually get up before noon.'

'I'm feeling much better,' Alice returned with a wan smile. Veronique thought she still looked drawn and pale. 'Michael is the one who wants to stay in bed. I'm glad. If he can sleep, perhaps he will forget what he saw. Paul tried to pretend we were all playing a game . . . hide-and-seek.'

'I know; he told me. Would you like some more coffee? Have you had breakfast?'

'Not yet.'

'Where is everyone?' To get to the stove, Veronique had to pass a long, wide window which overlooked the river. Motionless figures stood beneath the overhanging trees. She came to a sudden halt, exclaiming, 'Why, that's where the d'Estainvilles bury their dead.'

'Sarah died early this morning,' Alice observed, getting to her feet. Veronique's lips trembled as she turned.

'Dominic?'

'He's very tired—he stayed with her until the last. Won't you patch things up with him now?'

'I told him I loved him and he didn't believe me. Why should he do so now? He'd laugh in my face. I've lain awake at night aching for want of him, yet done nothing. Now I can. I can stay here, Alice, here at Moonshadow; fight for this place he loves above all things. Perhaps when it's over he will be able to look at me differently.'

It was still raining heavily when Dominic returned to the house. He stood in the doorway of the kitchen watching the two women who were cooking over the stove, shaking water from his hair.

'Come in and take off those wet clothes,' Veronique ordered, placing a fresh pot of coffee on the table and making a search for cups. She had never had to do such menial work before. 'Where are Cook and Belinda? I haven't seen either of them yet.'

'They ran off with that no-good Thomas last night while you were all busy upstairs,' Michelle returned, easing her way past Dominic to take charge of the laying of the table correctly, 'and they weren't the only ones.'

Veroníque saw that the hem of her skirt was covered in at least two inches of thick mud which was leaving a trail on the clean floor. 'For goodness' sake, leave that, Tante. Have something hot to drink and then change into some dry things before you catch your death. You too, Dominic, and you, Micah. Don't stand there in the doorway.'

Dominic eased himself out of his sodden coat and tossed it into a corner. He took the steaming coffee she handed him with a brief nod. Grey shadows of tiredness accentuated the unusual pallor of his features.

'When you've changed, take four of our best men and go after them,' he ordered Micah. 'I warned everyone what I'd do if there were runaways again. It's time I started using the whip. At least that way I'd keep my slaves.'

'But not their respect,' Alice said quietly, and he wheeled on her with an angry oath.

'I mean it. Why send good men after two worthless women and a troublemaker? Tante Michelle and I can manage.'

'And I can learn.' Veroníque added her voice to the argument. 'Is it worth it, Dominic, when there is so much to be done here? We have so little time. As Alice says, three slaves are unimportant when we have thousands of Yankees about to descend on us.'

'I'm too tired to argue. Besides, I'm outnumbered. Tante Michelle, you'll organise things as best as possible.'

Veroníque allowed him the oversight of excluding her, without comment. As he turned to look out of the window, towards the fresh grave which had been dug beneath the protection of the trees, she moved to his side and said in a low tone, 'I'm sorry.'

'Thank you. We buried her beside my father. She'd have wanted it that way.' He looked down into her face with a soft exclamation. 'Of course, you don't know. She killed Elizabeth. She should had died by *my* hand.'

'Could you have lived with the knowledge you had cold-bloodedly taken her life?' Veroníque asked, frightened by this part of him which always seemed to accept death so calmly.

'She deserved to die. Can you shed tears for her?'

'No—no more can you. I'm just glad you didn't kill her.'

His thoughts were hidden from her behind an expression which told her nothing. As she turned towards the door, he said:

'I've discussed with Paul the possibility of sending you all to Macon. It's possible Moonshadow may never see a blue uniform, but if it does, you'll all be safer behind the protection of the Militia.'

Veroníque's steps froze. She turned slowly, her eyes becoming decidedly stubborn as she saw Alice shrug her shoulders as if to say—'Well, that's that.'

'I think it's a very good idea for Paul to take Alice and Michael to Macon,' she returned. 'Alice and I have already discussed it. I'm staying.'

'To do what?' Dominic asked, his voice growing harsh. 'You heard what happened at Pinewood when the Negroes got free. Do you think the ones here are any better? Micah reckons we could rally twenty reliable men if it comes to a fight. The rest will run, or turn against their own kind, or join the Union army and come back here bent on burning this house and everyone in it, to ashes.'

'I'm not sure you're afraid of the Yankees so much as of my cooking,' Veroníque taunted, and turned again towards the door.

'You'll do as I tell you, or I'll . . . Where the devil do you think you're going? Come back here, I want to talk to you.'

Micah stood in Veroníque's path. She gave him a challenging look and he stepped aside. Over her shoulder, she saw Dominic watching her in amazement. 'First I'm going to find Paul and ask him what he wants for breakfast, which Alice can then prepare. After that I'm going to start hiding some of our grain and vegetables. Someone around here has got to start doing something positive.'

'What in heaven's name has got into you?' Dominic demanded, banging his cup down loudly on the table. Across the room he saw Michelle's face deepen into a knowing smile.

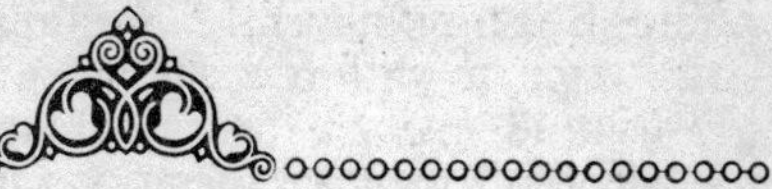

CHAPTER ELEVEN

MOONSHADOW PLANTATION continued to function as usual during those tense November days. With everyone taking on extra work, somehow they managed to keep things running smoothly. It was a strange kind of existence. They knew each passing day brought the Union army closer, but no one spoke of what could happen. During the daytime they were too busy to spend valuable time in idle speculation, and at night they crawled into their beds too exhausted to do anything else but sleep.

Moonshadow was a little world on its own. Whatever was beyond the boundaries seemed a thousand miles away—and very unreal.

It brought a mass flight of slaves one night to bring it home to all of them. The stark reality of burning barns, shots echoing through the still night air, and in the morning, the reckoning. Less than thirty Negroes left. Ten wounded and confined in the slave huts under lock and key. They could never be trusted again. A barn filled with cotton totally destroyed. Another, containing feed for the animals, without a roof, open to the bad weather which December would bring before much longer. Six chickens, two geese and two pigs missing. No matter how hard each of them worked now, severe hardships would result from that night.

From an upstairs window, as she tried to make her workload less exacting by putting away unwanted linen and closing up unused bedrooms, Veronique watched Dominic and Micah repairing the barn roof, using wood from several pine trees which they had cut down from behind the house. Both men worked themselves harder than anyone else, and her heart ached to see Dominic's drawn features at night. They never quarrelled these days. The uncertain future and the close harmony in which they worked had brought them together. She had at last taken her place as mistress of his home. But their new relationship ended when they went to bed—each to different rooms. Often she sat in here to finish some sewing before climbing into bed, exhausted and desperately lonely for the arms which had once held her.

Preparations had been made to evacuate the house if the Yankees came through Pinetree County. Paul would take the women to Macon; Dominic and Micah would remain.

No one in Pinetree County had any doubt that they were to be burned or starved into submission by the approaching army, probably both. Sherman's threat, delivered before he left Atlanta after destroying a large part of the city by fire, was horribly clear. It was his intention to 'make the interior of Georgia feel the weight of war'. Most of the families in the County had already felt the 'weight' of war by the loss of husbands, sweethearts, brothers and relatives. Still unbroken, despite their grief, these people began slowly and methodically to hide grain and livestock and winter food. Old guns were pulled from cupboards where they had lain for years, their stocks dusted and made ready for use. Muzzle-loaders from the days of Georgia's beginnings when the targets had been hostile Indians, not blue-coated soldiers. Long-barrelled squirrel guns, pocket Derringers which many Southern women now carried concealed in their skirts.

Veroníque made her preparations too. She had four sacks of grain buried beneath a magnolia tree in the driveway, and another two of root vegetables hidden beneath one of the baling sheds. Her jewellery and the most important silver items once belonging to Luc d'Estainville, she carefully wrapped in a clean sheet and took down to the river. The sheet containing its valuable contents was thrust deep into the ground beneath an old tree which stretched out over the river, its roots protruding some feet above the ground, thus leaving many cavities beneath. Earth and leaves were heaped on top of it, wedging it beneath the lower roots so that rain would not dislodge it and send it sliding into the thick mud at the bottom of the river.

No matter what happened, they would survive now. Food for the winter months, grain for a spring planting, and silver and jewellery to sell as a last desperate measure. If only she could have ensured that Pinewood would survive too!

She was curled up in a chair in front of the kitchen stove late one night when she heard Dominic return, listened to him talking to Micah in the hall, and waited for him to go to his study to have his usual nightcap. He probably hadn't eaten all day, she thought. There was a stew of chicken and vegetables still simmering on the dying fire. Wearily she climbed to her feet to fetch a plate. He came in as she was setting a place at the table.

'I thought you would be in bed,' he said in surprise.

'I fell asleep,' Veroníque confessed. 'The stew is hot. Will you have some?'

'I'm famished. Make it a large plate.' He left her for a moment, returning with two glasses filled with Bourbon. She kept the decanters in the study and the drawing-room always full. It was the only thing they never seemed to be short of.

'Sit down before you fall, and drink this,' he ordered, and stood over her until she had consumed half of the contents of the glass he handed her. Veroníque curled up in the chair again, feeling very comfortable, despite the fact she was desperately tired. The kitchen was a warm, friendly place at night.

'You didn't have the big fire lit again, did you?' Dominic looked up from his food with a frown. She looked lost in the huge chair. The calico blouse she wore was open at the neck. The skirt, although clean, was beginning to fade. Her hair was loose around her shoulders. It made her look very young and somehow vulnerable.

Damn her stubbornness, he thought. Why wouldn't she go to Macon with her sister? He tried not to think of what it could be like for her if she stayed, with Sherman's men twenty miles away. He hadn't told her the news yet. Only Micah and Paul knew what was almost upon them.

'I'm trying to economise,' Veroníque returned with a smile. 'Why light such a large fire to warm a room no one uses at the moment? Wait until the Yankees have gone, then we'll light it and invite everyone for miles to come and warm themselves by it.'

'Would you like that?'

'Very much.'

'You do realise, I suppose, that a fire could be all we have.' She smiled and he gave an annoyed oath. 'Why is it whenever I try to tell you what we're in for, all you do is look like the cat who stole the cream? Dammit, *ma belle*, there are times when you are a complete mystery to me.'

He ate in silence for a while. Veronique could see he was wanting to broach some subject which was either distasteful to him or to which he knew she might object. At last, pushing aside his empty plate, he swallowed his Bourbon and looked across the table at her.

'I'm going to the Folly tomorrow. I'm bringing Melissa here.'

Veronique stared at him in horror, and the unspoken accusation in her blue eyes prompted an explanation. The days had passed when he wanted to use his mistress as a lever between them.

'Benevolent Uncle Billy Sherman, at this moment, is less than twenty miles from Moonshadow. I didn't want to worry you with this right now, and I'd be glad if you didn't tell Alice yet, but you see why I've got to get Melissa here. Her place is directly in the line of advance. They've already overrun the Walker place, burned it to the ground, freed the slaves. The old man himself and his two sons were killed. Mrs Walker and her four daughters have gone to the Carsons, over at Dempsey. There are Yankees camped all along the Altamaha from Atlanta to the Sans Souci Plantation, and that's only six miles from Melissa. Are you saying you won't have her in the house?'

'I said that the day Paul and Alice were married, and I meant it,' Veronique said quietly. 'Under normal circumstances she would never come here again, but you know I can't turn her away. Just don't expect me to be civil to her, Dominic.'

'I'm bringing her here in order to save her life, not usurp your position. There isn't a woman on this earth who could do that,' Dominic returned quietly. 'It's getting very late and I have to make an early start in the morning. I'm going to leave Micah here. He has the keys to the gun cupboard just in case.'

'Did you manage to get the last of the cotton picked?' Veronique climbed stiffly to her feet. Another few moments and she would have been asleep.

Dominic shook his head with a grimace.

'We need at least another three days of good weather and

hard work, and at the moment I don't think we can expect either. It was trying to rain when I came in, and the boys are just about played out. We shall just have to let it stay where it is. I need what labour we have to finish gathering up the last of the vegetables, just in case you're thinking of hiding any more.' A smile curved around his lean mouth. There was no mockery—perhaps a little pride. 'By the way, where have you put them?'

'Somewhere where they won't be found.' By now Veronique had over half-a-dozen places to hide essentials. She was becoming more secretive about them with each passing day, afraid one of the Negroes who remained on the plantation might be persuaded to reveal the whereabouts of their secret caches to enemy soldiers, and ruin days of back-breaking work and the plans for the future which remained locked in her heart.

Her labours were not yet over, she thought as she slipped into bed. Someone was going to have to pick the last of the cotton, and if there was no other way she would do it herself. Her poor father would turn in his grave. To gather cotton like a common field hand, after he had raised her to be a lady. Would those happy times every return?

She watched the light beneath the communicating doors until it was extinguished, and she heard the huge canopied bed creak as Dominic climbed into it. Tomorrow she had to face the appalling prospect of Melissa's presence in the house, but it had been made possible by what Dominic had said in the warm comfort of the kitchen when, for a brief moment, they had both relaxed and enjoyed each other's company without qualms of conscience. 'I'm bringing her here to save her life, not to usurp your position. There isn't a woman on this earth who could do that.'

How wonderful it would be if she allowed herself to believe he meant those complimentary words. No woman on earth . . . It was almost as if he cared.

'Work the fields!' Alice echoed. She stared across the kitchen table as if her sister had taken leave of her senses.

'Yes, work the fields.' Veronique stared at Alice challengingly. Dominic had left early that morning. She had watched him ride away just after seven o'clock. She was in control now. She had to make everyone realise how important it was to pick the last of the cotton bolls before bad weather destroyed them. The South had been born and flourished through cotton; it would survive because people cared. 'All the field-hands have gone rooting for vegetables. I need volunteers.' She saw Paul grin and her cheeks flamed with indignant colour. 'Yes, even you. I need all the help I can get. There's work to be done.

Around noon, the dark clouds which had been threatening rain since first light allowed the deluge to descend on the three stooping figures in the middle of the last field of cotton. Veroníque's shoulders ached from the additional amount of bending and stretching which was necessary, and the large bag on her back was full of fleecy soft bolls. Miserably she looked across to the half-full cart on the edge of the field. Even the weather was against them.

'You're soaked,' Michelle declared, looking at her wet hair and the rain soaking through the thin calico blouse. 'We can do no more here. We can do no more,' she repeated insistently, as Veroníque continued on along the long rows of unpicked cotton.

A few more steps and she halted and turned, and the Creole woman saw tears mingling with the rain on her cheeks. Arm in arm they walked back to where Micah waited beside the cart. He offered no words of consolation. He knew there were none. As soon as they reached Moonshadow he began to unload what cotton had been collected and stored it in one of the baling sheds. Veroníque returned the horse to the stables, sending Michelle to the house to change herself and set out dry clothes for her when she came.

'What the hell do you think you have been doing?' Dominic's startled tones jerked her out of her deep thought. He stood at the far end of the barn, unsaddling two horses. He left what he was doing and strode across to where she stood. 'You haven't answered me. Where have you been? You're wet through. Dammit, you didn't risk going over to Pinewood after all my warnings?'

'I've been picking cotton,' Veroníque said slowly. She leaned back against one of the stalls, uncaring of her aching back or rain-sodden clothes. She wanted to watch his face at the news, hoping for some sign of pride or gratitude for what she had tried to do.

He wheeled on her with an oath, his dark eyes narrowing as he stared into her expectant features. 'Are you mad, girl?'

His apparent lack of understanding stung her. 'I hoped . . . I hoped you would understand why. Perhaps even be pleased.'

'Pleased?' he echoed, with a frown. 'Do you think it pleases me to see you straining your eyes each night sewing clothes, spoiling your hands with tasks Michelle once used to do, wearing calico instead of silk? One day I'll dress you in silk again.'

'In a manner befitting the wife of a d'Estainville?' she asked challengingly.

'Only if you're here, of course. I can't do it if you persist in the crazy idea you had of living at Pinewood after the war.'

Her freedom! She had forgotten how important it had once been to think of being free.

'Is that what you still want?' Dominic asked. He stepped closer, his gaze sweeping over her body outlined against the wet calico. 'Is it? Haven't you ever lain awake, wanting me as much as I have wanted you since that night? Just because I haven't touched you again, that doesn't mean I haven't thought about it—wanted it.'

Veroníque caught her breath, turned her head away as he leaned forward, expecting to be kissed, but he placed his hands both sides of her against the stall, imprisoning her between them and stared deeply into her eyes.

'If you say no, you're a liar, *ma belle*. I can read the truth in your face. That's why you are so afraid I'll touch you—because you know you want me to.'

'I'm not made of stone, Dominic. Of course I want to be loved, but not your way. Why couldn't you leave things as they were? I came with the house, like a slave, like Sarah. The only difference was that Sarah was loved by her master—made to feel a whole woman, not an object to be used and discarded at will.'

She broke off at the sudden fire which leapt into Dominic's eyes, turned and tried to push past his outstretched arm, but he refused to yield. 'So you want to feel a woman, do you?' he muttered.

The fire which leapt between them had been suppressed too long to be ignored. Dominic kissed her slowly, expertly, intent on drawing a response from her stiff lips, holding her face in both hands, her body imprisoned by his against the wooden rails of the stall. Veroníque's hands reached up to push him away. Instead they caught his shoulders, drawing him closer. Her lips parted and her kisses contained a hunger to match his own. She felt his hands on her body, burning her skin like fire through the thin material of her blouse, heard him utter a surprised expletive as she allowed him to draw her closer against him without protest. He half-lifted her and bore her backwards into the mound of hay piled behind them. If he said he loved her, she would believe it at this moment, because it was the one thing she wanted most in the world. Dominic drew back, lifting a hand to brush wisps of hay from her tangled hair.

'Don't you ever lock your door on me again, *ma belle*,' he said, in a low tone. 'If you do, I swear I'll tear it from its hinges.'

'Our house guest might object,' Veroníque answered meaningly.

'You little fool, are you blind?' he demanded in a harsh whisper. 'Melissa has never meant anything to me. I've never lied to you about that, have I?'

'No, but . . .'

'No, buts. I haven't touched her since before Alice and Paul were married. I haven't wanted any other woman since the night we spent together.'

'Yet you still went to her . . .'

'You sent me to her, remember? And half a loaf . . .!' He gave a wicked grin and then kissed her again, almost roughly. 'You're more than enough woman for me to handle.'

The sound of laughter from the direction of the doorway brought Dominic up on to his knees. All the good humour vanished from his face, and Veroníque watched his expression grow cold. She knew who stood in the doorway even before she gained her feet, making hasty efforts to tuck her blouse back into the waistband of her skirt.

Melissa wore a brilliant red riding outfit. It should have clashed with her hair, but it didn't. She looked immaculate, and made Veronique even more conscious of her own appearance.

'I came looking for Veronique. Michelle is worried she will catch a cold. I can see there's no chance of that.' Veronique heard a slight tremor in her usually controlled tone. Anger, or jealousy perhaps? she wondered. Melissa's eyes considered the younger girl with an almost disdainful smile before she switched her attention to Dominic, and added maliciously: 'I didn't realise you had your father's habit of tumbling wenches in the cotton sheds.'

With an inarticulate cry, Veronique brushed past Dominic and ran from the barn. Melissa's laughter floated after her, followed by her husband's harsh tones, but she did not catch the words.

She wanted to believe Dominic had broken off the affair, but as they all sat at dinner that evening, she saw nothing in his attitude to confirm that he had spoken the truth. In fact he seemed to pay special attention to their guest, and as the evening wore on she was aware of the smile on Melissa's lovely face, deepening in satisfaction. She said nothing and somehow behaved as if nothing was wrong, until she was at last in the sanctuary of her own room. There she unhooked her dress so roughly that she tore two of the hooks from their fastenings, and Michelle reprimanded her for her carelessness.

'You didn't see her! Damn her, Michelle, I won't let her have him! Not now—not after this afternoon.' Beneath Michelle's curious gaze she faltered, and then slowly told her what had passed.

'About time too,' was the only comment she received.

'How do I fight her?'

'You both have the same weapons.'

'Why must it always come down to that? He wants me, he told me so, but he doesn't love me.'

'It will be a beginning, and more than you have shared with him in the past. If you still love him, *mignonne*, you will fight for him any way you can. Her way, if necessary.'

Veronique ran across to the closet and threw open the doors. From the drawer at the bottom she took out the delicate pastel-coloured nightgown and wrap Michelle had made for her wedding night—as yet unworn. The Creole woman said nothing as she helped Veronique to finish undressing. She left her nursing her aching limbs in a hot bath and was gone for over twenty minutes. When she returned Veroníque saw she had brought with her numerous jars of sweet-smelling ointments, aromatic lotions whose perfume filled the room as she allowed the whole of her body to be annointed with them. Her hair was brushed until it shone, one hundred and fifty strokes, and left hanging loosely down her back. The nightdress felt like heaven against her skin after the cold, wet calico she had worn earlier that day.

She lay on her bed after Michelle had gone downstairs, determined not to fall asleep, but the exertions of the day had taken more than their usual toll of her strength and she slept soundly for over an hour, awakening to the chimes of the Louis XVI clock in Dominic's room. Twelve o'clock!

Her bare feet made no sound as she crossed to the communicating door. A faint light still showed beneath it. She hesitated for a moment, unsure again and then she had turned the handle and swung it open.

The room beyond was dark with shadows. Only a single light burned beside the canopied bed. A faint movement came from that direction and she moved closer, her eyes gradually becoming accustomed to the dimness. Dominic lay with his hands tucked beneath his head. He was still fully dressed—and awake. She stopped, realising he had been watching her since she entered the room.

'Can't you sleep?'

'No . . .'

'You were sleeping like a baby when I looked in an hour ago,' he returned, sitting up. His eyes inspected her appearance, widened slightly in surprise.

'If—if you knew the door was unlocked . . .' Veroníque began.

'I wasn't sure what kind of reception I'd get,' he interrupted. 'Come here, you'll catch your death standing there in a draught.'

'Were you waiting for me?' she asked.

'I hoped you would come.'

'I couldn't be sure you would be alone.'

'*Touché*—a trifle low, but I'll allow you that one.'

'You preferred her sparkling conversation this evening.'

'To keep her mind off what had happened today. The

Yankees reached the Folly an hour after we had left. We were on high ground above the bend of the river . . . the fire could be seen for miles.'

Veroníque sank down on to the bed, her cheeks paling. 'The Folly burnt? I can't believe it! What will she do now? Where will she go?'

'To relatives of her husband's in Augusta.'

'Her home has gone, Dominic. That wasn't very important to her, I know—and Melissa being the kind of woman she is, she'll survive no matter where she is—but . . .'

'Your soft heart still pities her,' Dominic broke in quietly. 'Save it for those who may need it, *ma belle*. She doesn't. Melissa is a survivor.'

'Like you.'

'Like I thought I was. I seem to be having second thoughts on the subject.'

'Why?'

'You ask me that—sitting on my bed at gone twelve at night, wearing the most provocative ensemble you possess? No man in his right mind could concentrate on the business of running a plantation when faced with such a challenge.' His eyes narrowed sharply. 'I suppose you do intend to stay? I mean, this isn't a way of getting your own back, is it, for this afternoon—or before?'

Mutely Veroníque shook her head. He lay back again, watching her expression grow puzzled by his apparent lack of interest.

'Why—why are you making it so difficult?' she whispered.

'Because I have to be sure this time. In a peculiar kind of way, I think you know me better than anyone, Veroníque. But that isn't going to be enough for us to base a marriage on. Gran'père Luc used to say, "attempt everything—regret nothing." He said it should have been the d'Estainville motto. It must be that way for us. All—or nothing. I can't change the way I am. I can only hope age will mellow the pain and disappointments I can't forget right now.'

He stretched out a hand towards her. Without hesitation she slipped her own into his firm grasp, the hand on which he had placed his wedding band. A sudden chuckle rose in his throat. 'Dammit! If only the old man could see us now

. . . holding hands like young lovers. He would wish us well, *ma belle*—do you believe that?'

The heady scent of musk invaded his nostrils. His fingers tightened over hers, drawing her down beside him, his body beginning to ache with the longing to possess her. She had come to him of her own free will, breaking down every barrier which separated them with the offer of her love. The love he had refused to acknowledge, had been frightened to accept until this moment.

'Veroníque,' he whispered.

Veroníque raised her head and looked at him. Her eyes were shining with happiness as she pushed away the wrap and nightgown covering her body. Her arms locked around his neck and she pressed her mouth to his.

. . . As they lay in the warm, contented aftermath of love-making, Veroníque became aware of an unfamiliar sound invading the silence in the early morning. It was barely light outside the windows. Even as she searched her mind to identify it, Dominic leapt out of bed, grabbing his clothes and struggling into the harness which held his throwing knife, as he ran to the window which overlooked the river.

'What is it?' Pulling on her wrap, she followed and stood at his side, staring out into the grey sky, streaked with the first rays of light.

'Cannon fire. The Yankees have crossed the river. I didn't expect this until tomorrow at least.'

'You knew.' Veroníque looked at him in amazement as he pulled on the rest of his clothes and boots. 'Why—why didn't you tell me?'

His face softened as he took her by the shoulders and gently kissed her trembling mouth.

'And ruin what we had last night? No, *ma belle*—it was too precious. Get dressed, quickly now. Don't worry, you'll be gone before they arrive. I had Michelle pack some clothes for you and Alice, too, while we were all at dinner. Paul has the rig already hitched and ready, just in case there was a sudden emergency. Thank God we thought ahead. Hurry now.'

He pushed her towards her own room, but she stopped, refusing to accept what she knew he was saying.

'I won't leave you. I want to stay.'

'You're going to Macon with your sister. Do you think I'm going to let you risk your life here—more than your life. Be sensible, Veroníque—I'm prepared to give armed resistance to whoever sets foot on my property. We both know what that means.'

'No—you can't. Not now—not after—after last night. We have each other, Dominic—isn't that enough? You said it was—precious.'

'Why else would I be sending you away, you little fool? Get dressed and then come downstairs. I'll get the others ready.'

For a brief moment he caught her up in his arms, bruising her mouth with the fierceness of his kiss, then he pushed her through the door into her own room and slammed it behind her. As she reeled unsteadily towards the dressing-table, she heard him scurrying downstairs, yelling for Micah at the top of his voice.

She dressed herself in a warm blouse and a divided riding skirt, which seemed the most sensible garment at that moment. It had a large pocket, large enough to accommodate one of Dominic's pistols. They were where he always left them, in the top drawer of his study desk. Her hand trembled as she selected one, already loaded. The last time she had touched them had been the day of Elizabeth d'Estainville's visit.

'Sensible,' Dominic remarked from the doorway. 'You may need that. As far as we can tell the road is open, but there may be Negroes loose in the woods.'

He advanced into the room. She felt a chill of fear run through her as she saw he had put on his jacket and hat. Did he intend to go out and meet the soldiers before they even reached the house? There was a new English rifle with a fine wood stock which he had brought back from his travels, propped against a chair. He picked it up and handed it to Micah, then took the twin of the duelling pistol Veroníque held and pushed it into his belt.

'Paul and Alice are waiting in the rig. Michelle too. Micah will ride ahead as far as the turn-off to Macon, and then he's coming back here with me.'

'They may not come. Dominic, you can't send me away . . .' It was a plea from the heart. Véronique ran to him, caught his arm, but he put her firmly aside, knowing if he weakened and took her in his arms he would be defenceless against her entreaties.

'Paul is waiting,' he said heavily.

'No.' Doggedly, Veroníque stood her ground.

With a savage oath he grabbed her by the wrist and dragged her outside. The sound of cannon fire sounded louder to Veroníque as she was lifted bodily into the waiting rig, where Paul sat with Alice beside him, white-faced, holding Michael in her arms. There was another sound too, one she recognised as the ominous crack of rifles. Were they that near? Somewhere over to her left, the sky was darker than elsewhere. Not with rain clouds, but spiralling smoke.

'Dominic!' she screamed his name as Paul whipped up the horses, and only Michelle grabbing her around the waist prevented her from throwing herself out of the seat.

'Wait for me in Macon. I'll find you, I promise. . . .' The rest of Dominic's words were lost to her and then a bend in the driveway obscured him from her view and she sank down against the Creole woman's bosom, sobbing, and threatening Paul with every dire atrocity she could think of between each sob, if he did not stop.

He ignored her. She thrust away Michelle's protective arms, her eyes blazing with angry tears.

'I will never forgive you for this—any of you,' she cried.

'When you've seen as many dead bodies as I have, you won't be so anxious to throw your life away,' Paul flung back over his shoulder.

'He's my husband—my place is with him.' Veroníque was suddenly aware of a missing face. 'Melissa?'

'Monsieur Dominic is taking her to the Cartwright farm. Mrs Cartwright and her grand-daughter are going to Augusta. She can travel with them,' Michelle said soothingly. 'Do not agitate yourself further, *mignonne*. He will be safe with Micah to watch over him. Do you think he will risk his life unnecessarily when he has so much to live for?'

Somehow she knew, Veroníque thought, looking into the bland brown face. Dominic had not told her, yet she knew. 'I came into this world with nothing . . . I will leave the same way.' Dominic's words hammered at her brain as the rig rumbled down the dusty road. Each mile took her away from the house she had grown to love—the husband she had only known for a brief night. It wasn't fair . . .

Where the road joined the main Macon road, Micah took his leave of them. They had gone less than another hundred yards when they came upon another wagon beneath the trees. A woman was bending over the prostrate figure of a man, trying to staunch the flow of blood pouring from a wound in the arm. Without hesitation Paul drew rein and jumped down to give help. Alice turned her face away, obviously remembering a similar scene. Veroníque gave her shoulder a reassuring hug before climbing down to see if there was anything she could do.

The woman was explaining how the road ahead was blocked by Union soldiers. A dozen of them had dragged a tree-trunk across to block it completely and were stopping all who tried to pass. Those who refused to stop were shot out of hand. Others who halted their wagons had them searched, often looted—were forced to stand by while their precious possessions were flung to the ground—their persons searched by rude hands for jewels and weapons. There were several Negroes, the woman added, slaves freed by the advancing army. If they pointed out anyone of importance in the county, that person was immediately arrested.

Veroníque looked at Paul in dismay. How could they go on now?

'We have to go back,' she insisted.

'To what? You heard what was said. Do you think we'll be treated any better at Moonshadow than up ahead? This poor man was shot because he turned his wagon around. He's losing blood fast—he needs a place to stay. We all do.' Paul's eyes were centred on Alice as he spoke. Veroníque knew that her safety would take precedence over everything. There was only one place she could think of.

'Go to Pinewood. Perhaps the Yankees haven't got there yet. They may not bother—it's off the beaten track and deserted . . . Michelle, come and give me a hand. We'll put the man in the wagon and his wife can drive. You will manage, won't you? My brother-in-law will take you with him.'

The woman nodded vigorously, willing to attempt anything that would take her and her husband away from the blue-coated soldiers barring the way ahead.

'You too,' Paul ordered Veroníque when they were ready to start off again, and she still had not climbed back into the rig.

'I have to warn Dominic that the soldiers have gone around behind him. Don't you realise he's cut off? He could be on the road from the Cartwright place right now, heading straight into more of them.' As he moved towards her, his hand reaching out to take her forcibly by the arm, she stepped back and he found himself looking down the barrel of the duelling pistol. 'Please, Paul—take the others to Pinewood. I'm going home.'

'You wouldn't use that on me, and you know it,' Paul snapped, wishing he had two good arms, so that he could wrench the damned thing from her and give her a sound spanking for being so stupidly irresponsibly, wonderfully brave.

'I'm not your responsibility. No, I couldn't shoot you, but I will put a lump the size of an egg on your head, and if you're unconscious, who's going to take care of Alice and Michael?'

She gave him no further chance to argue and as she saw Michelle begin to climb down, she whirled about and ran for the cover of the trees. She had often ridden in this part of the country and knew every cart-track and back road. Within half an hour she had reached the boundary of Moonshadow Plantation.

She had run as fast as she could until a painful chest forced her to slow down. At once she felt cold, and for the first time since she had left the others, aware of what she was doing. Alone—with only the protection of a pistol containing one shot. The knowledge that Dominic was in danger urged her on, instilling new life in tired legs, fresh air down past a throat raw with exertion.

She fell on to her knees at the top of the hill which overlooked the main house. It seemed a million years ago since she had ridden this way with Dominic, racing their mounts from Pinewood through the woods to this very spot, where he had held her in his arms and kissed her and so calmly asked her to marry him so that he could regain possession of his lost inheritance.

Something moved in the trees below her. The first soldier

did not see her, but the two following close behind stopped and wheeled towards her, began to run in her direction.

Veronique swung off left into the trees. As she came out on to the bottom of the driveway she heard the thunder of a horse's hooves and found a mounted soldier in a blue uniform bearing down on her. At the same time as she screamed, she lifted the pistol in her hand and fired. Her pursuer fell from the saddle stone dead and she found herself wondering, as she ran, how such a small hole could inflict death.

More horses! She could hear them in front of the house. Dear God, where was Dominic? She leaned heavily against a tree, faint with exhaustion. She wanted to lie down and rest, and knew she could not. And then she saw them, darting from behind the barn towards the house. Dominic, crouched low, pistol in hand, followed by Micah, carrying his rifle. On her knees, beside the barn, Melissa watched them. Her clothes were covered in dirt. Her loose red hair fell untidily around a face devoid of all colour. Even from where she stood, Veronique could see the naked fear in her eyes. They had not reached the Cartwrights!

The yard was full of soldiers, moving towards the two hidden men. She gave a choked-off cry as she saw the furtive figures sidling around behind Melissa—their black faces portraying the hatred they felt for this woman who had once owned them and whipped and starved them.

'The house—get into the house, for God's sake,' she heard Dominic shout. His voice was drowned by a volley of rifle fire which immediately forced him to duck back out of sight. At that moment four pairs of hands reached for Melissa—choking back her terrified scream—dragging her backwards out of sight.

Veronique began to run again, uncaring of the danger ahead.

'Mister Dominic—look!'

It was Micah who first saw the figure reeling blindly towards them. Dominic wheeled about and sprang from his hiding place, swearing at his companion's attempts to restrain him.

'Let me go, damn you! Oh, my God—Veronique. Go back—go . . .'

The first bullet took him squarely in the shoulder and

sent him staggering back against the side of the yard wall. The second, aimed at his heart by the same soldier, put an inch-long furrow across his ribs as Micah grabbed his leg and pulled him down to the ground.

A young soldier stepped out in Veroníque's path as she started across the yard. She lifted her hands, intending to beg if necessary in order to reach Dominic's side.

'Please—let me pass. Let me go to my husband.'

She had totally forgotten the useless pistol she still clutched . . . remembered too late . . . did not even have time to cry out as the rifle menacing her barked and the bullet entered high above the left breast.

'Can he understand me?' Even the burly sergeant who stood at Micah's side, a veteran of the Mexican War and countless bar-room brawls, felt uneasy when he looked at the man kneeling over the woman's body. He would not let anyone attend to his wounds, or touch the inert form over which he crouched like a protective watch-dog. 'The boy had no way of knowing the pistol wasn't loaded . . . he had his orders . . .'

'To murder helpless women?' Dominic's eyes were as cold as death as he raised his head and stared into the faces of the soldiers who surrounded him. He felt no pain from the wound in his shoulder—nothing but the numbness that always followed death. This terrible feeling would remain with him for the rest of his days, haunting him.

He had not cried for his father—or even Sarah, whom he had loved dearly. But he cried unashamedly as he gathered Veroníque into his arms, hiding his face in her long hair to shut out the sight of the red stain spreading over her blouse. The sound of his weeping made several men—men with wives they were suddenly remembering—turn away, so that they did not also see the murder mirrored in the depths of his eyes. Each and every one of them however, heard the terrible oaths which fell from his lips. Some began to fidget nervously with their weapons, not knowing what to expect next, and then, without warning, Dominic's mood changed. Looking up at the sea of faces around him, he said quite calmly. 'I am taking her home.'

'Home?' the sergeant queried suspiciously. 'Don't you live here?'

'Pinewood,' Dominic muttered as he staggered to his feet, cradling Veronique against his chest. 'She belongs at Pinewood—she was happy there before I took her away.'

His voice trailed off. He turned away and began to cross the lawn, oblivious to the command to stop echoing behind him or to the men who stepped out in his path. He stared at the blue uniforms dispassionately, without emotion of any kind expressed on his face, or in his voice when he spoke.

'I'll kill anyone who tries to stop me.'

They had taken his pistol when they first overpowered him, and the knife from the harness beneath his arm, but he still had Grandfather Luc's stiletto, pushed inside his sleeve. Even if he could have reached it, he was still outnumbered four to one. The men who faced him knew instinctively that he would carry out his threat and die without a second thought.

'Let him go, haven't you done enough to him already? You've just killed his wife,' Micah said tersely. 'He's no danger to you now. Look at him—half out of his mind with grief.'

The sergeant stared after Dominic, his hand on the butt of his pistol and then he looked into Micah's black face, demanding harshly, 'Who are you? Do you belong to him?'

'I belong to no one. I am a free man. He freed me because he is a man of honour.'

'Honour!' The man spat into the red dust in disgust. 'What is it about people in this part of the country? They worship that word.'

'And live by it. Die for it, if necessary,' Micah returned with a dignity that suppressed the sergeant's intended sarcasm.

'Go after him then—make sure he gets where he's going—or come with us if that suits you better.'

'I prefer to stay where I belong,' Micah returned with a half-smile. He had tossed away the rifle when Dominic was first shot, and when the soldiers had pounced on him had cowered away from them, pretending he had merely been hiding. If he had not been black, he knew they would have killed him.

The sergeant was no fool. He guessed the veteran soldier harboured his suspicions, and this was borne out by the threat which followed.

'Don't let me see your black face around here again, d'you hear? I'm good on faces, bucko—I remember them for years. Your pretty speeches won't help you the next time you're caught aiding a rebel.'

By the time Micah had found a cart which hadn't been appropriated for taking away the livestock and whatever else they could carry, and caught up with Dominic, the latter's strength had given out. He sat on a grassy bank beside Veronique. His eyes had lost that glazed look. Pain had restored both his senses and the awful reality of what had happened.

He stared at Micah without speaking, and then at the other person in the cart. Michelle had been unable to keep up with her mistress in her condition, and had reached the house in time to see Micah leaving. She too had declined the sergeant's offer to be 'freed', and had climbed up beside her man.

She fell on her knees beside Veronique's inert form and immediately anger blazed into Dominic's pain-ravaged features. Savagely he knocked aside the hands which were reaching for the blood-sodden blouse.

'Leave her alone. Don't you understand? She's dead. Dead! And never once did I ever tell her how much I loved her . . .'

His eyes flickered over Micah's shoulder—to the tell-tale pall of black smoke rising over the tops of the tall pines. Moonshadow! Why didn't he feel anger? Loss? Why was there nothing? He struggled up on to his knees. He felt light-headed from the blood he was losing and swayed perilously up on to his feet. Micah stretched out a supporting hand, but he brushed it away. He wanted no one—nothing any more.

Attempt everything—regret nothing. The words mocked him. He regretted so much—had left so many things undone—unsaid. Veronique's white face swam before his tortured vision. Michelle was bending over her again, muttering in a voice too low for him to comprehend in his fuddled state of mind. 'Blast you,' he had never spoken to her that way before, 'take your filthy black hands off my wife.'

He flung himself forward, but Micah was quicker, averting the blow he aimed at Michelle's head and felling him to the ground with a blow to the body.

'Stop it, both of you,' Michelle hissed. '*Bon Dieu*, are you both blind? Do you only believe what you think you see?' She gave a long-drawn-out sigh and held up blood-stained fingers to them to see the bullet her long nails had dug from Veroníque's breast. 'There—that is what would have killed her had I left it there any longer. Dead? Fools! One of you tear up your shirt, I need bandages, and then bring the cart here. We must be gentle with her, or the shock of moving her will do what a bullet could not.'

Dominic sat in the cart, with Veroníque's head supported in his lap. He could not believe life still throbbed in her still body. Even her hand was cold and limp in his grasp.

'We'll go away, if that's what you want,' he whispered to the silent figure. 'Anywhere—to California perhaps. It's a new country and we can start again. I love you, *mon amie*—God knows how much I love you—and when you're well enough, I'll prove just how much.'

A tremulous sob broke from his lips. He bent his head low over her face, as if to bring her back to him again with the touch of his tears on her skin. His eyes closed. He was so tired—drained.

Slowly—very slowly, Veroníque's long tapered fingers began to stroke his hair.

Melissa's body was not discovered until the army of occupation moved on from Moonshadow, and one final inspection was made of the place in order to either destroy or appropriate anything worthwhile which remained and could be useful to the enemy. Her corpse was found in some bushes behind the burnt out stables. Her throat had been cut.

The Union army moved at a rate of ten miles a day, spread out across sixty miles of Georgia countryside. It left behind it a trail of devastation the South would never forget—or forgive. Homes and property cruelly, needlessly destroyed. The empty wagons of the soldiers quickly replenished with corn and oats taken from people who were already near starvation point. Looting prevailed throughout the army, despite strict orders to the contrary. At Macon, flooded with refugees from hundreds of miles around, Sherman tore apart the railroad and then bypassed the Militia fortified town.

The news of the fall of Savannah did not reach Pinewood until after Christmas, brought by some soldiers on their way back to Atlanta, which had been retaken by the Confederacy.

Veroníque knew nothing of their visit, or of the anxious people who came and went like shadows from her room all through that month and into the first weeks of the new year. During the fever which racked her body, she wandered in a frightening world of grey shadowy figures who turned away from her whenever she asked for help. Paul's knowledge and Michelle's two skilful hands retained the weak spark of life in her body—fought to stop it being extinguished—and won.

When she grew stronger, Dominic carried her down to the room which had been converted into a parlour. It had once been George's study. She discovered the house had been spared a visit from the Yankees, although deserters and marauding Negroes on the rampage had left their mark. Her father's beautiful jade collection had been stolen, together with other valuables. Furniture had been smashed, curtains torn down and windows broken. From a window, she could see where horses had been ridden over the lawn and garden. Her heart ached at such wanton destruction. She had not been told about Moonshadow.

By the time she was strong enough to ride again, Dominic knew he could keep the news from her no longer. She listened to him with tears in her eyes and then asked him to take her there. He baulked at the idea, but she insisted, and in the end he gave way.

At the sight of the gutted upper floors which had once housed her bedrooms, the blackened, charred beams open to the elements, Veroníque wept openly. A brickwork shell was all that remained. A wild hog, probably one which had escaped the fate of his brothers, ran across the yard as she stood on the lawn staring with horrified eyes at the destruction.

Dominic's face was a closed book. She knew he often came here alone, to stand and look and remember, but he never spoke of the future. They should be making plans for the spring, she thought. Already Alice and Michelle had begun to plant a vegetable garden at Pinewood. They could do the same here, and with the seed she had so carefully hidden they would be able to grow food to support themselves until the war was over. Why had he not bothered to dig up the sacks of vegetables and grain?

Daffodils and brightly coloured spring flowers were beginning to flower at her feet. Behind her, the trees were budding with new life. New life, like that which even now was beginning to stir inside her. Dominic turned and began to make his way slowly to the horses, and she stifled the impulse to blurt out her wonderful news, afraid he would immediately curtail her future plans.

'I shouldn't have brought you here.' He sounded tired, Veroníque thought. He always did these days. 'I meant what I said, you know. We could go away. What is there here for us now? Paul's talking of settling in Atlanta. He's been offered a job with a newspaper—still intends to write that book, I think. It's about time we put all this behind us too.'

'Will you humour me a little longer?' Veroníque asked. It hurt her to see him turn his back on the place she knew he still loved. He wanted to go away for her sake. He had told her as much, blaming himself for the accident which had almost cost her her life. And if he had sent her away, she realised, he would have remained and fought and perhaps have been killed. She would have lost not only a home, but a husband. 'Go and wait for me on the hill.'

He looked into her thin face curiously, but with a shrug of his shoulders mounted and rode off towards the river. When Veroníque rejoined him, she held two dirty sacks across her saddle. She herself was splattered with mud, and the sight of her grimy face brought a reluctant smile to Dominic's set features.

'I wondered how long it would be before you started digging those up. Let them stay hidden, *ma belle*. You don't know what you are doing.'

'Yes, I do. We're going to plant this corn seed here at Moonshadow. I noticed the overseer's cottage doesn't look too badly damaged. We could live there.'

'We?' Dominic echoed thickly.

'Michelle and Micah. You and me. We don't need all these pine trees in front of the house either, they shut out too much light. We could cut some down to start rebuilding—clear a road directly to Pinewood—even make it one plantation. You never know, we could end up in the timber business. There must be hundreds of families like us . . .'

'For God's sake! Rebuild—with two pairs of hands?'

Smiling, Veroníque opened the second sack she held. The river had flooded once since she had hidden it, soaking the contents, but they were still intact.

'Silver—and that means a new beginning,' she said proudly, 'and my mother's diamonds. We will sell it piece by piece as we need the money. New cotton seeds, furniture; but that isn't too important right now because we have everything we need at Pinewood . . .'

'Then why try to do the impossible? Why live here?' Dominic demanded. He tried to sound disinterested, but already there was a familiar gleam in his eyes. Of course he had made plans, secret plans when he had stood among the ruins, but he had never intended to implement them. Veroníque had suffered too much. How could he ask her to endure the added hardships which would surely follow if they returned to their old home. The overseer's cottage, small and primitive after the elegance of the rooms in Moonshadow: barely enough to live on while they cleared the fields and began planting again. Months of back-breaking toil—months of waiting—hoping—perhaps destroying their dreams.

'Why?' A faint spark of anger glowed in Veroníque's eyes as she climbed carefully to the ground and put down the sacks. 'Why? Because it is our home. The d'Estainvilles have always lived at Moonshadow Plantation—they always will.' Taking him by the hand she made him follow her to the top of the hill. The memory of her flight from the soldiers from this very spot faded as more pleasant thoughts returned.

'This is where you first asked me to marry you, do you remember?' She threw back her head and looked up at him and he felt his heartbeats quicken as they always did when she looked at him this way and made him realise how deeply she loved him. Her enthusiasm was beginning to reach him. He wanted to believe it was possible. She pointed to the ruins of the house below them. 'Close your eyes. See it as it was—as it can be again. Don't turn your back on it because of me, Dominic. I want what you want. I am your wife—and I love you so much. Moonshadow belongs to the d'Estainvilles—to us—to the son I shall give you.'

'A baby?' Dominic's hand closed tightly over hers at the unexpected shock.

'You aren't pleased?'

'Are you?' His dark eyes searched her face expectantly, and with relief sweeping through him like wildfire, saw the smile which gave him his answer.

'Yes. You don't know how much. Now we are complete—a real family. New life, Dominic. We have to stay now.'

With a soft expletive he gathered her against him and kissed her.

'When did I first begin to love you, I wonder? When you were a chit of a girl, determined to tell me what a bad character I was? Or during those long hours we used to ride together? They would have been lonely times without you at my side—as lonely as my life would be if you ever went away. God! I feel I've only just found you, and now I am about to lose you to somebody else. I don't think I can bear that, *ma belle*. I need you.'

'We will bring our son here, to this very spot, when he is old enough to appreciate the inheritance his father has saved for him,' she said softly, proudly. 'Yes—we will bring Jean-Luc here.'

'Jean-Luc?' Dominic queried, his eyes narrowing at the name.

'Yes—after my grandfather and yours. A formidable combination, don't you agree?'

'It might be a girl.'

'No, a son first. Perhaps a girl later.'

'Jean-Luc,' Dominic echoed. What a moment that would be. Side by side with his son—and the wife he adored. She would always be with him. It was no longer possible to think of life without her. 'The name is perfect.'

Veroníque took his hand and laid it against her stomach with a sigh of contentment. So much work lay ahead of them, but it would be worth the long days of toil, the uncertainty until the first crop grew, the days of waiting for Moonshadow to rise again from the red dust.

'See how he grows inside me already,' she whispered, turning her face up to his. 'He's going to be a real boy. Jean-Luc d'Estainville, heir to Moonshadow Plantation.'